THE

ANATOMY

LESSON

THE ANATOMY LESSON

 A NOVEL

Nina Siegal

NAN A. TALESE | DOUBLEDAY

NEW YORK LONDON TORONTO

SYDNEY AUCKLAND

All rights reserved. Published in the United States by Nan A. Talese / Doubleday, a division of Random House LLC, New York, and in Canada by Random House of Canada Limited, Toronto, Penguin Random House companies.

www.nanatalese.com

Doubleday is a registered trademark of Random House LLC. Nan A. Talese and the colophon are trademarks of Random House LLC.

Page 267: *The Anatomy Lesson of Dr Nicolaes Tulp* (1632), by Rembrandt van Rijn. Canvas, 169.5 x 216.5 cm. Reprinted by permission of the Royal Picture Gallery Mauritshuis, The Hague.

Jacket design by Michael J. Windsor
Front jacket images: top and inset © The Bridgeman Art Library / Getty Images; bottom © traveler1116 / Getty Images; tulips © IgorGolovniov / Shutterstock. Back jacket image © DEA / G. DAGLI ORTI / Getty Images.

LIBRARY OF CONGRESS CATALOGING-IN-PUBLICATION DATA
Siegal, Nina.
The anatomy lesson : a novel / Nina Siegal.
pages cm
1. Rembrandt Harmenszoon van Rijn, 1606–1669—Fiction.
2. Amsterdam (Netherlands)—Social conditions—17th century—
Fiction. 3. Medical fiction. I. Title.
PS3619.I37A53 2014
813'.6—dc23
2013034642

ISBN 978-0-385-53836-7 (hardcover)
ISBN 978-0-385-53837-4 (eBook)

MANUFACTURED IN THE UNITED STATES OF AMERICA

1 3 5 7 9 10 8 6 4 2

First Edition

For Joseph, Cameron, and Sonia

Dumb integuments teach. Cuts of flesh, though dead,

for that very reason forbid us to die.

Here, while with artful hand he slits the pallid limbs,

speaks to us the eloquence of learned Tulp:

"Listener, teach yourself! And while you proceed through the parts,

believe that, even in the smallest, God lies hid."

—CASPAR BARLAEUS, 1639

AUTHOR'S NOTE

I knew Rembrandt's masterpiece *The Anatomy Lesson of Dr. Nicolaes Tulp* as a child, for a print of it hung in my father's study, but I never knew its title or its origins. During an art history seminar in grad school, I was assigned to "read" a painting—i.e., unravel the narrative within it. We were allowed to pick any painting; and as my professor clicked through slides of potential examples, it showed up on the screen and I thought: That one! I'll finally find out the real story behind that painting.

I moved to Amsterdam, drawn by the idea of writing a novel about the dead man in the painting, Adriaen Adriaenszoon, or Aris Kindt. I had a grant to research the period and to walk the streets and absorb sights of Rembrandt's world. I lived in a house built in 1624; I worked in an office that was once the warehouse for the Dutch West India Company. Horses clip-clop through the still-cobbled byways of the Old Center, now packed with international sightseers, who, if you squint in a certain way, could be sailors and traders. And in Amsterdam's city archives, I was able to find the complete dossier of the crimes committed by a recidivist thief named Aris Kindt.

One afternoon when I was sitting in front of the original Rembrandt portrait in the Mauritshuis in The Hague, I looked at the nearly naked corpse on the dissection slab and I thought: Before he became the centerpiece of this anatomy lesson, someone had cared for that man. Someone had touched that body, loved that body. That someone was a woman. I named her Flora. And that's where my story began.

THE
ANATOMY
LESSON

HANGING DAY

THE BODY

At the first toll of the Westerkerk bell Adriaen Adriaenszoon bolts awake in a dank stone jail inside Amsterdam's town hall. He is shivering and sweating at the same time. Shivering because winter gnaws through his meager leather jerkin, sweating because of the nightmare out of which he's just awakened.

What he remembers is no more than an assemblage of symbols—a dog, a wall made of doors, an old woman with a pail full of sand—but fear is pounding through him insistently, demanding he return to sleep to see out the dream. There is the promise of solace through one of those doors, and a bed to lie on, something tells him. But his eyes will not close again. His other senses are already registering the day.

Horse's hooves tromp in the puddles somewhere nearby. There's a whinny and the sound of clacking steel on cobblestones. The street, which he can see only through the tiny window, is glistening from last night's downpour. The air smells of mineral soil, sweat, and piss.

He crosses himself before remembering where he is, then glances around nervously in hopes that no guards have seen this. He presses his callused palm through his coarse hair and slumps against the cold wall. There's only his cell mate, Joep van de Gheyn, the fishmonger killer, still asleep on the plank against his own wall. Aris wipes his sweat from his brow with his left hand, then rubs the stump over its bloody bandages, stifling the throbbing of the limb, which pulses with every heartbeat. "That's all right now. Easy there," he says, massaging the limb.

Hearing the bells ringing out the final chimes of the morning hour, he slaps himself to full wakefulness. This is his last day living. Each time the bells ring he's one step closer to the gallows.

⤞✳︎⤝

Outside, there's a festive feeling in the frigid air. Damp and cold as it is, with clouds that hang so low they form a ceiling over the city's tile rooftops, there's still a raw excitement that pulses like a current through Amsterdam's quiet canals and byways. Some would call it bloodlust.

The streets echo with silence, hollow and expectant, like an empty tankard waiting to be filled. As dawn starts to creep across the water and the wharves from the swampy eastern marshlands, workers from the docks arrive with wood planks to build the hangman's scaffold. They drop the boards like pieces of a coffin on the square and the hammering begins. Nearby, vendors are setting up their stalls to sell delftware, wool mittens, or fresh-baked bread to all who'll come to gawp.

Tacked to the town hall door is the Justice Day schedule:

- R. Pijnaker, age fifteen, will receive a birching for willfully stealing from a tavern keeper's till.
- Brothel madam S. Zeedijk shall be beaten upon her neck with a rolling pin for general lewdness, moral corruption, and running a house of debauchery.
- Three burglary conspirators, R. Tolbeit, A. Schellekamp, and F. Knipsheer, to be flogged and branded with the Amsterdam *A* on their chests before being banished from the city for their brazen attempt to break into a diamond cutter's shop.
- A confined convict H. Peeters shall be whipped and marked with burning spears for his violation of confinement and other evil acts before his lifelong imprisonment is renewed.
- German convict E. Eisenstein caught smoking in the rasp house and, when scolded, cursed and spit at his jailors, shall have an ear sliced off. He will return to the rasp house to work the twelve-blade saws cutting brazilwood for the dye works until his hands are as good as his ears.
- The hanging of J. v. d. Gheyn, the notorious murderer of good fishmonger Joris van Dungeon.
- The hanging of A. Adriaensz, alias Aris Kindt, evildoer and recalcitrant thief.

Adriaen Adriaensz, Adriaen, son of Adriaen of Leiden, alias Aris Kindt, Hans Kindt, or Arend Kint: he's used different names in different towns where he was arrested, then banished, then arrested again. Arend was his father's nickname for him, meaning "eagle."

These days he goes by Aris, which means nothing. It was others who tacked on "Kindt" or "The Kid" years ago, on account of his small stature and since he was still lithe and smooth-skinned when he committed his first crimes.

⌀⁂⌀

Aris draws his jerkin tighter, clinging to it with his one hand making a fist over his heart. His nightmare has already fragmented into shapes—the terrible slimness of a starving dog's back, a room of doors leading onto still other doors, his own hands painted gold, clutching a goose feather pillow. A goose feather pillow.

Beside him, snoring, is Joep van de Gheyn, the fishmonger killer. By profession he is a tailor—a fact that Aris finds secretly ironic, since he has spent much of his own adult life stealing fine coats from tailors' shops. Still asleep like a babe in his mother's arms, the tailor has his hands pressed together in prayer under his pulpy jowls, his left foot kicking an invisible attacker.

Idiot, thinks Aris.

Still sitting, he extends his foot out toward his cell mate and nudges Joep in the ribs, not gently. "Sleep when you're dead," he says.

The cell mate's eyes open, and without knowing that he's just been victim of a minor assault, he comes coughing out of sleep. His hacking continues until he sits up straight, only to emit two consecutive sneezes. He pulls a dirty rag out of his pocket and blows his nose profusely.

"Well, then," he says, blinking his eyes to daylight.

The two convicts sit in their small cell, neither one fully awake.

In the idle haze of this first hour of the last day of his own life, Aris thinks: A pillow? Has he ever laid his head on a goose feather pillow?

Flora, comes the answer. When she'd mended him those months after he'd got that beating in the tavern. Flora. There she was, her proud, sturdy shoulders, the catlike curve of her neck, that comforting broad backside. She had cradled his bruised head and placed a pillow underneath, hadn't she?

Flora. Would Flora be out there?

THE HANDS

The tolling of the Westerkerk bell can be heard more distinctly at the stately canal-side mansion belonging to Dr. Nicolaes Tulp, who is pacing across the checkered marble floor of his sitting room. He is preparing himself to recite the speech he intends to give tonight, his wife, Margaretha, as his test audience. She is propped up in a high-backed wooden chair in front of him, with an enormous swath of damask silk she's embroidering in her lap, her hands motionless, waiting.

How lovely to have the new church so close by their home, she thinks, though she doesn't always love the half-hour bell. What she does love is when the organist plays something special at the hour, like her favorite, Sweelinck. She would like to go and see that carillon some afternoon soon if Nicolaes could be persuaded to join her. The churchwarden from the Westerkerk has invited them personally, because of her husband's position, of course, but he hasn't yet accepted. Of late, he has been so preoccupied with politicking that he has no time for any leisure activities. Tomorrow will be election day at last, and tonight he has the opportunity to convince the city's current burghermasters and aldermen that he is sufficiently learned and stoical to be elevated beyond a mere magistrate.

She hopes her husband will accept the warden's offer. It is a rare thing that such a grand church should be erected so close to their home, and she could use a small diversion from the household and his five children. Perhaps she will suggest the warden as a useful ally in his campaign. They might even be among the city's first visitors to the beautiful tower. What a view there must be from up there!

Tulp takes a ceremonial step forward. "Most excellent and ornate men of Amsterdam: Honorable Burgomaster Bicker, Amsterdam burghers, gentlemen of the Stadtholder's court, magistrates, inspectors *Collegii Medici*, physicians, barber-surgeons . . ." he begins a bit shakily.

"Welcome to the second public dissection of my term as praelector of the Amsterdam Surgeons' Guild . . ." He continues, and Margaretha follows the rhythms of his inflections and gathers the melody of his voice, working its way up and down the scale. She begins drawing her needle back and forth through the fabric, looking down on each stitch to check her progress on the tulip she is incorporating into the damask curtains of the entry hall.

She has based the design on the potted admirael over on the mantel, a recent gift to her husband from Roemer Visscher, in appreciation for treating the poet's gallstones. So far, she has managed to complete the white of the petals and now she is continuing with the red parts; her embroidered flower has no stem. She is considering adding a stem now, but that would involve going back upstairs to get the green floss in the basket that she'd absentmindedly left on the landing. The green floss. If only she'd remembered to bring down the green floss. She doesn't want to disrupt her husband, who's lost sleep for several nights already in anticipation of the important evening ahead, but if she had the green floss she could perhaps finally finish this tulip while listening.

"At the request of the governors of our noble guild, I do humbly come before you to offer my annual lecture upon the human body and the fabric of nature . . ."

He has commissioned this new painter at Uylenburgh's studio to commemorate his dissection tonight. It's his second year as praelector, but this follows a tradition. Each of the previous praelectors has commissioned a portrait of the guild when they've taken the helm, with themselves at center stage. She hopes the artist will focus on his kind, almost innocent eyes, which were what attracted her to him and which she still finds comforting whenever she looks up from her embroidery. He is a doctor of great compassion and skill, willing to rush out in the middle of the night to see any patient. He is a good man. A man of character.

The painter, she hopes, will capture his full head of dark hair and an ample beard that makes him look still so young. His eyes are just a tiny bit dreamy, though he works hard to appear stern and eagle-eyed.

Perhaps the painter will notice the deftness of his hands, which are, she has always felt, a touch feminine, with long elegant fingers that he often presses to his lips when in thought. He is no hearty man of the fields, certainly. The blue tint of his veins is visible through his pale skin; he's always had a kind of ethereal pallor that made her think he was closer to the angels. When he gives his lectures, he attempts to mask it with a touch of her rouge. The men he seeks to impress—like those who will assemble tonight in the Waag chamber for his annual anatomical display—are not worthy of such self-concern.

She knows, as well as she can recognize the dull end of the needle now pressing against her thumb, that he will rise to his natural position in Amsterdam society in due time. Already he's chief praelector of the City of Amsterdam, Dr. Nicolaes Pieterszoon Tulp, occasionally referred to by the Latinate: Tulpius. She sees how eager he is to rush this process along. Perhaps the portrait itself is even a bit premature.

He clears his throat—the sudden evacuation of a busy lecture hall—and begins reading his speech again from the beginning, this time trying out a slightly lower vocal pitch, more sober and authoritative.

"Most excellent and ornate men of Amsterdam: Honorable Burgomaster Bicker, Amsterdam burghers, gentlemen of the Stadtholder's court, . . ." he says, glancing up to notice that his wife is still quite attentive, though her fingers have begun to work her floss through her embroidery. "Before me, gentlemen, lies the body of a notorious criminal sentenced to death by the honorable magistrates of Amsterdam for wrongdoing and evil deeds and hanged by the neck this very day. . . ."

She adds a few more red details to this tulip instead, and muses to herself about whether the tulip curtains might not be one step too far in the florescence of their home. There is garishness to it, Margaretha thinks, especially as the tulip has just now become such a ridiculous craze.

When they had moved into this mansion it was just a bit of silliness. There was a gable stone with a tulip just above their front door and so when he'd purchased the carriage for his nightly house calls, he had a tulip painted on its side. Soon enough he became known around the town as Dr. Tulp, and the name stuck. He eventually adopted the name instead of his original, Claes Pieterszoon. After all, there were already a few Pieterszoons in town but only one Tulp.

Since then, friends and grateful patients often arrive at the house of Tulp with tulip-shaped gifts: tulip vases and tulip dishes, tulip-shaped silver cups, and actual tulips, too, sent from wealthier patients in earthenware vases with many small spouts, which the servants arrange on mantels positioned beneath oil paintings they'd been given, too, of tulip bouquets. All these beautiful flowers signify love and respect, Margaretha knows, but every once in a while she can't help feeling she resides, not in a home but in a tulip nursery. She draws the needle through the fabric until it stops.

Her husband has paced away again, but now he is moving toward her. Margaretha isn't listening exactly, and he has noticed. She hopes he will not take it personally, but she can see that he is agitated, looking for some way to capture her attention. He flips through the pages of his manuscript. Seeming as though he has a new idea, he shifts the papers from one hand to the other, then raises his free hand and begins to gesticulate. He's making a strange movement, rotating his wrist in a somewhat comical twirl, his index finger pointed toward the ceiling.

"Observe the motion of my right hand," he tries. "The hand, with its opposable thumb, as the great Galenus has revealed to us, is unique to mankind. To what do we owe to this appendage that sets us apart in form from all other barbarous creatures and brutes?"

He pauses to address her. "I have heard tell that the chimpanzee may also have opposable thumbs, though it is not yet confirmed. I wonder if I should mention this? Or does it confuse the point?" He muses to himself, drawing his hand across his beard, and then raising his hand again.

She suppresses a smile that wants very badly to form on her lips as her husband's hand continues to histrionically twirl in the air, like some grandiloquent rhetorician of the Egelantier's. He doesn't seem to notice, but he abruptly paces away from her, dropping his head and muttering something to himself. He holds his fist to his forehead and remains silent for some time. She looks down to check the red detailing, which has gone amiss.

"Don't you think it's quite fascinating that we associate so many negative things with the left hand?" his wife observes idly, after the silence has gone on for a while. "Think of it: the Latin *sinister*, which you use so often in your speech, for the left hand, means 'evil or inauspicious,' 'foreboding.' And when someone is left-handed, we fear they have powers of witchery."

She glances up to see his exasperated expression, before he drops his arms to his sides and some papers flutter to the floor. "My love, are you paying any attention at all?" He shakes the remaining pages of the manuscript at her. "I must memorize the speech by this evening. So far, I have not even completed the writing. I shall embarrass myself and our whole household."

Margaretha takes in the plaintive look in her husband's eyes. She'd heard him rustle in the adjacent chamber at least three times in the night. She should've gotten up to heat milk for him, or at least forgotten all about the green floss and not mentioned the Latin just now.

She runs her needle into the fabric, just where the stem will eventually reach the blossom, and leaves it there. She reaches out her hand to take her husband's. "You're absolutely right, my love. I shall not interrupt you again. Please start again from exactly where you left off."

THE HEART

Flora can hear no bells, not even the distant chiming of those of her own cathedral ringing for the fourth time since the dawn, only the quiet rustle of the rushes as the wind blows across the Rhine. She crouches on the ground behind her home, holding her belly and vomiting into the tall grass.

It had come on of a sudden, her stomach cramping, her mouth filling with salty bile; and then, in a second, her throat was convulsing. Six months along and still she suffers from morning sickness, running from her own home into the garden to erupt into the grass.

She brings foods to her lips and the smell is revolting, as if everything, all at once, has gone sour. A boiled egg, perhaps, she can manage. The smell of cooking goat can make her gag, the scent of cheese is overpowering. In the mornings, though, it comes on without the help of any food or smell.

It comes again, her stomach heaving, and again it is over sooner than she'd expected. Once she finishes, she turns onto her back and lies there. Her belly still aches, but the feeling will lessen, she knows. Flora opens her eyes to see the full globe of the sky. It was a luminous dawn, and it will be a clear day, she tells herself, and now that the demons have escaped her body, she will be able to work. Her stomach, at least, in peace.

She thinks on Adriaen again and imagines what his reaction will be to her news. He'd told her once that he thought he wasn't the right kind of man to be a father. Adriaen doesn't ever think very much of himself as a potential anything. Adriaen has his troubles, and he has his wandering, but maybe the babe would bring about a change in him. Once he will look into eyes that contained such love and innocence, maybe he'll see his own innocence as well.

It is then that she hears the yelling and the loud crack that follows. She sits up. No, it sounds more like something being smashed. It is fast, and now it is over. A cry, a loud crack, and the sound of feet running. Boys, making trouble. She pushes herself up, still holding her belly, and starts toward the front of the house. If she can glimpse the back of their heads as they run away, their clothes even, she'll know them. She knows all the boys in this town. All the boys and their mothers.

They'd screamed something. *Gekke heg*, she thinks: crazy hedge. What a strange thing to scream before throwing cobblestones. Was there something in the yard, with the bushes? No, she realizes as she turns onto the path that leads to the front of the house. One boy is still standing there, though the others have run off. He is a small boy, with bright blond curls. His mouth is gaping wide as if he's spotted a sea monster.

Heks, she thinks. That is what they'd cried. Witch. A witch, they'd called her. A crazy witch.

"Crone!" The small boy cries now again, before running off to catch up with his friends.

She stops where she is, a rock under her toe. She takes a few steps of retreat, fearing that perhaps they didn't really run away. Maybe they are waiting. Maybe they are hiding behind a tree, waiting to see if a man was in the house to protect her. They'd called her a witch. The neighborhood boys had come to taunt her.

But why? She'd been called other names, and maybe less flattering names. But never this. Stones thrown, curses hurled.

What had she done to offend someone? She could think of nothing. Since she'd gotten round in her belly she rarely left her property. A friend from a neighboring farm took her eggs to market for her, brought her goods back home.

Has something happened in the town? she wonders. She had heard rumblings of a renewed war between the Remonstrants and the Counter-Remonstrants, but what had this to do with her? Could it be that the Spanish have won the southern wars and have returned? It could be that. Spaniards.

She runs into the house to look around for anything that could condemn her. What will they look for? What will they take? What is there to protect?

There's another noise outside and she jolts. It is not loud; maybe it isn't anything but the wind. But she can't stay here. What if the boys return? What if more are coming? She grasps her belly and speaks to the babe inside, "We're okay. We'll be okay. I will get you somewhere safe."

There's nothing to take, she thinks, nothing worth saving. But where can she go? Who will protect them? When the Spaniards were here last, her mother and cousins had hidden at her church. But will they take her there, now that she carries a bastard child?

THE MOUTH

The distant Westerkerk bell mingles in De Wallen with the louder Oude Kerk bells and the Zuiderkerk bells—to make a thunderous racket between the ears of Jan Fetchet, lying in his hay bed in the storage loft of the Waag, the old town's weigh house, attempting to bury his aching head under a sack of millet.

Jesus, they chime as if to announce the world's end, he thinks, pulling his millet sack closer. There is a sudden eruption in the hay beside him, like the rising of Poseidon from the sea. He watches and soon recognizes the many folds of skirt and petticoat he'd crawled his way through last night, the undone blouse, the nest of blond hair falling out of the white cap. . . .

"Ooooh, ma poupée," the beast moans happily as she throws her arms conjugally about his shoulders. "There you are, you handsome charmer. Come back into my arms."

"My lady, my lady," he sputters, starting to push himself out of the hay, while attempting to ease her back to her side of the loft. "I don't even know your name."

"You make me laugh." She speaks hoarsely, her lips chalky with the dust of sleep. "You make me laugh," she says again before proving her statement with a series of great hacking laughs, like some kind of elderly mule coughing.

"Really," says Fetchet, as he pushes her off. "What hour bell is that? I was supposed to be up for the first. I'm late to my work, and, God forgive me, I remember nothing of last night."

He rises to discover he is wearing no pants, and spends several moments prowling through the hay to find them. His head pounds. He puts one hand to his temple and presses there to still the ache. His mouth tastes as if a rat has visited in the night. When he breathes into his palm, the full stink of the canals comes through his nostrils.

The wench in his bed keeps laughing as though he'd made another joke. As soon as he's located his pants, though, she sits up soberly for a moment and remembers: "But you owe me seven stivers." To accentuate her demand, she claws her abundant curls away from her face, holds her nest up like a flaming crown, and blinks her narrow yellow eyes to seem fierce.

Fetchet stands with one leg in, one leg out of his pants, his right hand still pressed to his aching head. "Well, that makes perfect sense," he says, while he attempts to pull the second pant leg into its rightful place with his free hand. Finding it impossible to tie the drawstrings into a knot with a single hand, he at last removes the hand from his temple and a powerful moan escapes his lips. His pants fall again. He reaches down and riffles through his pocket and finds his purse. He tosses it to her, but she doesn't reach out to catch it. It clanks to the floor, full as it is with the money he has lately earned from setting up all the provisions for the festive anatomy. "Take what you will."

"Better cover up that scrawny little bum of yours," she says, grabbing it and counting out her coins, pocketing a couple extra. "Or I'll take another bite out of it, fee or no fee." She begins to crawl toward him, tossing her hair about like a pony. Fetchet grabs his purse before she can filch another coin and tosses on his cloak, then climbs down the ladder of the loft, into the busy weigh hall, through the room full of traders and merchants, even as she's still following, pulling on her own clothes, taunting, "Come on back and I'll give you the next romp for free!"

Out in the brisk air and the busy square in front of the weigh house he has just exited, he stuffs his purse back into his pocket. He passes the line of horses tied up before the building, cups some water out of their trough, brings it to his lips, and gargles, spitting onto the dirt. One horse startles and he uses the mane to dry his hand. The trollop follows him into the square and when she catches up with him, she says, "Aw, you rush too much," trying to administer a parting kiss.

He pushes her off, saying, "Come now. You already earned your stivers."

She manages to plant one on him nonetheless, right on his lips, and after she pulls away at last, he watches her saunter off, dizzy and smiling, as though a love affair has begun. When she waves her plump fingers at him in final parting, he suppresses the bile in the back of his throat. He is reminded yet again of the sins of too much beer.

This time he dunks his full head into the horse trough, lets the frigid water wash over his face, and scrubs his mouth with both hands. He shivers, but he's awake now. Just as he's straightening, and feeling the stiffness of his aching back, he hears a voice calling from across the square. A young messenger is upon him. "You are Jan Fetchet, are you not?" says the boy.

"Who's asking?" Fetchet replies.

"I have a note from one T. Rotzak, a sailor on the East India ship *Lioness* for the curio dealer Jan Fetchet. A vendor on the market pointed me toward you. Are you Jan Fetchet, mister? If not, can you tell me where I find him?"

Fetchet knows the name Rotzak well; it's one of the sailors who supplies him with curiosities. "Yes, yes, you have found the right Jan. Did he already pay you for your troubles?"

"He did, sire," says the boy, before slapping the note into Fetchet's palm. The boy shifts from foot to foot as Fetchet reads the note, which is short and to the point.

"Take down two notes," he tells the messenger. "One is to Rotzak, the other to Master van Rijn on the Sint Antoniesbreestraat, the painter who runs the academy in the House of Uylenburgh."

The uninterested boy scribbles two notes that are dictated to him, shows them to Fetchet for approval, and then extends his hand for payment. Fetchet reaches into his still-heavy purse and hands the boy two doits. The messenger bows and speeds off through the crowded square. Within seconds, he has vanished.

Now, on to business, thinks Fetchet. The meat from the butcher, the cheese from the cheese market, breads from the baker, vegetables from the grocer, and then corpse from the executioner. When the fishmonger killer Joep van de Gheyn dangles from his rope, all they'll have to do is cut him down, so he'll drop right into Fetchet's cart.

Poor doomed Joep, thinks Fetchet as he starts out of the Nieuwmarkt. Well, at least there is one man in Amsterdam who's wickeder than me.

THE MIND

"Ah, there you go," says René Descartes, who is in the midst of negotiating the price of a lamb on the Kalverstraat with the cheapest of the half dozen butchers when the Westerkerk bell rings, its chimes reverberating down the narrow alley and through the shambles. "The church bells are tolling once again, which means it's a half hour now that we've been haggling."

The ringing of the bells incites a sudden lowing of the cattle up the byway. "Remarkable," says Descartes. "The animals are more attuned than the men."

"I agree, sire," says the butcher, a pleasantly ruddy-cheeked man with a giant belly and shock of white hair. "As they say, a friend is always better than money in the purse."

Descartes isn't quite so sure what level of sarcasm was intended with this axiom, since he never met a Dutchman who'd choose a friend over a guilder. He stands for a moment, contemplating his response as the bells finish their tolls. "Then friends we are," he finally answers.

The butcher smiles, revealing the large gap between his two front teeth.

A city of so many Remonstrants and nonbelievers and yet still this constant catholic ringing of the bells, he muses as the butcher waits for his payment. They mount a revolt against the church, build a capital on the worship of the mighty guilder, and still they continue to count out their hours by the church tower.

They are prosperous, though, these Amsterdammers, beyond all imagining. Yet so damn cheap—one has to wrangle over everything. He counts the coins in his palm one more time. Hadn't he paid half this amount not two weeks ago to this selfsame butcher?

Wait, though. His servant had mentioned the new exchange rate from guilders to livres, and he has just received payment for his "Meditations" in livres. Did the servant say the markets had crested? Was that the word he'd used: "crested"? Everyone in this town speaks the tradesman's argot, don't they?

Now then, he was becoming confused. Was *he* the one being stingy? Perhaps it was the other way around, and a week ago he'd paid twice as much? Descartes, a world-renowned mathematician, baffled by this utterly simple matter, hands over all his coins. "You're right. We must not waste our youth in bargaining."

The butcher nods with a smirk and, after pocketing the money, leaves to collect the animal. He should learn to put the servants in charge of these tasks, Descartes berates himself; they're more familiar with simple mathematics amid such trading chaos. Still, it is so troublesome to have to explain to them repeatedly that it isn't the *meat* he's after.

While the butcher is collecting the carcass, the mathematician leans down to pick up one of the stivers that fell from his purse onto the street.

"Monsieur Descartes," comes a voice from behind, immediately followed by a heavy clap on the back. "I see you're returned to the metropolis from the bog. Well, at least you don't look too much the peasant."

The man addressing him is so tall that it takes the diminutive Frenchman a moment to look all the way up to his face. On the way there, he takes in the silky finery of a true Dutch dandy: his black French silk shoes adorned with black flowers, white stockings and breeches, a doublet of glazed linen with paned sleeves, and a cloak adorned with loop lace, thrown open as if he is not the least bit cold, plus a wide-brimmed hat embellished with feathers from . . . well, yes indeed, a peacock.

"Good afternoon, Mijnheer Visscher," says Descartes, not yet placing this acquaintance's first name. "What, may I ask, brings a man of your high breeding into this bloody byway?"

"I should ask the same of you, my friend. It's rare that I bump into intellectuals in the butchers' quarter. My excuse is that it's an easy shortcut to Sint Antoniesbreestraat, where I am to join an art connoisseur's circle at the Uylenburgh academy. We are to hear from a painter whose name is on everyone's lips, some Harmanszoon or other. Do you know the name?"

"I don't believe I do."

"Apparently he's impressed Huygens with his biblical paintings and now he's doing burgher portraits. Truth be told, I've arranged all kinds of activities for myself today simply so that I can avoid the festival. The streets are too thick with foreigners."

The comment stings, since Descartes himself is, of course, a foreigner, but he suspects the dandy doesn't mean this as a slight.

"My excuse is, as usual, work. I'm doing a little amateur anatomical research to help with my search for the soul in the body," says Descartes. He sees his companion's face contort into what could be disgust for either the subject matter or the academic pretention. He adds, "I find the sights and smells of the Amsterdam markets pleasing, and the butchers are such clever tradesmen."

Meantime, Descartes has managed to place the name: Nicholas Visscher. That is it—the cartographer. Cousin to the merchant poet Roemer Visscher. They had all met last winter at one of those grandiose parties at one of those oversized Amstel mansions.

"Speaking of which, I presume we'll see you tonight at the anatomy?" Visscher continues. "I believe you will appreciate our Tulpius—a kindred spirit. He intends to elaborate upon Galen, I'm told."

Ah, Tulp, yes. Descartes has frequently been assured that he has much in common with the town praelector, a comparison he finds to be more than a little irksome. For he is a great mathematician, destined, he is sure, to transform scientia, and the praelector is a mere city doctor, dabbling in autopsies.

It is at this moment that Descartes realizes he has caused himself some trouble by leaving his lodging at the Oud Prins today. The city's chief praelector, that selfsame Tulp, had in fact invited him to the annual anatomy lesson and he had declined, saying he had planned to spend the week in Deventer with his friend and fellow researcher Henri Reneri. Now he had been spotted by Visscher, though, who no doubt would mention the encounter in passing to his cousin Roemer, who was sure to mention it to Tulpius, his own doctor and dear friend. Word traveled too quickly in these elite city circles.

"I have heard a great deal of praise for your praelector, though we have not yet had the opportunity to meet," Descartes answers. "I declined the invitation because I thought I should be out of town this week. Of course, I would not pass up such an important opportunity otherwise. Alas, I have already missed my chance."

"Don't be silly. I will arrange a seat for you," announces Visscher, "right in the front ring with the nobility. My cousin will be very glad to see you again, as well, I'm sure. And I suspect you and the great Tulpius will have quite a bit in common."

"I understand he sets about to debunk William Harvey's blood circulation theory," Descartes continues pleasantly, though he wishes Visscher might've curbed his generosity just this once. "One finds it hard to envision the way he imagines the heart to pump, but these are indeed very important discoveries he is making across the Channel. His logic is a bit Aristotelian for my tastes, but we must credit him."

"You would know better than I," Visscher says, as if it made no difference to him one way or another. "I say, it's good that you're in town. An educated man should not be keeping company with goats and country women for too long." He winks, clapping Descartes on the back once again, this time so hard it almost makes Descartes lose his balance.

"It is not idle time," Descartes defends himself, though he has no need to. "I'm working on a response to Golius at the moment, which might interest you, as it concerns his observations on refraction."

"Indeed, I should like very much to read it," says Visscher. "Though when will I have time? I spend all my daylight hours hiring new shipping men and managers. Who could have guessed a few years ago that we would grow so quickly? Everyone in the world, it seems, now needs to own a map."

Descartes considers how he will change his plans to get to the anatomy tonight. He had intended to spend the day in his quarters writing and dissecting his carcass. Now he will not have sufficient time to do both.

As if on cue, the butcher returns with the dead lamb slung across his arms. He lays it down at Descartes's feet.

"Do you plan to sup before the grand feast?" Visscher wonders aloud.

Descartes's answer—reminding the cartographer of his amateur anatomy—is drowned out by an eruption of shouting voices at a nearby meat stall. A boy guiding a drove of sheep shoves past the men, cursing them for blocking the way. Visscher shakes his head in disapproval.

"These men are too much like the beasts they handle," he declares. "I have no business here; I must not tarry. Do not worry about your ticket to the anatomy. I will get it for you and meet you there. We will count on you tonight, then."

"Yes, I appreciate that," Descartes answers. "Yes, of course, until tonight." He bows low before the Dutchman, who is already making his way down the lane.

THE EYES

Rembrandt Harmenszoon van Rijn is meanwhile in the studio in his painting academy on the Sint Antoniesbreestraat, examining a bolt of linen he bought this morning from a sailcloth merchant by the wharves. He is impressed; it is a strong, smooth, fine weave, though he will need to cut it down to the size of canvas he intends to paint. It's a vast amount of fabric for a single painting—a much larger piece than he's ever used before—and it was a huge disbursement.

Usually, he'd have bought two strips of ticking and joined them together using a slightly thicker ground, and saved those guilders, but he doesn't want any faint lines to mar the continuity of this particular work. It is the biggest commission he's received since he's been in Amsterdam, some six months already, and he can't afford to let the little things destroy its promise.

The bells are ringing in the Zuiderkerk, just across the Oude Schans. It's a reminder that the *liefhebbers* will be arriving at any moment for their weekly studio visit with the master. This is yet another one of the tedious requirements of his new station as the master of Uylenburgh's academy. He must appear to be pleased and courteous when these moneyed art lovers come to traipse around his studio; he must kiss their gloves and smile and bow, in hopes that someday they might deign to buy a painting.

It's infuriating to the painter. He took this position in Uylenburgh's academy, thinking he'd sell better in this art-loving city than in his mill town of Leiden. As it turned out, joining Uylenburgh's studio wasn't exactly an appointment. He had to "lend" his dealer a thousand guilders to become an "investor" in the business.

He recently learned, too, that he wasn't technically allowed to work as a master in Amsterdam, because of city regulations that prohibited outsiders from joining the Sint Lucas Guild, the artists' guild. To keep a painting practice in the city, he had to work for a studio for a minimum of two years. In this sense, he is indentured to Uylenburgh for the time being until he can get his own membership in the guild.

In the meantime, Uylenburgh is taking 50 percent of every commission fee in exchange for "studio overhead, guild membership, room and board, and connections." And he still needs to pay for materials out of his own purse? Rembrandt feels queasy thinking about how much money he's laid out for all these supplies, between the sailcloth and the minerals.

At least some of the money from the group portrait should start to roll in later this week. Four members of the guild have already posed for their portraits, Tulp and two more are scheduled for sittings, and an apprentice, Jacob Colevelt, has been in negotiations with Uylenburgh about joining the group. At a hundred guilders a head for the ordinary members plus one hundred fifty from the central figure, Dr. Tulp, he calculates to himself, he's due at least eight hundred fifty guilders, or maybe nine hundred fifty if Colevelt joins in.

"Tomas, come help me lift this bolt," he instructs one of his apprentices, who is preparing the ground for the painting, using a recipe from Italy, with a great deal of red ocher, that called for rabbit skin glue. The rabbit was slaughtered at dawn and the fat extracted from its skin. The rabbit itself is now in the cook's hands for tonight's stew.

The apprentice wipes his knife on his smock and follows his master's instructions. "On the count of three," says Rembrandt. "One, two—now, let's bring it toward the easel—three."

They heft the long bolt, which in truth isn't heavy as much as it is unwieldy, and carry it to the center of the room, laying it on the floor between two easels Tomas has been using to make a study of one of Rembrandt's paintings. The original is on one easel. Tomas's copy is on the second.

Once he lets go of the bolt, Rembrandt straightens and takes a moment to observe his pupil's work. The subject is Christ's supper at Emmaus. It depicts the moment when the resurrected Jesus, who has traveled a long way with his disciples, incognito, reveals himself over a meal at an inn. Rembrandt isn't satisfied with his own painting, which shows the disciples in light and Christ in shadow, and he feels that this contrast seems too forced. But what can he do? Earlier work is earlier work. He can return to the subject later, improve on it as best he can.

Tomas, anyway, is progressing, it seems. There is a good sense of volume to the space in the inn; the two disciples and Christ are clearly fore-grounded and the apprentice has managed to create enough perspective in this cramped space so that the servant appears to be well in the background, disengaged from the action.

"You've come a long way in the last few days," he tells the youth, who he sees has turned slightly wan since his master stopped to observe his work. "You've done a particularly good job of rendering Cleopas's facial features." Indeed, the surprise on the disciple's face is palpable as he realizes that the man he took for a vagabond has risen from the dead three days after his crucifixion.

"You're still having trouble with the chiaroscuro," Rembrandt goes on. "This kneeling disciple is too light, if Christ is to be so profoundly silhouetted. You must think of all the characters in relation to the source of light and how and where it illuminates their features."

"Yes, master. It was my intention to get his features correct first, and then work in the shadowing."

Rembrandt thinks the apprentice is just defending himself and does not grasp that this is an important bit of guidance. "It's not simply a matter of technique, it's a matter of narrative," he elaborates. "Remember that the disciples have been walking with Jesus in the dark for hours before they came upon this village and sat down to eat. It is only when the innkeeper lights the lamp that their revelation comes. The light is central. The light *and* the surrounding darkness."

This time Tomas doesn't chance it. "Yes, I do see what you're saying. I will work on that, sir. I have quite a way to go with it yet."

"Do not be frustrated if you don't get it right away," Rembrandt says, putting a comforting hand on the apprentice's shoulder and remembering, for a quick instant, what it was like to be in this boy's shoes some dozen years ago. "It takes a while. Keep working on it." He takes a few steps back. "Very well; we'll need to move these two works off the easels to have enough room for the new painting's stretcher. We'll put your painting in the ancillary chamber so you can continue there. Think only about the source of light. That will create all the drama you need."

His other apprentice, Joris, is standing at the pigment table in the corner, surrounded by ceramic bowls and glass cups containing his ordered minerals: Kassel earth, umber, red lake, vermilion, yellow ocher, red ocher, plus the lead for white and a particularly large quantity of bone char for the black. Some of the minerals have been precrushed and the apprentice just needs to mix the linseed oil into them, using a stone muller and palette knife. Others must be ground to a fine dust before they can be mixed with the binding medium.

He takes a few steps forward and looks at his own version of the supper at Emmaus. He went too far with the contrast, he thinks again. One can't see Christ's face; it's only Cleopas's reaction that can be seen clearly and that reaction is pure fear. That's how he had read the story in Luke when he was younger—imagining primarily the shock and terror of facing a man revived from the grave. A few years older now, he thinks perhaps he miscalculated Cleopas's reaction. He might have been just as awed as he was fearful; he might, at least, have looked more convinced of divinity.

Rembrandt lifts his own *Emmaus* from the easel and carries it into the room where Tomas has taken the copy. There, on a divan, is a completely nude woman leaning on a pile of pillows. Her hair is drawn back loosely around her head, and a few flowers have been woven into her messy curls. A sheet covers her ankles, and that is all.

She barely notices the intrusion, as she's busy biting her lips to bring out more red. "Your new boy is too nervous," she tells Rembrandt blithely, barely glancing across the room at the apprentice holding the sketch pad and charcoal. "His hands are shaking so much he won't be able to draw a straight line."

Rembrandt leans his painting against a wall and crosses to her, seating himself next to her on the divan. He inches his fingers up her thigh and then grabs a fistful of her flesh.

"Well, luckily, there are no straight lines to draw here." She squirms but doesn't pull away. "Curves all."

She giggles and falls onto her back. He kisses her breasts in full view of his pupils. Then he sits up and surveys her body. "Your skin is too olive. Let's get some powder. I want a pale Danaë. Very pale and virginal."

"Though we know I am neither."

"We are working in allegory, my dear."

There is a knock at the door. "Enter!" Rembrandt calls, sitting up.

His maid, Femke, calls from behind the door, "Master, the *lief-hebbers* have arrived."

"Thank you, Femke," he says without turning to look.

Femke clears her throat. "Also, master, young Isaac would like me to relay to you that he will continue with the etching plates, but he requests permission to join you in the studio now, if it is not too early. And also, sire, the surgeon Nicolaes Tulp will arrive in an hour for his sitting. His wife sent a note requesting you return him to her promptly after he is done. By then the town center will be mobbed for Justice Day."

Rembrandt turns to see the terrified expression on his servant's face as she enters the room and curtsies to him. She is accustomed to his women by now, but still she blushes.

"I have been expecting the *liefhebbers* since the hour mark, so perhaps they can wait for me a moment," he answers not unkindly. He stands, brushes off his shirtsleeves, and moves away from the model, to ease Femke's discomfort. "I will not detain Tulp; please send word to assure his wife. Tell Isaac he's free to come upstairs after he has checked the etching press, but I believe we're low on wax. The visiting artists arrive in the next hour, do they not?"

"Yes, Master Rembrandt," she says. "They will want a tour of the studio."

"Please ask Sabine to lay out suitable attire for me. And explain to them that we use real models for our mythical figures so they are not shocked by our model here."

Her mouth turns up into the hint of a smile. "Can I bring you some beer, master?"

"Yes, Femke, my tankard has gone empty. Send the *liefhebbers* in after that is done."

Femke curtsies again but she doesn't leave, though her gaze fixes on the floor. "I'm sorry to prolong my disturbance, master," she adds.

"Yes? What else is there?"

"A note has come for you from that scurrilous wharf rat they call Fetchet."

Rembrandt laughs. "Femke, what has he done to you?"

"Nothing, master. It's just what I hear about him from the other girls."

"He's a curio dealer, Femke, which means he's required to be a scurrilous wharf rat. How else would he manage to scavenge those exotic oddities I seek?" He holds out a hand so that she will bring him the note.

Femke takes a few steps forward and holds a piece of paper out to him as if holding a dead mouse by its tail.

He laughs, accepting it. "Now I'm amply intrigued."

Rembrandt passes out of the room and back into his main studio. He reads what it says, then uses a piece of charcoal to write a response on the back of the note, and hands it back to Femke. "I've agreed to welcome him before noon. Let him up when he arrives."

First, to make himself presentable. He is still in his painter's shirt and black wool breeches, sans doublet or jerkin. Perhaps he should put on something more befitting of this elegant audience. On the floor to one side of the studio lie several items of clothing he's borrowed from Uylenburgh to pose for a new self-portrait: a black cape, a fur-lined cloak, a pair of long black riding gloves, a soldier's pewter gorget, and a bright red embroidered cloak. All of them look like costumes rather than clothes: too pompous and absurd.

He finds a hand mirror on the side table and inspects his face. He tilts the mirror to try and catch some small amount of light from the dour sky. His face seems pinched, his nose too bulbous, his lips too pursed, his brow already wrinkling at twenty-six. The dark curls of hair on his chest sprout about the untied neckline and his chin could use a shave. His hair is not kempt either. Boundless, red, curly, it's always a thicket through which no comb dares venture. He places a small amount of etching wax into his palms and presses his hands against his hair, attempting to give it shape. Perhaps a cap would help keep his hair in place, he thinks.

He uses the remaining wax to pat down the stray whiskers on his chin. Wild as his hair on his head can be, what emerges from his chin is stubborn, unyielding, and patchy as a mangy dog's. He always tries to trim off what comes in except for a thin shelf of hair under his bottom lip and the red fuzz that manages to find fertile soil over his top lip. He finds a white scarf and wraps it around his neck, adding what he hopes will be a touch of formality to his attire—since no ruff is to hand.

One last glance in the looking glass before someone catches him in the act: let us try not to be too vain.

THE BODY

Joep and Aris sit in silence, unable to ignore the sound of the crowd assembling outside in the square. The sound builds and builds until they either have to put their hands over their ears or else talk to each other.

"I guess they'll be jeering at us?" says his cell mate, Joep the tailor.

Aris looks up from the floor to see if his cell mate is asking a question or making a joke. For the first time since they've been together in the cell, it occurs to Aris how frail and small his cell mate seems, and how his shoulders curve inward as if to armor his chest. Or maybe all those years of sewing have bent him this way.

The tailor adds plaintively, "It's unnecessary, don't you think? We're already damned."

"You've never been to a hanging?" Aris asks.

The tailor shakes his head, frowning, as if the suggestion is absurd. "I would find such a thing very unsavory."

Aris laughs.

"What?" asks Joep. "What's funny?"

Seeing the truly earnest expression on the tailor's face, Aris laughs even harder. "So, today's your first hanging and it's your own. You have to admit it's a little bit funny."

The tailor shifts across his plank of wood, not finding any comedy in the matter.

"I've performed on many a Justice Day," says Aris, a little proudly. "I was even hauled up in Haarlem once. They whipped me and branded me and put the noose around my neck and just left me on the rope. Public exposure for three days."

Joep has turned pale, as if he's just realized he's been condemned. He tugs at the collar of his shirt. His breathing is shallow and Aris thinks he might start to cough or sneeze again, or both. "The magistrate will still hear me, won't he?" Joep says, mostly to himself. "I didn't really speak my case when I should have. I still have time, don't I?"

"The magistrate can't do anything for us now, tailor. But don't fret. If you're innocent as you say, you'll soon be welcomed in glory. Or if you're guilty as sin like I am, you'll have a good time in perdition with me. At least this way, you've got witnesses to your death, and you won't be freezing in an alley all alone."

Aris's voice has turned hoarse and weary. He has not comforted the tailor, who still looks pitiably afraid. The poor man nods slowly but keeps clutching his collar. He rocks back and forth.

"If you don't mind, I'm going to kneel and pray," he says, after some consideration.

Aris shrugs. The tailor moves slowly from the bench to the floor, his knees finding the impressions in the dirt they've made several times already. Once he's clasped his hands together, he looks over his shoulder at Aris.

"Why don't you join me?" he says.

"I told you before, tailor, I gave up that bad habit in my youth."

"I know you've had your disagreements with God, but remember that he cares for all souls, and he is always listening. If you repent now, he will hear you."

Aris shakes his head. "I hear you when you're down there, Joep. You're not repenting. You're still telling God that he should know you're innocent. What kind of redemption are you going to get with that?"

"God knows the truth. He knows I am no sinner. He will protect me."

"Go to it then, tailor. Time's a-wasting."

Aris has been in many a cell with many a man who's claimed his innocence. He's done it himself when he was innocent, and sometimes when he wasn't. He knows what desperation looks like. This tailor is so fragile and timid it is hard to imagine that a fly would be concerned in his company, let alone a burly fishmonger. For himself, Aris has nothing to say to God. He made his peace with his fate a long time ago.

The tailor begins to pray in a whisper: "O God, holy redeemer, who wills not the death of a sinner but rather wills that he be converted and live, I beseech you, through the intercession of the blessed Virgin Mary . . . hear my case. I have sinned, Lord, I have coveted a married man's wife, but you, all-seeing God, know my sins have not transgressed beyond thinking. Lord . . . if you hear me now . . ."

Looking at the tailor's back, Aris thinks of his father's back—so often curved into that same posture, hands cupped into pious striving. The last time he'd ever prayed had been by his father's side. But that was a lifetime ago.

"Oh merciful Jesus, lover of souls, I beseech you, by the agony of your most sacred heart, and by the sorrows of your immaculate mother, wash clean in your blood the sinners who are to die this day . . ."

Aris stops listening to the tailor. He had not tried to retract his confession. He knew that this crime was bad enough that they'd try to put him back into the house of corrections again, and he couldn't live like that, like a man in a cage. Once in Utrecht when he'd got eight years, he'd planned to stab a guard so they'd give him the rope. Better that than to live in a rasp house. He would've done it, too, if he hadn't felt sorry for his jailors.

"Look down, Lord, upon the sinners in this cell. See my innocence and redeem this sinner who sits beside me, refusing to seek your forgiveness. It is his ignorance that makes him proud. He is a weak sinner, like me, Lord, and deserves your utmost compassion—"

"Hey," Aris breaks in. "Don't waste your breath on me, tailor. Save yourself, and let the rest of us damned be damned."

Joep opens one eye to see how angry he's made his cell mate. His hands are still clasped and his head still tucked. "I beseech you for the grace to move this sinner, who is in danger of going to hell, to repent," he continues tentatively, closing his eyes again and bowing lower to the ground in case Aris decides to hit him. "I ask this because of my trust in your great mercy. Amen."

The tailor makes a final bow to the floor and sits back on his haunches. When he opens his eyes, he turns and smiles serenely at Aris. That smile with all its solace makes Aris want to spit at the tailor or say something cruel to put him back in his place, to remind him they're equals: both destined for the hangman in a matter of minutes.

"You waste your prayers," says Aris.

"Compassion is never wasted," Joep says calmly. "You can join me in his glory. But first you must repent. You must confess with an open soul."

Aris doesn't answer the tailor. He moves across the bench to get some distance, so he doesn't hit the prayerful bastard. Then, finding this is not far enough, stands and walks to the corner of the cell. "I'm finished with this life. I'm ready for my executioner."

"You can still receive God's glory," says the tailor. "Confess and you'll be redeemed."

Aris feels vengeful blood rushing through his whole arm down to his bandaged stump. His phantom hand tightens into a hard fist, the nails of his nonexistent fingers digging into his imaginary palm. He feels the muscle in his forearm tighten, and the subsequent pain of the stymied force. He's standing in the corner of the cell, his back toward his cell mate, when Joep's name is called from the hall.

The tailor stands with dignity and puts a hand on Aris's shoulder. When Aris turns around, the tailor reaches for his good hand to shake it. "I will see you on the scaffold. Do not waste these final moments. If you confess all before the Holy Father, your soul will fly free to heaven and your human vessel can be left behind."

Aris regards his cell mate coldly, as he hears the jangling keys and their footsteps drawing near.

"If not for yourself," the tailor adds, hearing them coming for him, "at least say a prayer for my sake."

At last, the guards are unlocking the door, the sound of it unbearable for both of the convicts. Joep steps back to admit them into the cell. He doesn't fight them when they grab him by the arms and yank him into the hall and put the leg-irons on him.

"Hey, tailor," Aris says.

Joep turns. Aris wants to say something comforting, something that will make the tailor go bravely to the scaffold. Instead, he winks—a conspirator's wink, one condemned man to another. Joep looks as though he's been slapped. He shakes his head in befuddlement as the guards shove him down the hall.

Painting diagnosis: Rembrandt's *Anatomy Lesson of Dr. Nicolaes Tulp*, 1632

The painting is secured now, its breadth balanced between the two easels, its full bulk resting comfortably on their wide pine planks. I'm so pleased we decided to use the two easels instead of just one. Looking at it here in the studio, there would've been no other way for it to balance. It is such a big body.

I'm impressed all over again by its sheer bulk, which dwarfs me, and even Claes, who is six foot two. When he was seated before it this morning with his scope, for a split second it appeared as though he himself were among the surgeons. I prepare myself for many such strange, passing illusions.

You forget, when it hangs on the gallery wall, that the figures are all life-size. Nine life-size men, including the corpse. Today I begin with the painting diagnosis.

I have parted the curtains on the skylight to allow daylight to fall upon its surface, as per my instructions. Claes says twenty minutes max each day for two weeks. "Let it breathe," were his words, actually, as if it were a young Bordeaux. His approach is ninety-nine percent science, one part mysticism. It's that one percent that worries me.

Yet, I have drawn back the shade. And there is miraculously sun today. On the way to work the rain ceased. It has been four hours now and still it has not started again. Here we both are. The painting and I, soaking in daylight.

So, we begin.

Day One, painting restoration. Mauritshuis, the Royal Picture Gallery, under the direction of Claes van den Dorft. My name is Pia de Graaf and I'm senior conservator for the museum. Today we begin a two-week restoration of the Rembrandt van Rijn masterwork *The Anatomy Lesson of Dr. Nicolaes Tulp*, the cynosure of the royal collection.

The painting was commissioned by the Surgeons' Guild of Amsterdam in 1632, and hung in their guild chamber in the Waag (weighing house) along with other important paintings, next to the chimney. This museum, then called the Royal Cabinet of Paintings, acquired the work in 1828 after a kind of ideological bidding war against the Rijksmuseum. Though it was passionately argued by that institution that the painting should always live in Amsterdam, where it was painted in 1632, our director countered successfully that it was in fact a key treasure of the Dutch state, one of the most prized works of our Golden Age. Both are true: this is the first painting that catapulted Rembrandt to fame, back in 1632 in Amsterdam, making him a famous painter in that city and also a prized son of Holland. Of course, it could just as easily be argued that it deserves to be in any collection in the world nowadays; it is the first major work that made Rembrandt's name.

The painting was lined three times from 1785 to 1877, and then wax lined in 1877 and 1908. The varnish was regenerated five times and there is a record of ten cleanings, the last four in 1877, 1908, 1946, and 1951. The last time we took it off the wall was in 1996, so while we are cleaning it and removing some of the darkening varnish, this is an opportunity to examine the work and possibly to make a number of new observations.

We have secured funding for the current restoration and examination based on new evidence that leads us to believe we can make certain new discoveries about the painting. Recently, researchers in Amsterdam discovered in a 1632 *justitieboek* that details the entire criminal history of the dead man in the painting, one Adriaen Adriaenszoon, alias Aris Kindt (or Aris the Kid).

At the same time, a physician in Groningen has recently conducted a medical experiment to dissect an arm so he could compare it to the dissected arm in this portrait. Contrary to the opinion of medical historians heretofore, who criticized the painting for certain anatomical inaccuracies, this recent study reveals that Rembrandt actually got it mostly right. Together, these new pieces of evidence give us reason to believe that Rembrandt may have worked from life on this painting. That is, he used a real cadaver as a model, and it's even possible he may have known the dead man in question.

Therefore, the purpose of our current restoration is twofold: first and most practical is to remove a layer of old varnish, which has dimmed aspects of its coloring and possibly obscured certain elements of the painting. We want to bring the painting back to life, give it more vitality—health—as it were. My strategy will be to do as little to the painting as possible. Only to repair what needs to be repaired and to remove anything that's been added that appears to be unnecessary. To bring out the painting that is already there and to eliminate any obscuring values.

The second purpose is investigative. We seek to explore how this new evidence informs our understanding of the painting. People sometimes invent stories about works of art based just on other stories; but as conservators we use the painting itself to tell the story in the same way that a forensic scientist might—looking for evidence of different possible scenarios. I will try to get a response from the painting itself. To look at it in good light, to write down what I see.

Claes likes to say we are conducting our own dissection of the dissection masterpiece. Rembrandt, as it were, under the surgeon's scalpel. The first step, the most important step, is simply to look at the painting. The work this first week is really about looking. To see the painting in natural light, with a torch, a head loupe, a scope, and much stronger light to get a sense of its physicality.

Then we can compare what we see with the naked eye to what we discover using x-radiographs. To figure out what is there. We already have an image in our minds from looking at it on the wall, but what can we discover from the brushstrokes? From the palette? From examining the painting technique, the use of pentimenti? The ground, the underpainting? Were there parts that changed over time? Or when he was painting?

Sometimes, as a conservator, I spend hours and hours just looking at a painting and very little time actually working on it. Every day, I come in and I look at the painting and I try to understand it a little bit more, before I do actual painting of any kind. I try not to do any painting at all, if I can avoid it. It is the painter's job to paint. It is the restorer's job to resist painting. You try to still your hand, to avoid using the brush. You must do as little as possible for the maximum possible effect.

You look and you look and you look, and then you have to decide what the goal is. For me, the decision to use my brush at all will be limited to fixing damages. But to get to that point, I first need to understand what's meant to be in the picture and what's not. I can't be too speculative. I have to stick to the facts, to be able to talk about what you can prove or what you can see.

The doctors of the seventeenth century used to talk about "ocular testimony" when they looked at a body. That's what we're seeking here, too, with this technical study. We can devise our story, but it has to be based on what we can actually see.

II

THE HEART

So many stones came. They broke big things and small things. Bowls my mother made, the milk jug, eggs ready for market. There were never much to break and there's nothing left to break anymore, that's certain.

Everyone in Leiden knew Adriaen were to be strung up before word got to me. That's why the boys called me witch. That's why the stones came. They pulled cobblestones out the lane and threw them at my house. Broke windows. Sent things flying. "Witch!" they called me. "Crone!"

The voices weren't just boys'. Some I knew from market, other times selling their wares. They were the same voices that shouted, "Clay pots, six for a stiver!" or "Goat's cheese! Goat's milk!" I could swear I heard Hendrijke the potter, and Maartje the wagoner's wife. Them were voices I knew. "Hag!" they screamed. "Whore."

There were no one else there but me, and, well, the babe in my belly. I've lived alone since Adriaen went. Mother died years ago and father left before her. I hired a man once to tend the mill for a time, but when the earnings dried up he left, willing. The mill didn't yield much and so I just tend to the animals, grow my patch of garden out back, manage the barn, and feed the chickens. The eggs bring a few stivers, and what little rye there is from the mill I ride to the bakers for barter. I never took money to lie with a man, no matter what them townsfolk like to say. Nor crafted any magic.

When I heard the first shouts, saw the stones, I ran to Doc Sluyter's. His family were the one sheltered my great-aunt in the Alteration. She were a Catholic, you know, and they accused her of idolatry. The doc were surprised when he saw the bulge under my apron. That's how long it's been since we've seen him. He hushed my screaming and said it weren't Spaniards this time. He sat me down and told his servant to leave us be.

"Adriaen was arrested in Amsterdam," he said, after I'd caught my breath. "They sentenced him to death, Flora. He's to go hanging. That's the news from Amsterdam."

He said it so quickly I didn't get his meaning.

"Your Adriaen," he said very slowly, "been caught in Amsterdam. They'll hang him now. That's why the townsfolk stone you. That's why they curse your house."

I said to the doc that he had to be wrong because they don't hang a man for fighting and thieving and that's all Adriaen ever did. Doc Sluyter shook his head. "He's gone too far this time," the doc said. "Tried to steal the cloak off a burgher. Used violence, they say. Tried to kill the man." The look on his face were like a closed door. "The hangman will string him up and feel no remorse."

I still don't know why he said that part, the part about "no remorse," because what does Doc Sluyter know about the hangman's heart? I knew Adriaen didn't try to kill someone. That weren't who he was. He were a weak and lost soul, my Adriaen, but he were never a cruel man, never like that: empty.

Then that door opened in the doc's soul and he looked into my eyes and his own eyes went moist.

"That child you're carrying," he went on in his deepest voice, nodding to my belly, "is going to be the child of a hanged man. The bastard child of a murderer."

That's when I put both hands on my belly to protect my unborn child. I got angry, 'cause a doctor knows that evil words over pregnant belly can split a babe in two and make it come out two headed. I told him, "Don't you talk so in front of my son."

I've always known he'll be a boy. From the way he sits in my belly and from the way he kicks right up against my ribs. I know, too, he'll look just like Adriaen. I already named him. He is Carel, a free man.

Doc Sluyter kept talking, but he turned his face away from me this time. "There's more," he said. "They won't bury him in Amsterdam. They'll put him to the gibbet."

I guess I fell down then, because when I opened my eyes next I were on his table. There were a lot of other men around me now, hovering like crows, all shaking their heads and clucking as if I were down with the black death. I could feel my chest and neck cupped. I could feel my skin tight and my wrists tingling where they'd stuck me. I heard one of them saying, "Isn't it a pity for that child?" The rest of them murmuring.

I pushed myself up from that table and brushed off the cups, the glass cracking on the ground. Doc Sluyter shushed me and told me I needed rest, but I told him I didn't want my unborn to be cleaved to pieces with their ominous words. The other men tried to hold me down, too, but I pushed back.

"It'll be dangerous at the mill house," said Doc, when I got to standing. "There are sure to be more stones."

Another one of them said, "We're only trying to protect you from the senseless fools out there who intend to hurt you. We know it's not your fault that your man was a murderer."

I told him, "Adriaen is no murderer. I knew him since he were a boy. You knew him, too. He were a child of this town, of Leiden. If the townsfolk won't claim him, they're as coldhearted as the executioner."

They stood in silence and not one of them tried to correct me.

"A mob is cruel," were all Doc said. "No reasoning with a mob about evil and goodness."

I left Doc's house, telling all them other crows not to follow.

The boys with their stones were there when I got home, like they'd said, so I went in through the side yard. That were Adriaen's yard once. We lived side by side in them houses by the Rhine.

I went in the back door, hiding in my own house. For the rest of the morning, when the peltings came, I moved behind the wall and wrapped my belly in a blanket to drown out the shouting.

Some of them stones came through the windows. That's how hard they threw, them boys. Them maids. They came into the house, thud, thud, crack. We don't have much and now so much is broken. But I could stand behind the hearth and the stones didn't hit us.

When it went quiet, I fixed things. I picked up the shards, the fallen chairs, overturned pitchers and mopped what had spilled. I collected the pieces and put them on a mantel.

Then it would start again and I would wait by the wall, singing to Carel in my belly. When it stopped, I'd tidy. When there were too many shards for the mantel, I put them into my apron. I took them out back so I could use them to border my garden.

There were a long stretch when the pelting stopped, and I thought maybe it were over. I listened to the silence. Then came a dark figure in the doorway. A black hat and cloak, a long carved cane.

With the light behind him, I could see no features of his face. I thought: all them curses have done their work. Death has come for me and the babe. Maybe from weakness, I mustered politeness. I said, please to come in and sit with us. I got up to heat the kettle.

Death walked in and sat at the table quietly, and when I brought him the cup of cider, I saw it were Father van Thijn from our church under that great black hat, that long sad face with his gray beard.

I got tired all over again, because I didn't want to argue with the priest or have to ask his blessing.

The father didn't take my cider. He looked around and saw all the broken pitchers and plates, shards on the mantel. It must've been him who'd told them to stop because finally it were really silent. I went flush with shame for us, me and Adriaen and our babe. Things are not right when a man of God has to visit a poor woman's cottage.

"We are in the Lord's hands," I said quietly. "He will protect us."

The father shook his head. He blurted out how it were wrong for people to believe in superstitions, witches, omens, and curses. He said it were wrong that the world were so backward and godless, even now in this modern century.

"The boys don't know better, but the townsfolk should," he said. "After all we've already been through, they should know." Father van Thijn talked about Jesus and love and compassion. He said, as he does in sermons, that the greatest sinners benefit most from forgiveness. "It was his crime," he said. "Now it's his death. But that'll be your cross to bear." In his old age, he said, he sees that only great love can overcome man's cruelty. Only true hearts, people with courage to love, people with a mind to forgiveness.

"You will need strength," the father said, as if he were coming to something, "but you must make the journey."

Then Father van Thijn took out his purse. He put coins on the table before me. It were more money than I'd ever seen all at once. My first thought: a man of God should not have such money.

"It's from the collections, Flora. For charitable works. Today it is for you. To help you and your family. Our church can spare it."

I thought he meant for the pots, the broken glass.

"For the sake of the child that will be born," he said. "You must leave this house. There will only be more stones and more curses. You must go to Amsterdam. To the town hall at the Dam. Tell them you are Adriaen's betrothed. Show them your belly. Tell them about our church, and take this letter I've written." He reached into his pocket and pulled out a note, sealed and stamped with red wax.

His betrothed? I were not his betrothed. Could a priest lie like that?

"And if you cannot prevent the execution, then at least you can . . . You'll bring him home to Leiden for a Christian burial in our church."

"Doc Sluyter said they call him a murderer."

Father van Thijn looked into my eyes. "Sometimes they do terrible things to make a man confess."

It hurt to hear that. "Confess? But fighting and thieving. That's all Adriaen ever did."

"Then perhaps there will be mercy." He touched the coins on the table. "Say that to the magistrate. Stand strong. Tell him what you know of Adriaen."

"You think words can save him?"

The answer in his eyes weren't certain. "You can take a barge across the Haarlemmermeer and be there before noon. That is what the money is for—for your journey."

To Amsterdam. "I've never left Leiden."

"I am going to send a boy from the church to accompany you. When you arrive in Amsterdam, hire a coach or a boat to take you both to the town hall. Time is short, but if you leave quickly, you can get there before the hanging. The boy will be outside waiting."

He lifted the coins from the table, one by one, took my hand in his hand, and placed the coins in my palm. "You must go, and you must go now, Flora. You must use your words carefully with the magistrate. You must convince him that Adriaen's soul can be swayed to goodness. Either way, you'll bring him back to Leiden."

"I never spoke to any magistrate."

He spoke very slowly. "You must do this, Flora. Only you can do this." He pressed the final coin into my hand. "Please." He placed the purse on the table.

I nodded, though I didn't fully understand what he meant. He stood and put a hand on my shoulder. "I'm sorry I didn't come sooner."

He stood up and put his hat back on his head. The shadows across his face made him look like Death again. I sat on my stool and wondered if it were all real or a dream. God does his work in so many ways, but we must never doubt him.

I knew that I had to do as the father instructed.

III

THE MOUTH

Ask any burgher in Amsterdam and he'll tell you: if there's an oddity or rarity you seek, I can put it into your hands. I'm a barterer,
a trader, and a broker in God's great bounty. Should you desire a
clawless otter from the Cape of Good Hope or a bull's horn to be
played like a trumpet, merely inquire here. Maybe you want a tortoise shell worn as a German helmet in our roiling Spanish wars? Just
say my name: Jan Fetchet.

Most curio dealers get their specimens stuffed or dried like market prunes, but I deal in live beasts. Seafarers in my employ bring
me armadillos, crocodiles, and wild boars, which I house in the East
India Company stables on the quayside. If you went there right
now, you'd find a rhinoceros as big as three donkeys and a peacock
as colorful as a Haarlem sunset. I can get a sunset for you, too, given
the right price.

That's just a jest, my friend. Just a jest. If you'd like to take a
look at my museum of curiosities, it's this way, up these stairs.

No, curio dealing isn't my sole vocation, of course, for while there is money in rarities and oddities, it comes and goes like galleons, with the tides. For steady pay, I work as the *famulus anatomicus* for the Amsterdam Surgeons' Guild. A splendid title, is it not, for a rather ghoulish post? Simply put: I'm the one who collects the corpses for our chief anatomist, that famous Dr. Tulp. On the streets they call me skinner's assistant, or, if they're punsters, the skinner's right hand.

I can tell you the whole of the tale. Everyone wants to hear it now that that painter is the talk of Europe. Since that picture he made caused such a stir. But you'll have to bear with me, for I've been told that a long wind blows across my tongue, and my story may digress. Let's settle in then, take some beer and vittles, and afterward you'll come see my *kunstkamer*.

That morning when I awoke, my beard brittle with chill, I thought it was fortuitous. Cold weather is always good for the dissection. I get a clean cut of ice from the canals for my corpse bed and the body stays fresh longer. We like to do the annual festive dissection on Justice Day; that's the guild's chance to cull whatever body the magistrate strings up at noon, as fresh as a pig from slaughter.

My body was named Joep van de Gheyn, the fishmonger killer. I read the court papers on Joep's case, where he'd admitted, without even being put in leg-irons, to murdering the monger in cold blood out of lust for the man's wife.

I'd had my doubts, you know. When I went to visit poor doomed Joep in the rasp house, I found him to be a gentle and devout soul who'd sooner say he was too warm than send cold soup back to the cook. If I said it was raining, but the sky was perfect as the sheen on silk, he'd still nod his head and mumble, "Yes, the rain, the rain! I'm sure you're right; it will rain very soon."

Picture him felling a big burly fishmonger with a single swipe of a blade? Couldn't do it. But you never know a man, do you? From watching our anatomies over the shoulders of our physicians, I've learned that a fellow with the kindliest outward bearing often can contain the organs of a sinner. I've seen blackest livers removed from even the jolliest of tavern keepers.

Four days earlier, the mayor had entered the sentencing chamber wearing the dooming blood band and Joep's fate was sealed. The magistrate handed me the promissory note for his body just an hour after the butcher secured me a wild boar for the feast.

So, that morning I was in a good mood, indeed, what with the promising weather, all my orders placed, and a fresh body ready for collection. I was washing my face in the basin by my home when a messenger tapped me on the shoulder and handed me a note. It was from Rotzak, one of my suppliers, a deckhand who works the Australasias for the East India Company. He's Amsterdam's most reckless curio hunter, going off on his own to chase alicantos and fabled apes. Once, he brought me a sea unicorn, which I sold to Martijn de Groote, who used its horn to cure the bulbous goiter that used to mar his famous neck.

The note read: "Living Bird of Paradise netted in the Australasias. Fifteen stivers. Today only at the company stables. Shipping out tonight. With feet!"

The bird of paradise, that true rarity of rarities! *Avis paradiseus.* A bird so beautiful and strange it could join the Italian commedia as Harlequin. No paradise is like another. One might have the plumage of a king, a red crown, and velveteen breast, while another wears a canopy of purple feathers around his fat black neck. A female might have feathers that trail behind her like a fine courtesan's train. Each one can inspire awe not just through its beauty but also by the fact that these birds, alone among winged creatures, have no feet.

Few men or women on this continent have seen a bird of paradise alive, for it lives its whole life aflight and does not deign to mingle with the lesser birds in the trees. It's almost impossible to capture the *paradiseus*, and when snared, it soon dies, so well does it love the free air. The great wonder hunters of all Europe have tried, and failed, to bring one back to Amsterdam.

A living paradise was certainly enough to divert me from my chores, and since this is a town teeming with greedy traders—all thieves, you know, every one a common crook—I knew I'd have to be excellently nimble not to miss this rare specimen. The greatest incentive: the word "Feet!" in Rotzak's note.

Impossible, I thought, though I have heard one local philosopher claim that paradise eggs are too large and heavy to be hatched in flight, so the bird *must* sometimes alight upon a branch to nest. I do not have a firm opinion on the matter. However, I knew a footed specimen could bring me at least fifty stivers.

I had the perfect client in mind: that one they now call Rembrandt. I knew him then as humble Harmenszoon van Rijn, a painter and etcher who runs the Uylenburgh studio on the Sint Antoniesbreestraat.

He has quite the *kunstkamer*, and pays top guilder for items to add to it—more, I suspect, than he can truly afford. Although now he can afford all he likes, I suppose.

I've delivered to him a death mask of Prince Maurits cast from his royal face, a gourd from a calabash tree, a Turkish powder horn, two Indian Mogul miniatures, and numerous coral branches and shells. He has no small interest in birds, and I've procured for him two dodos, a cockatoo, and a pelican from the Málaga coast, all alive and clapping their beaks. He has no aviary, but receives these specimens to sketch them and then gives them away—pure foolishness.

Van Rijn is a bit of a rarity himself, as you may have heard tell, and does not often leave his studio. I must call upon him at the Sint Antoniesbreestraat to bring him his wonders, and each time I visit him, I find him attired in some strange new garb. I've seen him don a beret with a plume; a gorget, though he never was a soldier; and the starched ruff, far above his station.

I conclude that he likes to play at theater and that he uses many of the curios I bring him as props. It is his choice, of course, and who am I to judge? He spends so lavishly on wonders that I compete for his attentions with almost every other curio dealer in town. The paradise would certainly help put me in good stead with this eccentric painter. I breathed in the beautiful wintry air and called myself fortunate.

However, trouble started to show its face soon after. At the butcher's shop, after I'd collected the wild boar, the side of beef, the sausages, and the last of my lamb, the butcher held out his hand and said, "That'll be seventeen stivers." My mouth was agape. I'd already paid him well in advance, as he knew. I told him so.

"*Nee*, that was just half," said the butcher, his face as innocent as the lamb's. I was baffled. I've known this butcher, Bart Oomen, for years and he's never been anything but straight with me in the past. It was still Bart Oomen: his eyes were just as blue, his teeth as crooked as ever. I concluded he was right and I must be mistaken. I handed over the additional seventeen stivers and went along my way, shaking my head in befuddlement.

At the baker's, my breads were still piping hot when I arrived, and packed and ready for my pickup. Just as I was turning to leave with the loaves, I heard, "But, Fetchet, you owe me ten stivers more." That was baker Essenhaas.

This time, I was certain I'd already paid. "Nienke, I may be older than I was last week, but I am not already demented," I told her. "I paid you in full last week and you shook my hand on it." She smiled a rather wicked smile, folded her arms across her vast bosom, and simply said, "How *is* good Dr. Tulp?"

That famous Dr. Tulp, the man who holds the forceps in that painting. I thought to myself: Dr. Tulp? What did he have to do with it? Ah, yes, now I understood the butcher and the baker and foresaw how the rest of the afternoon would play itself out as I went to collect my goods.

Publicly, Tulp's a man of the people, riding about all hours of the night in his carriage to cup and bleed and leech. That carriage with the tulip painted on its side and his grand mansion on the Prinsengracht make everyone in town think him a gallant spendthrift. When it comes time to actually open his purse for his purchases, though, it seems nothing falls out but dust.

Those who encounter him in the shops, too, find he's as puritanical and stingy as any of the Leiden Gomarists. I have seen him scold his maidservants for gossip, and berate his daughters for the slightest tinsel on their collars. They cry—*Oh, Daddy, but it's the fashion!*—and run off in tears. Even when he does buy sweets for the girls, the shop is left waiting for his payment for weeks. In short: were Tulp a horse, it wouldn't be his fine mane that people remember but his droppings once he's pranced away.

Last year, many farmers and butchers and bakers supplied the Surgeons' Guild with bargains for the winter fest. After all, it's the highlight of the season and usually the guild spares no expense. But this year, the local merchants wanted to get back at "Dear Tulpius":

what he'd saved from penny-pinching for his personal goods, they'd get back from the guild. The rest of the morning, whatever vendor I met, I could tell by their eyes even as I approached that the price of my goods would double.

What could I do? I could not walk away when the boar and the calves were already in the cart. Return the baker's freshly baked loaves? Should I refuse to pay or refuse to take the goods I'd ordered, it would be my problem; I'd be bad-mouthed all about town as a conspirator. So I swallowed hard and paid those exorbitant fees and hoped the good doctor would see his way to reimburse me.

Some more beer, then? Here. Take this tankard, and I'll refill the glass. Another slice of duck? It is all gratis, of course, and you have traveled far. You'll love this larded dove. No need to worry about expense; the guild fathers paid for it and there's plenty left over to last another year. Do you know we ordered twelve hundred tankards from the brewer? Those men drink heartily all through the night; after I finish with my work in the anatomy chamber, I always have to use my corpse cart to carry a few of those surgeons home. Every time I do that, some wife or other decides I'm the cause of all evil, and chases me down the canals with a rolling pin. I tell you, the poor man is never spared the rich man's ransom.

So, as I was saying, I was at the tallow merchant's shop being fleeced—a single bundle of incense for four stivers!—my purse was getting lighter and lighter with every passing moment, when the messenger returned to me with a note from the artist on the Sint Antoniesbreestraat.

"I'd be very curious to have this curiosity," he'd written. "Should it be what you claim it is, I'll pay you a guilder." A guilder was good enough, I thought, and if the bird was truly beautiful, perhaps he could be persuaded to pay more.

I calculated that I had just enough time to get to the wharves to fetch the bird and still make it to the execution at noon to collect my body. Off I went in search of my paradise.

IV

THE EYES

Let me be candid in my opinion of these guild portraits. I've never seen one that is in the least bit interesting. You've got a bunch of men standing in a line, or in a couple of lines, facing the viewer. It's obvious they've all come to sit for the painter separately and he's placed them on the canvas together.

Sometimes the portraitist has some fun by depicting the guild members while they point their fingers in different directions. With the doctors' guild they tend to use some obvious memento mori symbol, like a wilting flower or a candle that's just been blown out. I wanted to do something that wouldn't feel so damn stilted. Something that would breathe a little life into the subject matter. The question was: How?

I enjoy the preliminary work of conceptualizing a painting. Van Swanenburgh taught me to think in terms of architectural spaces and simple geometry. Lastman trained me in certain Italian perspectival techniques. These things I learned, though it's true that I never went to Italy—and they love to criticize me for it, especially now.

Since there were so many men to include in this picture I decided to start with a pyramidal shape, as I have done with my new composition of Christ's descent from the cross, the one I'm working on for the stadtholder.

There is a beautiful cohesion that comes from a pyramidal structure. If you've got the geometry right, every point in the painting seems to relate to every other point. As the viewer, your eye is encouraged to move back and forth between the elements before settling directly into a single focus.

You see different characters and give each of them your visual attention for as long as they interest you, and then your eye moves along to the next character, knowing that each one plays a role in the unfolding drama.

Eventually, your eye is compelled to the focus of the painting— which is somewhere at the center of the pyramid or else at the pyramid's base. The eye actually aids in the drama of the visual image, because it is drawn elsewhere first, building up suspense. I can't tell you why it works that way, but the masters have proved it again and again. Giotto, Raphael, and Leonardo—they all teach us that aesthetics are built on a foundation of hard mathematical principles.

If you get the basics of the equation right, you have a sturdy structure on which to construct a beautiful house. If your math is faulty, the pillars are weak and the house will totter and topple. So you want to think out the structural principles first, especially with a canvas this large with so many figures.

As a mathematician, I expect that you'll appreciate this perspective, even if it sounds somewhat naive coming out of the mouth of a painter. The aesthetic mathematics, if achieved, should quickly disappear into the background so that the viewer doesn't think about them at all. It should feel as if you walked into a grand mansion, confident in the knowledge that the architects have done their work, and you need not worry that the roof will fall.

I'd thought perhaps I would place Tulp at the top of the pyramid, since he was meant to be the primary figure and he would pay the most for the privilege. I'd put another guild member at each of the corners, perhaps two apprentices, gazing up at him with professional reverence. The other figures would all be positioned within smaller triangles inside this pyramid. I sketched all this out in my notebook and felt satisfied that it might work.

By the time I was ready to try it on canvas, the pupils were done with the preparations. All the minerals I'd instructed Joris to crush were now arrayed in tiny ceramic bowls on the table, like a detachment of civic guards. Those that he'd mixed with linseed oil were in small glass jars, plugged with muslin and corked.

The linen had been stretched and the ground applied. The canvas was a gray hue with a little yellow ocher and umber mixed in and enough chalk to give it texture. That was it: a blank canvas already primed but not yet touched. The pot of ground was at the foot of the easel, the Italian recipe laid under its base and my priming knife set by.

I placed a small amount of Kassel earth on the grinding stone with the palette knife. The apprentice had already mixed in the linseed oil, but I wanted it to be very thin, so I added turpentine to dilute it further. I ground it with the pestle until it was a very thin consistency, and then I placed a dab onto my palette. This part of the painting process is more like sketching for me. I try to put very little paint on the canvas at first.

I drew a wet paintbrush out of the *pincelier* and dabbed it into Kassel earth, deciding to add a touch of bone black, too. In this way, I could begin to outline the figures with general, open strokes. I wasn't going for details yet, just trying to find the overall shapes and composition—where the guild members would stand, how the bodies would relate to one another in space.

After a while, I became bored with it. All those identical-looking men on a single massive canvas? And for what? A waste of sailcloth, if you ask me. They should rather use it for an East India Company ship to sail off to Jayakarta. Then at least they can bring back something fascinating from across the seas.

My thoughts drifted beyond my studio, out of the academy, and out into the streets of Amsterdam, where I could hear the sounds of the crowds making their way to Dam Square for the executions. I've never had any interest in watching the hangings, though I do go to the gibbets at the Volewijk sometimes to sketch. I feel the city begin to boil with this kind of carnal energy and it makes me want to stay away from the mob.

Generally, I rarely escape the studio, but I envy those who exist within the swirl and tumult of real life out there, on the filthy, chaotic byways. Sometimes I pluck them off the streets and bring them indoors to sketch them. Once or twice, I have gotten to know them more intimately. But I am already, at twenty-six, a sad man who works too much, gets far too little sunlight, and stands beside the window, watching people pass by as if it were life itself at my window. I stood for some time at the window and watched people pass.

Then Femke came to tell me that Dr. Tulp had arrived for his sitting. I asked her to bring him into the studio, and while she was out I set up a place for the doctor to sit. I found my sketch pad and a piece of brown charcoal.

Tulp entered the studio, stepping into the room as though on tiptoes so as not to soil his shoes. You've seen him so you know: Will you agree with me that there's something overly preened about the doctor, every element of his attire tidy to immaculate, his shoes at a high polish, his silk collar straightened, his hose seams aligned? It is unusual for a city physic to be quite so, I don't know, unsullied.

He seemed ill at ease from the first. If he saw the nude behind the curtain, he did not acknowledge her. No, it was something else. And when we were alone in my painting studio, he handed me a package wrapped in dried leaves, tied up with twine.

"You must drink it to ward off the grippe," he instructed, "in this especially cold season. My wife suggested I bring it."

I took the package and turned it over in my hands.

"You brew it," he went on. "The taste is not terrible. It is not medicine. It prevents illness. Shortly you can read about it in my pharmacopoeia."

It seemed like he wanted me to inquire about his pharmacopoeia, so I obliged. "And what is that?"

"I have enlisted the city's best physics and barbers to work with me to assemble a book of reliable medicinal treatments." He paused, perhaps realizing that this all sounded a bit too prepared. "I am on a crusade to wipe out quackery."

It was an awkward kind of moment, because I got the sense he'd been coached in cordialities—perhaps by his wife.

I handed the package to Femke, and Tulp instructed her with many specifics: to boil some water, fill the pot only halfway, then brew the leaves for a good ten minutes, and then fill the rest of the pot.

"I'll drink some as well. So you'll trust it won't poison you," he added. This was obviously intended as a joke, so I laughed to please him.

I offered him the seat near my easel. "Please, make yourself comfortable."

He sat, but he didn't look comfortable in the least. "I understand you have had several guild members to the studio already for their sittings?" he asked.

"Yes," I said, pulling up a chair as well. "I have seen four of your members so far. Will the final number be seven or eight?"

"Jacob Colevelt has yet to make up his mind," Tulp said. "He feels a hundred guilders is a bit steep, as this is only his first year as an apprentice in the guild."

"From the painter's perspective, a face is a face," I said. "I should not end up leaving off his nose or forgetting to add an eye, simply because he has not yet finished his training."

That managed to cudgel a smile out of him. "Let's hope you do not leave off any elements of my face," he said, finally removing his hat and gloves. "Let's leave it to Colevelt to decide, and instead discuss the look of the painting."

"Very well. You had a particular idea for the image, then?"

"Indeed, I do. I have put a great deal of thought into the matter, since I know you will want firm instructions on how to lay it all out."

I had not expected him to direct me in the painting's composition, but I didn't see why I should inform him of this until I'd heard him out.

"Naturally, the painting should depict the current members of the guild who want to participate, but I feel strongly that it should also, in some way, represent the most current anatomical information. Since you are from Leiden, can I venture that you may have attended the lectures of Petrus Pauw there?"

"Indeed, I have."

"Ah, good. Then, is it also safe to assume you are familiar with Vesalius and his complete anatomical atlas, the *Fabrica*?"

I told him I was not only familiar with the book but that I was a great admirer of the illustrations and that my own library contained a first edition.

"Then you are more than just a tradesman painter!" Tulp said. "Not all artists own books."

"I have a small collection," I said. "The pupils can use them as references as well."

"You are, no doubt, familiar then with the frontispiece to the text—the image of Vesalius himself? The image representing the great anatomist standing with an arm that he has dissected."

"Let us take a look," I said, and called Tomas over and asked him to fetch the book.

Tulp went on casually, "You see a little bit of the torso, but it's mostly the arm. Vesalius often focused on arms and hands in his lectures. Unlike Galen, he believed that the structure of the arm and hand is what separates humans from all other species. He was the first to fully dissect the human arm. Indeed, the human arm is evidence of God's manifest wisdom. He gave us this limb so that we, above all other creatures, would be able to handle tools. Vesalius was very wise to point this out. To know the body is to know God's purpose, I always say. Well, I don't mean to play the pedagogue."

Of course, he did. I refrained from sharing my thoughts on the matter for the moment—and it seemed he did not require them. He went on talking about the wonders of the human hand, the ingenuity of the flexor tendons, the grace of the small bones in the fingers, the incredible dexterity that is allowed by the radius and ulna. . . . Tomas arrived with the book and we opened it on the large drafting table.

The woodcut of Vesalius is one of those by Jan van Calcar— perhaps you're familiar with him?—the student of Titian. The anatomist is posed, as Tulp had said, in front of a cadaver, but all you see is the dissected arm, like a kind of trophy. It's an unusual choice for a portrait, but as Tulp clearly hoped to convey, it was a choice guided by his moral philosophy.

"I like his expression in this portrait," said Tulp. "I think he looks both wise and approachable. That is how I'd like to be portrayed."

It was funny, looking at that portrait with the doctor standing next to me, because I saw very clearly that Tulp had fashioned his own appearance in the mold of Vesalius. Tulp had trimmed his facial hair into a similar cut. But there was more than that. They seem to have similarly round faces and a certain analogous seriousness. The more we looked at the picture, the more I could see it.

"So, you would like me to try for this type of expression? Enhance your natural likeness to Vesalius."

"Well, I don't think I look like him . . . not really. He was Flemish. I am of pure Batavian stock. But, yes, I think it would be useful to include a part of the anatomy, perhaps a dissected limb. I'd prefer an arm, if you wouldn't mind, in homage."

I laughed, for I thought at first this was another one of his awkward jokes.

"Pickenoy included a full skeleton in his portrait of the Sebastiaen Egbertszoon guild," Tulp made his case. He seemed to have anticipated my response. "The portrait is held in high regard."

"Indeed it is." Let me tell you, candidly, that I loathe Pickenoy. He is a very popular painter, but his pictures are comical in their falsity. I understood he meant for me to be guided by Master Pickenoy. "But do you not think a skeleton is somehow less, well, upsetting than a flayed, severed human limb?"

Tulp gave this a moment of consideration. "Perhaps you have a point. I suspect there are many—and women in particular—who would find flesh more objectionable than bones. We are familiar with the skeleton, aren't we?"

"And what would be the justification, in terms of narrative, for including just the arm?" I wondered aloud.

"Narratively?" He did not get my meaning. "So people will understand my adherence and respect for Vesalius, naturally."

I tried to imagine this picture he wanted me to paint: more than half a dozen gentlemen in elegant cloaks and ruffs, looking very dignified, standing next to a dissecting table with a man's flayed arm upon it.

"The difficult part, from your perspective, I should imagine, would be to make sure the anatomy is right."

"I see. You'd like me to paint the inner workings of the arm, as it is depicted here."

"Yes, precisely. Only better, hopefully. With greater anatomical accuracy. You see, Van Calcar was a fine artist, but there are certain mistakes."

"Ah," I said, considering this added dimension of the request. "But then I would need to be highly familiar with the anatomical structure of the forearm. As Titian and his pupils were when they illustrated the *Fabrica*."

"Well, that is easily solved. You'll attend tonight's anatomical lesson. And there I will dissect the patient's forearm and hand. If you observe with acuity, you should be able to depict the limb with far greater accuracy than Van Calcar did. It will not be so difficult."

I didn't argue with Tulp, for he seemed to have little under-standing of how the work of painting is accomplished. Observing a dissection from a seat in the theater would not provide me with the necessary source material for capturing a dissected limb in oil paint no matter how much "acuity" I applied to my observation in chambers. I'd have to be able to study the arm, to return to it again and again. Flayed skin, stretched tendons, ligaments, and bone—not easily captured by eye or by brush. I found the assignment both thrilling and confounding.

I thought about the question of the flayed limb while I sketched him. We drained about three cups of that vile brew he had brought me before I sent him home to his wife for the rest of the afternoon. He left my studio in relative good cheer; my stomach was already grumbling over that tea.

He repeated that he would welcome me at the anatomy lesson that evening and suggested I arrive early, as he suspected it would be a particularly popular event. I promised that I would attend, and I said it would certainly be helpful to have a good view—so I could observe the dissected arm with "utmost acuity."

Meanwhile, in the back of my mind, I was trying to imagine how I could get a flayed arm in my possession so that I would be able to bring it to life on canvas, to satisfy this Tulp.

Initial observations: daylight glances off the surface. What's
immediately apparent with the naked eye is the textural variables
in the lighter hues. Natural light pushes the darker hues into gloss,
almost glare. Perhaps that is the result of the darkened varnish.

I will move closer with my scope. The clothing of the figures
is worked up in subtle shades of grays, browns, blacks. I also see
evidence of some purple in one cloak. It is clear that Tulp's cloak was
repainted, although the original paint layer is still partially present.
It was fixed after heat damage from the fire in the Nieuwe Waag in
1732. We have notes here about its damaging the work, though not
severely.

Claes calls it a dissection, but I prefer to think of it as an autopsia
in the sense of the original Greek: *auto* (self) *opsis* (sight, vision). In
this case we look within the body to discover the self. What did the
artist intend to say about himself when he painted this? What did he
want to reveal to the world through this body?

Rembrandt built up the body using his brushstrokes, through
layers of paint. Later, he changed his mind and made certain
alterations to the body, going back and adding pentimenti to alter
the composition. I love that word—*pentimenti*—which comes
from the Italian word for repentance. I repent with my brush and
add dabs of paint to change the image. With the pentimenti, what
we can see is real evidence of the painter before his easel. The
painter, that is, thinking on the canvas. It is evidence of Rembrandt's
process—his mind at work—while he was crafting this.

We've noted in previous radiographs that Rembrandt has a great density of pentimenti in the dissected left hand, evidence that he worked and reworked that hand, trying to get the composition right. The radiograph reveals a light area partially painted in white lead, which links up directly with the X-ray image of the dissected lower arm now visible. Of course, it's only natural that Rembrandt would spend quite a bit of time reworking that left limb, since it must've been quite a challenge to figure out how to paint the inner anatomy of an arm with all its tendons, ligaments, and muscles and so on. He was not, after all, a doctor, nor had he any occasion to intimately examine the inside of an arm. He had to discern how to make a dissected limb based on what he could see. But where did he see it? What was he using as a model?

Previous researchers (De Vries et al., Schupbach, Heckscher) have posited that Rembrandt may have used anatomical textbooks—of which there were several circulating in Holland at the time—in particular Vesalius's *De humani corporis fabrica* (On the Structure of the Human Body). It's certainly very likely that Rembrandt had that at his disposal (I have proposed elsewhere that it is the folio volume lying at the corpse's feet in the foreground of the painting). But isn't it also possible that he used something more lifelike as a model?

Until now, it has been assumed that Rembrandt did not attend the anatomical lesson, but rather constructed a scene based on sittings with the individual medical "players." This is supported by arguments (Wood Jones; Wolf-Heidegger) that the anatomy of the dissected left hand is inaccurate in a number of ways.

The new Groningen medical study, "A Comparison of Rembrandt's *Anatomy Lesson* with a Dissected Left Forearm of a Dutch Male Cadaver," published in the journal *History of Hand Surgery,* however, siding with Heckscher, suggests that Rembrandt in fact gave a strikingly accurate depiction of the superficial flexors of the fingers. It concluded that the "details and realistic colorful appearance of the original painting suggests that Rembrandt used a real limb...." This seems to indicate that Rembrandt was working from life. That is, that he not only saw the dissection but spent quite a bit of time with the arm of the corpse, both before and possibly after Tulp's anatomical lesson, and used a real arm as his model. I think we must consider the implications of that discovery for a moment: Rembrandt used a real limb? Where would he have gotten a real limb for such an exercise? Off the gallows? From the anatomist himself?

What I intend to do now is to examine the rest of the body of the corpse to see if there might be any other evidence that Rembrandt saw this body in particular.

I'm looking closer now, with the scope.

The paint layer is relatively thin, especially compared with Rembrandt's later paintings, and built up with great economy as though he is trying to save paint. The pigments, especially warmer hues, are applied more thickly in the foreground; the background details and the figures in the back have cooler, more subdued tonalities. The warmer tonalities are in the front. The brushstrokes are also applied more summarily in the back, more detailed in the foreground. This is the beginning of the emergence of Rembrandt's technique: he draws your eye to where he wants it to go with lighter and thicker pigments. The figures of the doctors are relatively uniform in terms of hues and thickness of paint; however, the face of Colevelt at the extreme left has a more grayish tonality. He was painted later, but this has been discussed previously.

Now I am looking at the body of the corpse. There are some shadow areas in the head of the corpse that are overpainted. Perhaps he moved the head of the corpse a bit? The hues here are grayer but also warmer, with a greater density of pigment. There is an inordinate amount of light pouring onto the corpse, as if from a single source above. Still, the hues tend to the grays, to indicate death.

Here's something intriguing: it does appear that there is an uneasy transition between the corpse's right hand and the wrist. Wrinkles of paint occur together with a few premature cracks. This is the right hand—the hand closest to the viewer, not the dissected hand. Also, there is a shift in coloration between the right wrist and the right hand. The hand is grayer, and there is a greater density of pigment. It is a very unusual hand, an unnecessarily elegant hand, it seems to me, for a thief. I have thought that before, just looking at it in the gallery. Very intriguing indeed.

Please note that I will need to request permission to take a sample from this passage. Very curious. Perhaps I should also take a look at the '78 x-radiograph from De Vries and his team and figure out if this was there then. I will do that this morning.

V

THE MIND

January 31, 1632
Dear Mersenne,

I promised you that before the end of the year I would send you
my new treatise that explains heaviness, lightness, hardness, and
the speed of weights falling in a vacuum, and as is plainly evident
by the date on this missive, I have failed to keep my promise once
again.

   I beg your continued patience with me, dear friend, as my reason
for putting off sending it to you has been the hope of including
some of my recent observations for "The World." I wanted to
respond to your thoughts on the corona of the candle flame and to
advance my own positions on the question of the location of the
soul in the body as well.

   This morning, I bought a lamb from one of the butchers near
my lodgings, and I have been examining it in my rooms. Having

scrutinized its organs closely, and attempting to jot down my observations of vital functions based on the lamb's anatomy, I hope to learn about the digestion of food, the heartbeat, the distribution of nourishment, and the five senses. I cannot assume that these are corollary functions in a man, but they are a beginning.

Still, I'm afraid that I shall discover little in the lamb that I did not already observe in my vivisections with dogs and goats. The organs of animals are remarkably similar in shape and function; they are only different in size and sometimes in corporeal location. I searched this lamb for some evidence of its rational soul, but because it was already dead, I did not have much hope of discovering it. Animals are as complex in many ways as human bodies, yet I still do not find any explanation for the fact that they lack the powers of speech or reason.

Dear friend, my intention was to travel to Deventer this week to meet with Reneri and compare notes on these and other recent observations. However, it seems that I have been detained once again, both by the frigid weather, which makes many of the country canals and rivers impassable, and also by an event at which my presence is required this evening. I shall attend an anatomical demonstration and lecture of one Dr. Nicolaes Tulp, the praelector of this town's surgeons' guild—in Holland every profession must have a guild, for men here do not care to be singular but rather more like epiphytes that grow where other plants of their ilk have already found a ready supply of moisture.

Did you know that here they are also allowed to perform anatomies on criminals straight from the hangman's rope, in front of a vast public, which includes every merchant and shopkeep who owns a ruff? It is unlike anything I've heard about in Oxford or Padua. The Dutch cut round and lecture, discuss and debate, and then they feast openly and with public approbation. The festive anatomy is quite a bit more pomp than substance, however, almost like a drama on the stage.

Have you heard of this city's anatomical praelector who takes his name from this country's most emblematic blossom? Tulpius, they call him, like something out of Rabelais. He is the one who has been known to say, "I'd rather err with Galen than circulate with Harvey," as if betting on the ancients against modernity were some kind of hound race.

Tulp objects, I understand, not to the specific theory William Harvey presents on the pumping of blood through the heart but to the very notion of exploring the heart's precise function. I do not quite understand the logic of this. There are those, of course, who still consider the heart to be the locus of either the mortal or immortal soul, and perhaps his objection to Harvey's work stems from the fear that we would disturb that image of such a sacred organ. It seems to me quite clear that the heart has a mechanical function within the body, and one that relates in some way to the revitalizing of the blood. When blood leaves the heart it does not have the same qualities as it did when it entered. It is hotter, more rarefied, and more agitated. Are medical men afraid that the heart could no longer be the seat of the soul if it had a mechanical function?

I have my concerns about Harvey's conclusions, because his observations on the heart's movements differ substantially from the evidence I have accumulated during vivisections of live dogs. Yet Harvey deserves the highest possible praise for making such a valuable discovery about the pumping of this organ.

I may have something to learn from this Tulpius—and to discover our differences so that I might articulate my opposing position more forcefully—and at the moment some firsthand observation of a human anatomy may yield greater insights than my own amateur animal anatomies.

By the by, have I mentioned that they sell the bull's full hindquarters here, so it is possible to trace the veins and arteries directly from the feet all the way to the intestines? I find myself thrilled to discover it, and cannot wait until I have cleared a place in my lodgings to move ahead with my studies.

Many times I have sung the praises of Amsterdam as the perfect urban retreat, and how preferable it is to Paris or Rome, because everyone here is so engaged in trade that they ignore you quite entirely. It was not even a year ago that I boasted to Jean-Louis de Balzac that I could live here all my life without ever being noticed by a soul. However, time has worn out my anonymity and I have begun to be noticed . . . indeed, I have begun to have certain social obligations from which I cannot seem to extricate myself.

So, there it is: I will have to postpone my Deventer excursion once again. I remain here in my lodgings at the Oud Prins and I will share with you some new chapters from my "World" as soon as I have them.

Your true and loving friend,
René Descartes

VI

THE HEART

I never knew there were so much empty space out there between Leiden and other parts. I always figured one town ended and another began just across a dike or dam.

Mother talked sometimes about the lonesome stretches she'd walk when she went studding her bull, but they must've been lonelier than I ever imagined because there were nothing out there but fields and sky and crows. At least, that's all you could see from the barge that took us across the Haarlemmermeer to Amsterdam.

That breeze on the boat were something, though. When it rushed across my face, I thought, There's more in the world, more than cruelty and meanness. Adriaen told me once that he'd been on a galley. He were to row for eight years with other convicts for the admiralty of Rotterdam. That sounded important, but he said the admiralty were no better than them slave traders and it were his job to row them. I never knew how he got off that ship, but I thought about where it would have taken him. I thought, maybe, even on a boat like that, there were that breeze. If he felt that, I bet he smiled. That made me feel better, so I held my belly and thought on how Carel should get to feel that breeze someday.

The boy the father sent with me were a frail, ash-colored thing. He said his name were Guus. He reminded me of Adriaen when he were young: stringy and loose limbed. He might have been one of them boys throwing stones in the morning, though. When he came to me, he looked like he were sent to meet a ghost or a hobgoblin. Maybe he'd heard what they all cried. Maybe he had ideas about me.

I took his hand and I held it between my two hands and closed my eyes. I said, "Thank you, young man, for not being fearful. You are a good boy. We'll take care of each other."

He smiled weakly.

When we were close to land, the barge were drawn along the edge of the canal with a horse on land to pull it. But soon as we go out into the open water, they let the horses loose and the barge went to sailing. They hauled up the sheets and the wind flapped up against them, and you could see the strength of it, hard and fast, tipping our boat sometimes till it scared me. A ghostly power, that breeze. Nothing you could touch, but the force of it were something.

When the boat were out there in the *meer*, every once in a while the boy would look up and ask a question: "How long you lived in Leiden?" "How'd you meet that convict?" "Do you know how to read?" "What's it feel like to have a baby inside you?"

I took his hand and put it to my belly. We waited until the babe kicked. The boy jumped back when Carel moved. Then he laughed. We both did. Funny, how you can laugh at any time, any place, even through the worst of it.

"Did you get a baby from a spell?" he asked me then.

"No, I got it from a man," I told him.

"That man we're going for in Amsterdam?"

"Yes."

Guus took a step away from me. "They said he murdered someone."

"He didn't murder anyone. He only tried to steal a man's coat."

He looked confused. "But didn't he have his own coat?"

"I don't know," I said, to be honest. "Sometimes he had a cloak. Sometimes he were just in his jerkin. He had things sometimes and then he lost them. He weren't good with keeping things."

Guus thought about this. "He can have my coat," he said. "I'm never cold."

"That would be very nice of you."

He looked proud to have said it.

After that, he were less afraid of me. He called me "ma'am."

⎯⎯⎯ ✻ ⎯⎯⎯

The night before the stones came, I had a dream that we were climbing a tree with our newborn. Me and Adriaen. The babe in one of my hands. I were to make an apple tart for springtime and we were going all together to pick the apples from the tree in the yard. When I climbed, Adriaen lifted the babe into the branches, because he said the babe would only be safe up top. I were trying to grab an apple off one limb and trying to reach for the babe at the same time, and I got unsteady because of my reaching and I broke the limbs off below. Adriaen were on his way up and instead he fell forward, so we fell together and we fell far, we fell for a long time. In the dream I were calm about it, not screaming, but afraid for the babe.

Finally we hit a branch and landed in a giant nest, but it were thick with thorns and we were both cut and bruised and crying. The babe weren't with us anymore. He floated up to the top of the tree when we started falling, and as we went lower, he went higher, and finally we saw him up there, settled on a perch as calm as a lamb. Adriaen and I stayed in our nest and he held me and we watched our babe up in the high branches of the tree above us. I saw Adriaen's belly and felt where he'd been branded, and it weren't any of the shapes I knew. It were a bird this time, with wild many-colored feathers. I traced my name in that brand and my finger were a flame.

⌒⟆⁂⟅⌒

I thought about what I could say to the magistrate to make him grant a pardon. I did not know what my words would be to a magistrate. I'm just a poor woman with a broken mill and I'm tireder now than ever with the babe's heaviness.

I did not know if Father van Thijn's note would help. Except that they were calling him murderer and I knew that weren't Adriaen. The father knew it, too, even if he didn't say it. Adriaen were not soft or gentlehearted, but he didn't have that meanness. I knew all he stole and how he stole it. He were not shy to talk about his ways of thieving. He were proud of his way. He said he were always kind to men even when he were thieving from them. And if he were caught, he said he always showed respect to his jailors. He didn't mind what they did to him, no matter how much they did to him, he seemed to think it were coming to him. That were the way it all worked for Adriaen. He did his misdeeds because it were how he lived; they gave him his whips and brands because it were his comeuppance. But hanging? For murder? No, no. That weren't him.

Maybe I would've said this to the magistrate: Adriaen loved people. He talked to everyone like he never met a stranger. What were his were theirs; what were theirs, his; and if he liked something, he didn't mind to take it. But he never kept much very long and never had much from thieving. A gully knife for eating and a set of leatherworking tools his father gave him. That's all I ever know he had. He loved his vagabond life, too. He liked to warm his hands by a crackling canal-side fire with the other mendicants. He thought the wind were a song in his ear.

I knew him as a boy and I knew him as a man. We grew up in houses side by side on the Rhine. He were a sweet, spindly-legged boy. He looked after me when my father went drunk to the hayloft. I looked after him when his father went wild with his fists. He left Leiden when they lost the shop and spent years wandering.

When he came back to Leiden after all them years traveling, he were the tiredest man I ever saw, my Adriaen. It weren't just in his eyes but everywhere, like he'd been a sail on a high seas trading ship, where pirates climbed aboard and slashed. That were how he were when he came back to me after all them years wandering. He went out and got himself tired.

His body weren't beautiful no more, neither. But each of them flogging scars and brandings were evidence of the life he'd lived, and when we were in bed I used to touch them and trace my finger from one to the next like they were a map of his travels. That back of his were like the sloping hills of our marshland, and each long scar a canal, a passageway to his salvation. He let me touch them, though the skin were sensitive there, and I don't think he let anyone else do that, ever.

I listened and I heard about where he'd been. It weren't nice what he said, sometimes, but them words were a deep lake you walk into and stay in the bottom muck, your feet held in its murky sink, somehow just swaying. What I mean is, it weren't ugly down there inside Adriaen, just dark and different. I could stay there in that place for a long time without feeling any ways bad about anything.

⁕

Once we got through the *meer*, they hitched the barge back up to horses, and they pulled us along the bank up the Overtoom. When we got close to the city gates, they started to buck and whinny. There were too many mares in the sluice. Word spread through the barge that they had shut the city gates at the Leidse Port. They said there were too many outsiders trying to get to Justice Day. They had to keep back the crowds.

That were us, outsiders. That were the world, coming to see Adriaen hang. I ran to the captain and told him I had to go to the Dam to stop them, but he weren't hearing me. There were a racket with the horses and so many men shouting for the boats to turn back. They had to go around and sail it to the Haarlemmer Port, he said. That were the only way in. I told him Adriaen would hang if I could not get there with my letter. He said he were sorry. I'd just have to wait.

That's what they did. Turn back. The horses were wild with the chaos on the banks, but the shipmen whipped them till they quieted and backed out the sluice. I were getting nervous and Guus kept looking up at me and saying, "We'll be there soon, ma'am. Don't worry. I'll get you there." As if a young boy could fix everything.

VII

THE MOUTH

I didn't find my paradise at the quayside stables. I couldn't find Rotzak either, though I got there as quickly as my legs would run me. The stable keepers told me they'd seen a cage that they assumed held a bird and that Rotzak himself had picked it up a few moments earlier. He'd come and gone fleet-footed, and hadn't said where he was bound. When I asked them his direction, I was pointed toward the wharves.

Perhaps he'd gone back to his boat. I ran out along the piers and down to the water, not knowing on which ship he'd arrived, or whether he was already bound for the sea again. I climbed aboard ship after ship. I couldn't find him anywhere. One sailor told me to look by the herring packery, so I went there; a fishmonger pointed back toward the pier, so I ran out that way again. Back and forth I went, first inquiring politely, then calling out his name. The phantom Rotzak was "just here a minute ago" or "went down to get a beer, I think" or unsettlingly "was talking to some dealer on the pier."

I was frenzied, finally running about decks, shouting like a bloody pirate bent on revenge. At one point, I saw a man carrying something that looked like a covered cage, and without looking at his face I ran up and grabbed it from his hands. It was only a foul-smelling bucket of trout, and the fisherman I'd assaulted demanded it back with both fists.

This was like chasing the bird of paradise itself. I gave up, cursed the deckhand, and muttered angrily all the way back to Dam Square. I figured I would deposit myself before the hangman's scaffold, catch my breath, and wait for Joep to drop. It was then I heard my name ringing through the square: "Jan Fetchet, Jan! I've been looking all over town for you!"

The phantom I'd chased from ship to ship was standing there, wearing a big drunken grin. It hit me: I'd never checked the taverns. The cage was in his hands, covered with a tarpaulin, just as it'd been described to me. "Rotzak, you rascal," I shouted, and ran toward him. "I've been chasing you and that paradise. I should charge you for all I've lost in sweat!"

He wobbled on his feet. "It's yours, my friend, all yours," he said, holding the cage up in the air. "Fifteen stivers for the paradise."

I reached for the cage but he pulled it back, taunting me with the prospect of eluding me still. I could see that my anxiousness offered him a bit of a thrill.

"Here, then," I said, and pressed my stivers into his palm. "Hand it over."

He did, but not with out twirling it over my head one more time. I stomped on his foot once and he howled. Then I added, "Someday you'll pay me back for making me jump." The words were harsh but the exchange was merry. At last he put the cage in my hands. "Spend your coins on a nice young wench!"

So relieved was I to finally have that cage in my possession, that I didn't bother to check if the bird was footless. No matter, I thought, as I flew from the square toward the Sint Antoniesbreestraat—I had very little time to get there and return to the Dam for the hanging— I'll earn some profit for the brief excursion either way.

I was still wearing a ridiculous triumphal grin when I arrived on the Sint Antoniesbreestraat and rang the bell at Uylenburgh's shop. Something was troubling me, though, and I hadn't had time to think about it while I was running. It came to me just as the maidservant was opening the door: the cage was strangely light. There was no life energy within it—no noise, no rebellious wings.

It was too late to turn back. The maid, a pale-skinned young thing, was gazing upon me with gimlet eyes. "What's your business here?" she asked, since I had not spoken to introduce myself. "I seem to have knocked upon the wrong door . . ." I started to say, bowing to take my leave, but then she said, "Oh, I'm sorry, Mr. Fetchet, I didn't recognize you at first. The master said I must bring you to him soon as you arrived. Come along."

Now I couldn't leave for two reasons. First, because I had no excuse to leave now that I'd only just arrived. Second, the maid-servant had taken me by the hand, and was already leading me through the main chamber of Uylenburgh's house, full of paint-ings and sculptures he must've been dealing, along with fine drap-eries, porcelain from the Orient, and hand-carved wood furniture from Italy. I was doing a mental inventory, in case this information should prove useful someday.

She let go of my hand as soon as we reached the narrow stairs, only to allow me to steady myself on the railing while we climbed.

Yet as I padded up the stairs behind her, I became ever more aware that something was desperately wrong within the cage. She arrived on the second landing and motioned that I should enter the studio first. I hesitated and the girl came back down the narrow corridor and grabbed my hand again. A sound also fell from her lips, the kind of disapproving cluck I associate with New Town ladies, and then she reached out to release the door's iron latch. The door swung open so quickly I feared we'd burst in upon the painter unawares.

The studio was, in fact, already full of people. There was a boy of maybe eleven sitting before what looked like an apothecary's table, crushing minerals in a mortar with a pestle. Behind a curtain, I could spy at least two other people; at first I thought they might be two more assistants, though on second glance it appeared to be a painter with his model, who was only half-clad. Painters do have the jolliest excuses for frolics.

Van Rijn stood with his back to us, facing his easel. There was a rather giant blank canvas before him, which he was observing with intense contemplation. Another boy was seated next to the easel, with a small drawing pad in his hand, sketching out shapes of several men. The windows were flung open, perhaps to let in the sun or else to let out the reek of turpentine.

"Master, the curio dealer Jan Fetchet," the maidservant announced.

Van Rijn turned abruptly, clearly untroubled at the interruption, and when he saw my face he wiped his brushes against his smock. In a second he was before me, vivid and expectant. "Fetchet! What a treat! I've been eagerly awaiting your arrival."

The artist was dressed in a smock that covered his rumpled studio clothes, and his sleeves were pushed up above his elbows. His bushy red hair was springing out from all points on his head like a haphazard halo. "I received your note and was very pleased," he said.

Without waiting for my reply—for the painter was a busy man—Van Rijn removed the cloth from the birdcage. We both discovered, with one short swipe of the painter's hand, that I was a fraud. Instead of a living bird of paradise, the cage contained a stuffed and mounted sack of feathers on a stick. Dead, of course, and footless, too.

"What's this?" he said. "This morning's note said you had . . ."

The cheerful smile that had greeted me sank like a Swedish ship. The expression was more dismay than disappointment. Keeping one eye fixed upon my face, he undid the clasp on the cage, reached inside, and removed the feathery trinket. He drew it out of its prison with two fingers, by one wing, and held it before me. "Tell me, Jan. Is this bird, in your estimation, alive?"

"I am no anatomist, Master van Rijn, but I must admit, I do not think it is well."

"Not well?"

Why had I replied so saucily, too? "Not very sprightly, it's true."

"Not sprightly?" Van Rijn's eyebrow was raised and mouth turned to a mocking frown. He was beginning to find it amusing, I think. "I'd say not sprightly at all. I'd even venture to say entirely lifeless. As an exemplar of living beings, I'd say, quite poor. I'd even say desiccated. What do you think, Jan, am I getting close?"

I could not form words that were appropriately contrite, I know not why. I was sick with myself, after the running, after all the shouting for that lousy double-dealer. "Master" was all I managed at first. I took a deep breath and finally lowered the cage. "I was most egregiously misinformed."

Van Rijn called out to the young man who had been seated next to his easel, "Tomas, I need you a moment." The painter held the sad bird aloft by the useless wing, and the assistant came toward us with cupped hands, like a supplicant. Van Rijn deposited the dead paradise in his hands and said to the youth, "Tomas, we must be very careful when we deign to do business with curio dealers." The comment was certainly meant for my ears. "They offer you one thing and deliver something quite . . . other." Then, turning to look me full in the face, he added more gravely. "They raise your hopes only to dash them."

The youth nodded and took the bird over to a shelf by the window, which was already full of items he'd collected from me and my competitors—Roman busts and shields, masks and swords, shells and animal skins. I saw that in the corner there were also a few cages and in them winged creatures that moved. I felt all the more ashamed.

"There is not a very high price attached to this pouch of feathers surely?" He was rooting through his pockets for a coin.

"You owe me nothing, master," I said, finally finding a tongue for contrition. "I've made a terrible mistake." I didn't think it wise to get my supplier in trouble, for tattle travels too fast down these narrow byways. What other excuse had I? "Life and death live so close by in this city, I can only say that sometimes it's hard to tell which is which," I said rather feebly.

Van Rijn said, "Hum," and put a hand upon his hip in a pose of exaggerated consideration. "Now this confounds me truly, Fetchet. You say you cannot tell the difference between life and death? Have you spent too much time in the burgomaster's chambers, then?" He laughed, and I managed to join him in a half chuckle. "Why, I can show you life." The painter grabbed my arm and drew me toward the back of the studio, where the two unidentified people were sitting behind a sheet. It was a woman there, and she was, just as I thought, poorly garmented and being sketched by a young man. She did not cry out or cover up when we entered, merely pulled a sheet closer to her breast and giggled. Her cheeks were ruddy, her legs beautifully rotund.

"This," said Van Rijn, "is life." He leaned down and planted a kiss on the woman's bare shoulder. He did not stop there: he kissed three more times, all the way up her neck, until she was squirming and squealing. Then he walked across the room, drew me toward the window of the studio, and pointed out across the IJ.

"And there, my friend, is death." We could see the gallows field from that window, though it was not very close. We could make out only three figures hanging from the gibbets, while I knew there were other, older bodies, farther along.

"Indeed, Master van Rijn," I found the courage to say at last. "To the left is Bas van der Plein, who strangled his mother with his belt in the Nieuwe Heren Sluice. In the center is the former bailiff Bart Boatel, who knifed four men in the rasp house, just for the fun of it, and blamed it on other prisoners though he was caught in the act. To the far right is sad Sander van Dam, who tried to torch the landlord with a burning mop head, and hangs there six weeks since."

"Ah, now see. You do know something about death, at least. You seem to be its chronicler." He was a little impressed.

"I am, sire, in a manner of speaking," I said. "I am present at every sentencing and execution and know the names of all the condemned. Because I buy the bodies from the city."

"And what, pray tell, do you do with them?"

"I work as the *famulus anatomicus* for the Amsterdam Surgeons'

Guild," I added, since I thought I could recoup some of my dignity with this splendid title. "I choose the bodies that shall be used for the praelector's dissection, and then I cart them to the Waag. I'm late for collecting a patient just now."

His reaction was far more pronounced than I would've ever anticipated. "You work for the surgeons' guild, you say?" His attention shifted. "And what is that: *famulus anatom* . . . ?"

"*Anatomicus*, sir. It is a glorious title for a gruesome post. I arrange for the bodies for the public dissections."

"And you will do this today?" he probed further. "For tonight's festive anatomy with Praelector Tulp?"

"I am meant to be there now, as a matter of fact."

Then the artist's face seemed to change. "I am to be there tonight as well," he said, picking through what was in his palm for the small coins.

I paused before answering. "Why, I should expect as much, master. All the city's important men will be attending."

Van Rijn gave me a quizzical look. "I'm glad we had this transaction today," he said, handing me four stivers, which seemed to be payment, not for the bird but for the information about the gibbet.

Still, the coins felt paltry in my hand, since I'd spent so much in sweat to earn that damned paradise, and yet I took the money and bowed deeply. It was an absurd and unnecessary gesture, but a man has to stay in the good graces of his clients.

"Stand up, Fetchet," Van Rijn said. "We are not in Italy. Tell me: When will you have your corpse?"

I straightened. "In moments, I hope. It is a noon execution."

"Then you are already late," he said. "Be off."

I ran down the stairs and out the door and up the Sint Antonies-breestraat, and across Old Town and back to the Dam, and arrived in the square just in time to see the hangman raise the noose over Joep's head.

As I caught my breath, I felt relief. Though it would've been natural for me to have pangs of sadness for doomed Joep, I was more like a turkey hawk circling its prey. My hunger trumped my mercy. I thought: At least I will get this bird.

Just as the hangman tightened that cord, a shriek arose from the crowd so high and piercing it forced all of Dam Square to turn to look. The crowd parted around the font of this eruption, as it might be trying to protect itself from a rearing horse. There was a wench, dressed in tattered rags; her bodice was undone, revealing nearly her full bosom, and her hair wildly sprouted from her head.

"Stop, devil!" she screamed. "No man shall be hanged! Save the innocent!"

Oh, she cried and cried like a Greek siren so no one could ignore her. She screamed that she was a witch who'd already borne five tigers out of her womb, and "I'll birth ten more here and unleash them upon the square unless you halt this execution!" Though I have seen many a true witch in my day, there were more theatrics in her than sorcery. Her hands outstretched attempted to summon lightning but none came. Her eyes, though red and wide open, were not demonic, only at wit's end.

It was whispered through the crowd that her name was Trijntje van Dungeon, from Antwerp, the widow of the slain fishmonger. Some wenches pushed her forward, and a few men lifted her onto the scaffold next to the hangman to plead her cause.

We could all see her more clearly. Her face was round like a plate and smeared from tears; her hair was a mass of curly locks with threads of gray poking out among the fairer hues. She was like some kind of wild Medusa, writhing out of the sea. Her arms were like two great oars stolen off a war galleon. This was no witch, but some proud specimen of Nordic womanhood, who could crush a frail man as easily as a passing carriage wheel would flatten a mouse.

Instead of trying to press her back off the stage, the hangman seemed as awed by her presence as the rest of us. She did not go directly for Joep, as I anticipated, but instead took the scaffold as if it were her own stage and launched her soliloquy upon the crowd.

"This man is innocent," she cried out, now that she'd gotten the full attention of thousands of spectators. "He did not kill my husband." Seeing them standing next to each other on the scaffold, it was hard to believe that there was supposed to be a link between this fleshy Medusa and the timid, pious tailor. It was like imagining a bull wed a wood ant. "I stabbed my husband myself out of pure malice and without a moment's regret," she went on. "I hated him with all my guts and knifed him right in the throat and watched him bleed."

The crowds gasped but I doubt it was because anyone thought she wasn't capable of it.

"Oh, I hated him truly," she went on. "Joep loved me, and he stumbled in during the act and, poor blessed man, took the blame. The sheriff hauled him off and he never argued. All these months, he paid for my crime, now I am here to die for him." She turned and gazed kindly on her beloved. He exchanged the gaze and anyone could see it was real love between that twig and the hearty pea stew.

Turning back to her audience, she began to shout: "Take me! Take me instead. It is I, I, who should have the hangman's rope. I'm the murderer and I have no remorse. I was crazy with hatred. I killed him with my own hands."

She scratched at her breast with exaggerated histrionics to prove her point, crying that the crowd must prevent the unjust execution.

She would not be silenced unless the hangman removed the rope from her beloved Joep and put it on her neck instead. She even tried to push the masked man aside and to draw down the rope, accidentally beginning to strangle her own lover with this force . . . but here the scaffold carpenters and several men from the crowd stepped in. They managed to wrangle her off her stage, but she kept screaming and pounding her massive chest.

I was moved by this scene, I must admit. I was happy for Joep. I'd always found him to be a kind and gentle soul in the months I'd courted his flesh. I'd never wanted to pluck his eyeballs and put them in a cup.

The crowd would've been more than happy to see the hangman swap the rope from Joep's neck to Trijntje's. Soon enough the whole of Dam Square was chanting for his acquittal, and her damnation.

The cry went up as they were hauling her out of the square toward town hall: "Cut him down, cut him down! String her up! String her up!" Even I got swept up in foment. Waving my fist in the air, I chanted, "Joep, Joep! Free the innocent! Kill the damned!" I shouted and cheered, too, when the hangman started to cut Joep down from the rope, and even raised a child on my shoulders to give the lad a better view.

It was only moments later that I realized what had transpired: my cadaver—the one I'd spent so many months cultivating—was not going to die. Though the crowd demanded that crazy Trijntje be dangled from Joep's intended rope, the hangman wouldn't take action until the magistrates had a say, he said. What cowardice! She was clearly the murderess! She'd be a perfect Joep substitute, too. With the body of a woman for dissection, I could charge six or even seven stivers a head for door admission, and certainly her organs would be full of evidence of her ignominy.

I cried out, "Don't waste another moment!" with such fury a few people around me turned in amazement. The hangman didn't heed me. Trijntje was put in irons and dragged off to the Sint Ursula's *spinhuis* instead. As she was being led away in front of the chanting crowd, I climbed the scaffold myself and begged the hangman.

He shook his head at me. "Won't hang a witch," he said bluntly. "You never know what'll come of that."

So instead, this witch would sit in the *spinhuis*, sewing and knitting her days away rather than serve the noble purpose of scientia. It was a scandal.

My troubles were now grave, if you'll forgive me a pun, one obvious pitfall of this profession. What a day! Everything was turning against me.

"But what about my body?" I said to the executioner. "The papers are all signed! The fee paid! The annual anatomical lesson is this very night!"

"There's yet another hanging," said the hangman. "Talk to the magistrate."

VIII

THE HEART

That barge finally got to the Haarlemmer Port, and the gates there were still open, thank the Lord. But now they said we were far from the Dam and the streets were too full of carts to pass. We'd need a skiff to get to the square, and even so, the canals were clogged to bursting. It were getting closer and closer to noon, and my heart were jumping.

The boy said he'd find us a boatman, and before the barge were even docked, he'd jumped across onto land and gone to find one. I watched him run the shore while the barge slid into the berth.

I had to get to the Dam, but the city made me afraid. It were noisy and crowded and the stench of garbage were heavy like a mist. That port were full of sailors, tradesmen, militiamen, scavengers, vagabonds, and all kinds of foreigners in silks and velvets and turbans. Whoever weren't shoving down the lane were standing in the way, trying to sell something. This side, a toothless beggar barking out handmade wares; there a little lass no more than six selling caps and collars; here a bawdy lady tugging down her bodice, selling herself. Men pushing barrels of beer onto carts; boys handing out oysters still wobbling in their half shells. I were afraid in this city like I never were in Leiden.

Guus came back with a big burly fellow in clothes so tattered I took him for a galley slave. "I found him," the boy said breathlessly. "He's got a rowboat."

I could see there weren't no others who would take our fare.

"We must go quickly to Dam Square to stop the hanging," I said. I took one coin out of Father van Thijn's purse and pushed it to him. "We are already late."

The man nodded like he knew all about it. "Keep your money hid," he said. "These streets are teeming with thieves." He smiled a strange smile.

His skiff were close by. He offered me his hand to help me down, and I sat on the seat behind his. Then he climbed down into the boat himself, nearly tipping us all over, and took up his oars. "Are you ready?" he asked.

"Go as fast as you can," I said. "Please."

"We'll have to go around into the harbor," he said. "The canals off the port aren't passable. It'll take till sundown to get through."

"Take us so we get there," I said.

Once we were out of the port, the boatman got into a rhythm with his rowing. I could see he were strong and able, and that he were sure at the oars. He were facing us, his back to the open water, but he knew where he were going. He looked me up and down for a while, and I were sure he were judging me when his eyes fixed on my belly.

"You married to Aris the Kid?" he asked. I knew who he meant.

My Adriaen. "The Kid" were his nickname. The boy had told him our story.

"We never married," were all I said.

"I knew your man," the boatman said. "We were in the same house of corrections in Utrecht."

"Adriaen?" I didn't believe him.

"I got the brand of Utrecht," he said. Holding both oars with one hand, he loosened the strings on his shirt to show me a marking on his neck. His skin were paler than Adriaen's, and his neck were strong and wide. It weren't like Adriaen's branding. It looked longer and twisted, like he'd pulled away when they'd burned him.

Guus watched with an open mouth.

"You want to see it?" the boatman asked, motioning for the boy to get a closer look.

Guus slid forward in the boat. "Wow," he said.

I waited until the boatman tied his shirt. "You must've been saved, then. Because here you are a freeman and a workingman, and Adriaen is being readied for the noose." I felt a sudden chill in me. "Will we be there soon?"

⌒⁊⁎⁊⌐

The harbor of Amsterdam must be the busiest place in the Lord's kingdom. It were like a forest where the trees were masts and the birds were flags and ribbons whipping in the wind of ivory sails. Everywhere around us were giant galleons carved with wooden ladies and imperial crests. Sloops ferried men out from the shore, their shoulders burdened with trunks.

Ours were a small vessel, and we tossed side to side in the wakes of them bigger boats. I asked the boatman if we were to die out there. "Don't be afraid, lass," he said. "She's a small but sure craft."

That's when I saw it. There on the other side of the IJ waterfront. The gallows field where there were crosses lined up and bodies hung from them, they call the Volewijk. That's where they take the dead to let their bodies rot after a hanging. They were like a small orchard of weird trees. The bodies looked like black rags half fallen off the clothesline except when you looked longer they started to round out as they swayed in the wind. My heart started to race, and I could hear the blood come into my ears. I imagined Adriaen there among them, another drooping bundle of black rags, beaten by the sun, sinking in his flesh, the buzzards circling.

The boy at my elbow by the rail said, "He out there?"

I told Guus that Adriaen weren't to hang.

The boatman looked over his shoulder and saw what we saw. "Better close your eyes, then," he said. "No need for you to see such things now."

We followed the big ships down the main canal from the IJ they call the Damrak. The boatman were right. I could see that the smaller canals were all jammed up with skiffs and rowboats, and the banks were full to overflowing. We were just one boat in a sea of ships trying to get to the Dam. We clung close to the canal wall, and sometimes the bigger boats banged against us. The boatman put his oars into the boat and used his hands to push up along through the vessels. We held on to each other, the boy and me, as the boatmen all around us shouted and cursed, seeing who could get farthest.

If that were not enough, on all sides were those street vendors. Hands came reaching down at me as we moved through the stinking canals: smoked fish and cobbed corn and toys for the boy. Harlots raised their skirts to the boatman. Street vendors cried, "East Indies sugar and spices! Sugar from the New World. Spices from the Far East!"

I wanted to be there. We were late. We would not get to Adriaen in time. The boatman knew my thoughts. He saw the fear in my eyes and said, "Lass, we're closer than you think."

The buildings grew bigger and bigger as we passed through the Damrak. They were grand and tall, twice as high as buildings in Leiden. It looked like they were built one on top of the other, not even a garden or a simple path between them, and doors right on the street, so you step from your own rooms right into public, everyone on top of everyone else.

"I'll stop here," he said at last, "and walk you to the square. It's not far, but the Damrak's too crowded and we'll get there faster on foot." He turned and looked at my belly. "You okay to walk?"

I told him I were. He turned into a narrow canal, tied up the skiff, and we got out. I tried to hand him my coins again but he would not take them. He took me by the arm and the boy came to my other side. We went into a narrow alley and I could hear the crowds nearby. He were doing what he'd promised. He were tattered and hard, but I could tell he were a good man.

"I need to see the magistrate," I said.

But soon as the narrow alley opened into the huge square I feared we were too late. Everyone were already there and the scaffold were readied, waiting. I saw them drag a woman up the gallows in chains, and thought: If Amsterdam hangs a woman it'll hang a thief just the same.

The boatman said to keep our chins low and go direct to town hall. It were not far, just right there on the square. There were a posting on the door I could not read and the room were dark inside. I thought I'd missed the magistrate, but the boatman told me there were men inside. A man pushed open the door, almost hitting us with it as he went out, waving a scroll of paper in one hand. He were a short man carrying a burlap sack.

It were the boatman who opened the door for us. We stepped onto a marble floor and the heavy wood slammed it shut. A clerk came in and without asking who we were told us to wait. They sat us down in high-backed chairs covered in red velvet. They made that room for important men, and I felt small and dirty in there, like a field mouse sneaking in for cheese.

We waited a long time and I could hear the crowd outside the door get loud again before the magistrate's clerk called us in. He were a thin man with a long chin and bulging eyes. He wore a long white collar and a tall black hat. His face had small lines etched from his eyes to his lips.

The boy came with me to his desk. I did as Father van Thijn had told me. I said my name and showed my belly and told him I were Adriaen's "betrothed."

"Marriage papers?"

I shook my head. "We didn't marry yet."

He nodded in silence. "Birth record?"

I shook my head again. Adriaen were born around when I were born, too.

"Any papers at all?"

The boy stepped forward and put Father van Thijn's letter on the desk.

"What's this?" The clerk opened the letter and read it through one time. Then he eyed the boy. "Who are you?"

"Father van Thijn sent me," he said proudly. "I'm an orphan in our church."

Until then, I hadn't even thought on who the boy's parents might be.

The clerk looked at both of us. "Your intentions are noble, but I'm afraid you've come too late. There's only two men to hang today and the first one just got taken off the noose. Next one is condemned. I've just signed his body over to the Amsterdam Surgeons' Guild."

"Signed his body . . . ?" I said.

"They use convicts for the annual anatomical lesson."

"To the skinners?" the boy said.

"They've paid a goodly sum for his flesh." The clerk straightened and glanced at my face. "He's to serve medicine. His body will be used for public good."

"For public good?" I said. "But he doesn't need to die. He's not a murderer. He's only a thief."

The clerk looked down at a book in front of him where words were written and looked back up at me. "Yes, that's what it says here. A thief."

He read to me from his book: "Early in the morning about five or six o'clock, on the Heren Sluis in this town he joined two others to attack a certain person with the intent to snatch away his cloak and whom they threw to the ground while all the three pounced upon him and as this man, this victim, tried to cry for help, they gagged him, preventing him from making a noise. If the night watch had not discovered them in time, they certainly would have killed him."

He had put Father van Thijn's letter away, shaking his head. "All these evil facts and their serious consequences are not to be tolerated in a town of justice and honesty."

"But Adriaen. Adriaen loved . . ." I knew my speech would not be heard.

I pulled out Father van Thijn's purse and poured the coins out onto his desk. They made a sound like heavy rain. "What did they pay for his body? We will pay more." I did not know how many coins were there or what they were worth.

The clerk stood, pulling his hat tighter on his head. "There's nothing I can do for you now. The sentence was sealed four days ago. The hangman already pardoned the other convict on the word of his wench. And the Surgeons' Guild must have its anatomy."

"Adriaen weren't never cruel," I said. "Never violent . . ."

He had some pity in his eyes. "You should have come earlier. There's to be no more pardons on this Justice Day."

He stood and his chair screeched against the marble floor.

"But we have come from Leiden. The church . . ." the boy said.

"If you want to claim that body, I'm afraid you'll have to wrestle it from the surgeons." He were already walking out of the room.

"That man . . ." I said. "The one who just left? He's the one bought Adriaen's body?"

He didn't answer my question. "After the execution, you'll have to go to the guild, to the tower in the Waag. Dissections begin at sundown. I suggest you get there first."

I ran out of the town hall and into the crowd, looking for that short man, the one with the scroll. If he'd paid for Adriaen's body, he'd take my money instead, wouldn't he? He'd let them leave Adriaen alive. He'd let them hear me.

I ran through the square, and the boatman and the boy followed me. But I saw none of that short man and all of the other people. It were like wading into a river, the current against us, the tall grass grabbing at our ankles. It all went too fast. I lost so much so fast, so deep I were in sorrow. I could do nothing to stop them hauling him up on that rope. I nearly drowned in that square.

"I'm real sorry you have to see this," were the last thing the boatman said when we got to the center of that square.

The voices and the noise and the smells and the sounds were more than I could bear. I did not move forward but there I were right in front. I stood and I watched and I saw. Adriaen were bruised and cut and his right hand were gone.

The people parted and he walked toward the hangman's scaffold. His face were pale, sunken. His eyes were red and wild. He didn't seem to see anything, though he looked straight ahead. His legs were in chains that rattled against the ground, his arms held behind him in irons. There were a guard on each side of him, shoving, making him shuffle and clank. They were as rough as if he were a mule.

He did not resist them. He would not resist. He were trying to walk tall. He puffed out his chest and kept his chin high. But they shoved him through the crowd, and the people shouted his name, then the guards pushed and pushed.

He were beaten and weak but he did not let them see it. The hangman unlocked the irons, and they fell to the scaffold with a clank. Then the hangman asked him if he had any last words. He asked only if he could take off his jerkin and shirt. He stood there, in the whipping wind, his body cut and scarred and beaten, his lips dry and bloody, his pant legs torn. He raised his free arms into the sky and flexed them like a strongman.

"I'm not afraid," he cried. "I've been waiting for a long time. Death, I welcome your embrace. I do not fear you."

I looked up for some sign of mercy, but the sky were dull and dark and threatening. There it were, right before me, the dangling noose, readied for my Adriaen.

The boy's small fingers crept into my hand and I were glad, at least, for that. It made me think on Carel and how I had to live for him.

Then the bells began to ring. The church bells ringing out the hour. The deathly hour. The sound were hard and cruel. *Bong, bong, bong,* like a demand. Like the devil himself instructing the hangman to do his work. I felt every ring of that bell like I were on the end of the cord that rang it.

The hangman stepped forward and put the noose around Adriaen's neck. "Aris! Aris! Aris Kindt! Aris Kindt!" the people cried in time to the sound of the bells. It were not music. It were not chanting or singing. It were not the sound of God or Jesus or love or prayer. It were thunder crashing in your ears before a coming storm.

I felt the whole square close around me. They were all moving up to see it done. Now it were time. The bells rang, and it were to be done. It were so tight. There were nowhere to move, no air to breathe. I were ready to drown. The hangman stepped toward Adriaen. He were not a human but a devil with black holes for eyes inside his mask. I closed my eyes and kept them shut. My head pounded with every chime, every *bong*. I breathed in the foul smell of Amsterdam. The people, the square, the black sky. All of Amsterdam were roaring. They roared his name with a loud, wide throat. "Aris!"

Then there were silence. The moment that they put the noose around his neck, Adriaen stopped and stood still. It were only then, the moment before they hauled him up, that he saw me. Somehow he saw me.

He stopped looking proud. He stopped looking strong. The noose were on his neck and he looked down. That's where we were standing, right there, straight ahead. His eyes fixed on my face, but he saw my belly, too. He saw me and he saw his babe.

"Flora." He said my name.

"Adriaen." I said his.

Then the hangman covered Adriaen's face with a hood.

Painting diagnosis: Rembrandt's *Anatomy Lesson of*
Dr. Nicolaes Tulp, 1632

Earlier, I noted something that intrigued me when I began to observe the right hand of the corpse with a scope. I described it as an "uneasy transition between Adriaen's right hand and the body" with wrinkles of paint occurring together with a few premature cracks. This is the hand that is not the focus of Tulp's dissection (the one that has gotten so much attention from the medical community over the years) but the other one. I requested a copy of the 1978 radiograph from De Vries and his team and I have that in my hands now.

Over lunch, in the cafeteria, I gave the X-ray a great deal of my attention. I observed something no one seems to have noted so far in previous examinations of this X-ray or of the painting: remarkably, the underpainting of the right hand is a very unusual shape. It is not a full hand but a shape that is more like a curve, like a very large backward *C*. This seems to indicate that Rembrandt originally painted in a hand that is not quite a hand. This presents two possibilities, it seems to me: it could either be a kind of sketch for the hand, or it could actually be a depiction of a severed limb. That is, a hand that was amputated. A stump.

I'm quite surprised we overlooked this in the 1978 study, because it's right there, and quite easy to see, now that I'm looking at it.

Could this just be a way that he sketched out a location for the hand before adding more detail later? I suppose that's possible. But I've never seen him use that technique in other paintings. His underpaintings are typically quite detailed, especially in these younger years when he seems to never want to waste any paint.

When he does change things using his pentimenti, he typically moves objects or figures left or right or up or down—he makes some of his characters in this portrait lean one way at one point and then adjusts their position in the frame later, to make way for other figures, like Colevelt. But I have never seen him sketch out a hand like a club and then paint in a more detailed hand later. Nor a foot. Nor a head, for that matter. Rembrandt didn't sketch on canvas. He painted. And when he made a mistake, he went back and dabbed in pigments until he corrected his painting.

I am almost certain there is something else going on here. Perhaps what Rembrandt was trying to paint was indeed a stump. Because now we know that the dead man he painted was a thief, a recidivist thief. And in the seventeenth century, thieves were often punished with the amputation of their right hands. Corporal (corporeal) punishment. The next step is to check this *justitieboek* to see if he was in fact punished in this barbaric way.

Fascinating, really. It could explain why there is so much discussion of the left hand being quite distended. The right hand is quite a bit shorter, and it appears that the distal area of the hand has been painted over the shorter limb.

I am now taking a very small pigment sample from the right hand area, to examine it under a binocular microscope. I am also taking a small pigment sample from the overpainted section. I'll have to discuss this all with Claes when he comes in this evening. It could be a very exciting finding, indeed!

IX

THE BODY

I committed my first crime with my first breath, Lord Schout: I killed my mother as I came wailing into the world. My father never made mention of my name day nor year of birth, nor season. He only cursed that day and me with it, pronouncing me sinner from birth.

Yes, Lord Schout. I will tell you all. I will speak volumes. Only don't let them haul me up with weights, sire. I will tell you all you want to know. I will sing, Lord Schout, I will dance for you. Just do not haul me up.

Yes, Your Honor, it is true what it says in your papers. I'm a Leidener. I grew up in a cottage on the Rhine between a corn mill and the Kerkgracht Bridge. Father was a pious Calvinist by temperament and a sheath maker by profession. He supplied the civic militias with leathers for sabers and falchions, and holsters for daggers and muskets, and did trade with sword smiths and munitions men. He sometimes did handiwork on saddles, too.

We got scraps of hides from the butcher and the tannery, and irons from a nearby smith. The work of a sheath maker is only to craft the leathers, and it is not too hard for a child to learn. Since as early as I can remember he took me daily to the shop, where he taught my tiny hands to smooth the leathers, press in studs, and sew on straps.

While other children went to school, I was sent out into the woods to harvest oak and beech bark, or crack beechnuts for their tannins. We used that to soften the harder bits of leather. My father did the carving—fancy patterns all along the length of the scabbard—and then I'd sew the seams and add the belt loops. At the end, we'd add our shop's brand, a beechnut coming out of its husk. The nut is shiny and smooth, but the husk is a prickly burr. It was a simple brand, and he used a fire-heated iron for it—he'd leave it in the stove until it was red as a poker and then press the brand into the leather. I used to love the smell of that burning hide.

Inside the shop and out, my father was as devout and workman-like as a monk, and unless instructing me in skills of the trade, he uttered no words. I would be grateful if a yawn or a sigh passed his lips to break our terrible monotony. We toiled side by side all the day, all the week, year upon year, as I grew from a small sickly boy to a large able boy, his apprentice in every trade but happiness. I was a dutiful servant, never fighting, never swearing, never throwing bones or running off to the town square as the other boys did; and on Sundays I followed two paces behind him on his weekly pilgrimage to church.

I should have known no love at all in my life had it not been for Flora, the girl who lived in the house with the mill. She was as wild as the red corn poppy that grew among the heath. From my window

I watched her in the yard. I saw her putting out saucers of milk for the cats. I saw her in the shade of a juniper tree.

She did not live under the heavy hand of Calvinism. Flora's father's only religion was beer sucking, and he'd take to bed midday in the mill's hayloft. Because of his idleness, the mill had long ceased to spin and the grindstone never felt a chaff of wheat. Flora's mother, whose fingers were too fat to ply the Leiden linen trade, earned her family's way by hiring out studs. From break of dawn until lantern lit, she led the bull from town to town and farm to farm, leaving Flora to wash the linens and tend the garden and the farm.

If my father tried vainly to convince me of God, here at last was evidence. In church, if the scriptures mentioned Mary, I imagined Flora. And when I was told to consider the sins of the Magdalene, there I imagined Flora, too. But when Flora passed my windows and I saw the golden flicker of her sunlit hair, I dropped my eyes in piety as my father taught me to do.

Father believed in the strictest doctrine of predestination. When Maurits of Orange came, Father quickly fell behind the stadtholder's crusade to rid the Low Countries of the *waardgelders*, and as soon as the more pious Calvinists in his congregation took up arms, he was the first to call for outright war. He set out to supply their forces as a sutler, and planned to pack up from our home and leave me behind to tend the sheath-making shop.

The thought of living in that house alone, running the workshop without him, was frightening, in spite of his cruelty. I tried to prevent him, pleading, "But, Father, I will miss you if you leave." He only raised an eyebrow and told me a man does not use his tongue to stir honey.

The night before he left, we sat down to sup together for the very last time. Before our peasants' feast, I opened my mouth to speak and in a quavering, cracking voice, I started out slowly. "What is the use of fighting any war if we are predestined to our fates?"

His desired silence broken as a pebble disturbs the clarity of a windless lake, he steadied his gaze upon my face. "Say you something, my son?" he asked. "I didn't summon you to speak."

"I only said . . ." I hesitated but then mustered the courage to go on: "If God had predestined us to our fates, then it makes no difference whether anyone is a Gomarist, Arminian, Calvinist, or Libertine, goose or swine."

Anger bloomed in Father's cheeks. "Do you doubt our cause?"

That was all I ventured. My lips, which were now clenched to save me from my own destruction, could not utter even "yes." I looked back to my plate.

But my father, now stirred, would not let it rest. He repeated his question, this time strengthened by my timidity. "Would you have the Libertines in our church? Open the dikes to let flood in all those papists from the south?"

I focused my gaze even harder on my plate.

"Speak, son. You are so bold as to challenge our morality. I will hear it."

I knew he would goad me until I would speak again, so I tried.

"It's only . . ." I had worked on my logic for some time. "If we are destined each one for heaven or hell, what is the use of this war? Each of us will learn God's will by our own hand."

My father's expression was like that of a man kicked by his own horse. Then, with the full force of his wrath, he smacked me across the jaw, knocking me from my stool to the floor.

He stood above me and spoke with anger, masked by clarity and reason. "God forgive me, but now I will repent. Does that take away the sting of the blow? Does it raise you off the floor? If this is your belief, Son, tell me: Shall I repent for this act as your papists do? Or is it better had I not raised my fist to you at all?"

My father had never before touched me in the spirit of anger. He had almost never touched me at all. This blow rang through my whole body like a sudden revelation, and I did nothing but let tears fall from my eyes and run along my cheeks.

"What is better?" my father wanted to know. He seemed to think we were having a discussion.

I had no answer for him. I had never tried to argue with him before and now I knew why. I became aware of the taste of something like copper in my mouth. I moved my tongue and tasted it, and when my tongue roamed further, it found a tooth moving freely in the gum.

"Answer, lad," he said, kicking me in the ribs. "Does it hurt any less if I repent?"

I spat out some of the blood. "Repent not," I told him from where I lay. Now I wanted him to kick me. "Your place in heaven or hell is secure, Father. Kick me, if you must."

It was the only time in our lives together that I spoke back this way. And it was the only time in our lives he obeyed an order from me.

He kicked again. "Cannot keep shop, cannot carve or sew. Is this what God gives me in exchange for my Ilja? Why has God cursed me? I am a pious man. I have been a soldier in God's army."

I felt nothing for my father then. Not hatred and not love, and certainly not pity. I did desire to weep but gritted my teeth instead because I saw for the first time how much he hated me.

I won't recount all that did befall me at my father's evil whim that night, for every man knows the consequences of betraying a lord and master. But I will tell you that he used the tools of his trade to sear the memory of my disobedience into my flesh. He heated our brand in the stove and pressed that beechnut into my back. I do not remember when, exactly, it came to that, but I recall his words: "I might be gone a long time," he said, "but now I'll know you when I see you next."

By morning, I had succumbed to the force of his argument. I wasn't dead, but I could feel every inch of my body. I had been beaten and branded by my own father, but it was human contact and that was something for which I very strongly craved.

I awoke to the sound of his sobbing, as he crouched beside my cot and stroked my head. I let him cry, and didn't reveal that I was awake, for I preferred to see him at least manly in his rage. Then he left to wage his war. I didn't open my eyes until I heard his footsteps fade on the path.

Flora came to me for the first time that day, with her basket of bandages and herbs. She had heard it all from the mill house next door, and she'd waited until my father left me. She came and fed me, cleaned my wounds, dressed my cuts. She was the only person who ever touched me with gentleness, that Flora.

⋯⋰✳⋱⋯

My father went to join the Gomarists and I went to join the tankardists at the local tavern. As the year wore on, I spent more and more time there and I became a lax servant to the shop. Although I knew my new path was ruinous, life among the beer suckers, pickpockets, and thieves was far easier than attempting to become an upright man.

Those days, my Flora was very far from me, because she had become a slave to her father, who had finally given up his old religion, only to become one of the most austere Calvinists of our town, though her mother was a Lutheran. Poor Flora wasn't allowed to walk the circumference of her yard, unless she was fetching water or taking the washing to the canal. I saw her only from afar, now wearing a servant's scarf over her beautiful straw-colored hair.

But the more time I was without my father and without Flora, the worse I felt. For, among these damned souls, I was only securing my own doom. And yet, I reasoned, was it not unavoidable anyway?

On the third anniversary of my father's last night, the Leiden overseer posted a bill on my door, claiming the shop would be closed. I had failed to pay property dues. It was the fault of my idleness and depravity. I tried to find a man in town who would help me, some good friend of my father's—a former client or customer who had relied on him through the years—but none would help. A week later, they came and boarded up the shop. They posted another note on the door naming me and calling me a bankrupt and a coward.

On that same date, I got word from my father that he would be returning home to Leiden to work alongside me again, this time to take up the cobbler's trade. The trade in warlike goods was ended, he said, and he wanted to run a civilian shop.

I didn't know what to do, Your Honor. I dared not stay to show my father my ignominious face! I could not stand before the shop and see his view of me confirmed as he read the slanderous bill posted on the door.

I threw a few goods into a sack that night and ran as long as my strong young legs would take me; and when I could not run any longer, I walked until I was out of breath; and when I could not walk without limping, I slowed my gait; and when I could not walk at all, I crawled. At last, I found myself in a forest of stunted trees and there, bleary-eyed and tired to sightlessness, I cried until my eyes were void of tears, put my head down on a log, and fell into the arms of sleep.

I was awakened, just before dawn, by dreams of such a terrible nature that they sent my soul fleeing from rest: I was on the shop table, and my father was standing over me, holding a knife over my chest. I was immobile and unable to speak or to move and defend myself. I could see and hear my father, who was lecturing me about human frailty and moral turpitude. He spoke at great length, but I didn't understand the words he was saying, muffled as they were as if through a muslin cloth. Other men entered the room and looked on as Father used shears to slice into my breast. The men were awed by his actions, but they did nothing to protect me. They seemed to agree that I had sinned, and that was enough to justify this living torture.

I bolted awake to find my head swarming with black ants. The creatures were everywhere about my face, in my hair, within my ears, inside my nostrils, and climbing across my tongue. I soon saw the cause of this pestilence. In the darkness of the previous night I had made as my pillow a log that was rotted and emptied by vermin. And behind this log there was the body of a gray hair who seemed to have been taken by the black death. In the weariness and torment of the previous night, I'd lain, unawares, with a corpse. The insects had taken me for her companion and were already trying to make a meal of my flesh.

Once I'd shaken off the ants and the chills, I looked at this gray hair for a while. She was a curious cousin, curled into herself like a ball, her hands touching her face. Beside her was a metal pail, filled with sand. I didn't know where she had hailed from or where she was bound, for I could think of no beach near this forest, and concluded that she was a crone whose bucket of water had turned to sand.

All of this I took for a dark omen for my journey, but I didn't turn back to Leiden, for my greater fear was of my father's wrath. I searched the old woman's body, found two stivers in the pocket of her smock, and went fast upon my way.

X

THE HEART

They tell me I fainted when the deed were done. When I awoke, I were lying in the wet mud, the boatman kneeling over me, holding my hand. The boy were saying, "Ma'am, ma'am, ma'am," over and over, like a babe cries.

I moved my hand to touch my belly. All could go like that, all at once, everything. I didn't feel him there at first and I could not move, the fear were so tight in me. But then I felt movement—a hard kick up under my ribs. Once, then twice, and a third time and I cried, laughing, too. My boy. He were still there. We were still here.

Adriaen were gone. The scaffold, the guards, everything. He had seen us, and he knew, but now they'd taken him away again. The noose had been cut from the rope, the hangman were gone. The sky were as dark as midnight. It seemed like black night, but it were still day.

There were people standing over me, peering down to see my face. "She's carrying the Kid's child," I heard one of them say.

"She shouldn't be here, not in this cold," said another.

"Get her somewhere warm," said another.

"Let her rot out here," said someone else.

I felt Father van Thijn's purse. I drew a few coins into my fingers and held them out. I said, "I have money. Take me home. Please take me home. We have to go home."

"But, ma'am," the boy said, "ma'am, Father van Thijn said we should claim the body. For his Christian burial. If he didn't live. That's what Father van Thijn said."

His small hands found my fingers again. He made me think on Carel and how the two of us would go on.

The boatman helped me raise myself onto my elbows. He said, "They carted his body away."

I pushed up from my elbows in the mud. The people in the square got me standing. They helped me to walk a few steps, and then a few more until I were not too dizzy, until I could walk alone.

"The boy is right," the boatman said, once he thought I were ready. "If you want to claim his body, we need to get to the skinners."

Yes, I remembered. His body. That is all I would be able to save.

❧❀☙

I did not have the words to save Adriaen. They did not want to hear my words and I had no words to tell. I did not know they would take him from me like that, like that so fast out in that square. I thought there had to be some will of God in it for it to be done. But what God wills this? To hang a thief? If they knew he were just a thief, why did they hang him?

I had no words for the magistrate but I thought I could form words for that doctor who wanted to cut open his chest: He would find no hard heart in my Adriaen. No cold liver, no black blood. Adriaen had a sweet soul. Ever since he were a boy. I knew him then and I knew him as he grew. His body came to be a man's body but I never saw his soul change. He were a soft soul and a hurt soul, a soul in want of kindness. That's why they called him "the Kid." Them who knew him. Though I never liked that name. He just went simple from one thing to the next.

⳥⳥⳥

I want to tell you about how it started between us, because we were in love, and it were true. It started when his father beat him and left him to join Maurits. We heard it from the house next door, my mother and me. We held our hands to our lips to stop from crying out and crouched there by the stove. We knew the wrath of men when all the kindness has left them. We waited and when the father left, my mother said I were to go.

I brought him food and mended his wounds and stayed until it got late. The next week, he came to our house with wildflowers he'd gathered from our yard. I saw him out there picking them, and then he tied them up with twine. My mother said, "The boy's come to see you. Fix your hair." So I twirled my curls round my finger and went to the door. Adriaen were young then, his hair blond and fine. He asked me if I wanted to take a rowboat out on the river and I said I would if he were well enough to row.

I remember that day and every drop of light in it still, because it were then I fell in love. We walked down to the docks and he untied a rowboat and pushed it out into the water. His face still had some cuts and his eye had a bruise above it, but he looked strong and young, and his arms were lean and freckled. I were quiet most of the day and he did all the rowing. He took me out into the river and we glided along. The sun were shining and the air were crisp and there were birds to see just everywhere. He weren't turning around to see where he were headed. He knew where he would go. He were taking me somewhere and I were happy to go there. Wherever it were.

We landed on a small island just covered in trees. I never saw a place like that, with no houses anywhere, no paths and no walls or fences. It were all overgrown, untame, and we had to hold on to tree trunks just to scramble up through the weeds. He went ahead, but every time I looked up, he were holding out a hand to me. We went into it, this wild forest, and soon we were on top of a hill.

"There," he said, pointing upward.

There were nothing there except the sun, but it were the sun, and we could see it clear. The light rained down through the thickness of the trees and the light were cut into pieces, like small drops, falling onto us and into our eyes.

I sat with him, not touching, not kissing, nor any of the things young lovers do. He were shy, but he sat near me and he watched me and he said, "I wanted to show you this."

Something changed in me then. I grew up, I grew old. I saw him, this bruised boy, hurt but strong, proud but weak, tamed and yet wild, showing me the sunlight. I don't know how long we sat there but soon we left, and it were in the skiff on the way back from that trip that I looked at him and knew I loved him and knew we'd never be apart.

It were days before he kissed me, but eventually he did. It were years before we became lovers, but eventually we were. There were years and years in between, but Adriaen were always that boy to me. The one who rowed that skiff across the river and took me to that quiet, gentle place. Where he pointed up through the mess of leaves in the wild thicket and said, There. There's sun.

XI

THE MOUTH

It was no simple deed to get Aris all the way to the Waag in the corpse cart with that crowd upon me. I suffered a beating of cabbages and apples; my hair was yanked, my beard pulled, my sight nearly blinded by rotten eggs.

The police escort proved well worth the extra ten stivers the magistrate charged me for the "courtesy" of his company. There were hundreds of men and women and even tiny lads who wanted to put a hand on that dead Kindt. I haven't seen anything like it since they put Black Bartle to the rope—and he'd killed six men with an ax.

This is the worst part of the job of the *famulus anatomicus*. The rest—the eye plucking and bathing and burying organs in the churchyard—is mere dirty work compared to getting that dead man out of the square once he's been hanged. The women howl, the men grab your garments, and the children hit your shins with wooden spoons.

I swear, they would lift the corpse right out of the cart and carry him over their heads through the town, singing his name, if they could. I know not why a crowd is so capricious like that. One minute they're calling him a rogue and crying for his neck; and once he's fallen all is forgiveness, and they rush to greet him as if he were the miracle of Amsterdam itself.

I felt sorry for that Kindt, though, because he didn't need to go that way—on the rope and to the anatomy, too. He was a cloak thief and a vagabond, but it's rare to get the rope for robbery.

Oh, yes, I am the friend of all scoundrels, a lover of rapscallions. I have no lust for vengeance on any living soul, sinner or saint. There isn't a man in Amsterdam who can't be accused of burgling and beggary on some scale, small or large. Wrongdoing is what makes us human, you see, for not a single one of us is sinless. Show me a man over twenty who hasn't at least a hundred minor crimes to his name and it's sure to be a monk or a minister. Then show me a monk or minister who doesn't have fifty smaller trespasses, at least. Even that magistrate took a little extra out of my pocket when I had to buy Aris's body instead of Joep's. "Another three guilders," that long-faced officer declared as a cunning smile swept across his lips. As I say: every man in this town is a thief.

Once inside the Waag and cloistered with the body behind the heavy doors of the guild chambers, I felt, at least, secure. I began to consider all that had transpired that day: chasing Rotzak, getting the fake paradise, visiting the painter, seeing Joep set free, begging the magistrate for the new body, being harangued through the streets. The bird, the sailor, the artist, the corpses, the throngs. As soon as there was silence, my emotions pressed for some release. I'm not ashamed to admit I sat for a moment and cried like a babe.

Then I composed myself, for my work had to be done with some haste. The first thing I needed to do was to remove the dead man's shoes, a sad pair made of battered leather with holes through the soles and rotted wooden heels. Then, using a blade, I cut off the rest of his tattered rags, which consisted only of a coarse pair of wool hose and knee breeches. He no longer wore a shirt or the jerkin, since he'd stripped himself above the waist for his performance at the hanging. All that covered his upper body were the bandages wrapped too tightly around his stump. It took a little effort to get it free from all the caked-up blood and dirt.

Next, it was my job to trim the man's hair and beard. I think that mane had never met a comb, and likely he'd trimmed his beard only with his own folding gully. The whole of his head was mangy like a mutt's and let off a foul odor, like something between a dog's legs. I could've cut it with a pair of shears, but I managed with one of the surgeon's tools instead. I trimmed the mane down to a civil militia-man's cut and shaved all but the chin of his beard.

Once that was accomplished, I got my bucket and filled it with cold soapy water, then dunked my cloth and began to wash him. There was a thick layer of grit all over his flesh, and a line across his belly so thick you'd think it was drawn on him, right where his stomach would've met the hem of his jerkin. My cloth moved across his flesh slowly, because his skin was so coarse. I had to check for wax in the ears, globs of snot in the nose.

It's no small undertaking to make a vagabond look tidy. Think of it: he sleeps by the side of the city gates, bathes in the river or canals, sups by the side of a campfire, never a basin or sponge within reach. I had to press for a while in places to loosen the grime on his skin. I cleaned his feet, which were brown and blistered; under his arms, which smelled like mushrooms and charcoal; under his nails, which were encrusted with black. And I had to check in the private parts, too. A lot of them soil themselves when they're hanged, but not that Aris.

After I finished washing the body, I plucked out the eyeballs one by one and put them in a cup. I use a special tool for that, a kind of toothy spoon. I'm used to it now, after all these years, but I'll tell you that's the part I like least.

I gave him one final rinse and felt satisfied with my work. Then I put him over my shoulder and lowered him—shoulders, torso, legs, feet—onto the block of ice so as to keep him fresh. He was bigger than me, but I managed to heft him. I'm small but sturdy and used to carrying dead weight.

Then I had to adjust his pose before it stiffened into an uncomely shape. I know what happens to the man in the few hours after he's hanged and before he's dissected. The body stiffens and becomes cold and pale. The jaw won't move anymore, so if you haven't closed his mouth in time, he'll look startled throughout the dissection. The joints stiffen and the limbs won't flex. So that he doesn't go flat as a board, what I do is bend his elbows and prop up his knees with a stick to give him a lively look.

I stood back and judged my work. This thief could not have had a more solemn and stately bed. There was not much I could do about his scars, but at least I'd made him neat and tidy.

No matter how well I prepared him, though, I knew Tulp would not be pleased with this specimen. The scars, the stump, the rough rope burn. What could I do, though? There was only one hanging, and this was the one they'd hanged. We could not reraise the scaffold and noose someone else instead.

I got a white sheet I'd use to cover him—the same one I later use for the burial—but before I put it over him I let him lie there in the open air. I like to leave them like that for an hour or two till the soul of the dead man has time to ascend. Or descend, depending on how it goes. I learned that from Otto van Heurne, my second master. He said the Egyptians wrapped mummies up tight so their souls would join them on the trip to the afterlife. I like to let the soul get to the afterlife faster, and sometimes it's a bumpy road indeed. If you leave a dead body for a few days, you'll see and hear that soul escape. The flesh swells, the chest rises, foul winds escape its mouth. It makes other . . . emissions. I tell you this not so you will laugh. It's the body settling, while the soul finds its release. I think the soul must be like vapors, and when the body doesn't hold on to it anymore, it flies out through every orifice.

⸙

I was cleaning up my tools when I heard a faint rap on the outside door. Only one knock, and then nothing else. Then I heard the swinging of the bolt and footsteps, and a chill rose through my spine.

"There you are, Fetchet," someone said from the shadows. "Did you not hear me knock?"

"Yes, my liege," I said to the anonymous voice, for I did not recognize it. Master van Rijn stepped out of the shadows. "It's only me, Fetchet. I hope you don't mind I let myself in."

I reflexively drew the cloth over the corpse, and stepped between it and the painter. "Master, you should not have troubled yourself to come all the way here. You only need to send a messenger and I would ably arrive at your doorstep—"

He pressed into the room. "I'd like to apologize for being so brusque with you earlier," he continued as casually as if we were meeting on the street. "I rather berated myself after you left for my presumptuousness. Imagine, expecting fantastical creatures to appear on my doorstep. The fabled footed paradise. Only to order them up and think I can have them. As if I were some kind of king."

"That is the beauty of our modern times, sire. It's true that we can now get almost anything from anywhere, if only we wish it. I promise you, if there is a footed paradise in this world, I'll procure it for you."

The artist waved his hand in the air. "Indeed, and it's not why I've come. I came because I would like a little time with him."

He was talking about the body. "I don't expect he will be much of a conversationalist, Master van Rijn."

The artist laughed. "My business won't require an exchange of words. I have been commissioned to paint the commemorative portrait of Tulp's lesson."

"Then a true honor has been bestowed on you, Master van Rijn. The great Pickenoy usually paints the guild pictures." I could see this comment irked him, so I continued. "Of course, I'm sure that your portrait shall far exceed his."

"The point is, Fetchet, that I would like to have a bit of time to sketch the corpse."

I thought this a strange request. "He has no money, sire. If he had, I'd have found it in his breeches, I'm sure."

"What difference would that make?"

"I know what they say about curio dealers—that we'll take coins painted on the floor. But there are noble men in this profession, too, sire. I'd have given it to Professor Tulp, because it was he who bought this body."

"But I am seeking no money from him, Fetchet."

"Don't they pay you to be painted?" I asked plainly. "Otherwise, why paint?"

"I only want to have a good look at his arm, because Dr. Tulp has asked me to make a special point of portraying his arm in the picture."

"Has he?" I thought this over.

"Yes. It's, well, it's a longer story."

"The arm in particular? Did he happen to mention which arm?"

"Which arm? Does it matter which arm?"

"In this case it does, sire. For, you see the convict was a thief."

"I have to admit, Fetchet, I don't always follow the thread of your logic."

"A thief, sire, steals with a hand."

"Indeed, for he cannot steal with his feet."

"Unless he is a monkey, sire."

"Which he is not."

"It is the hand that gives offense."

"Well—"

"And that which gives offense must be taken."

"You mean his hand has been lopped off by the executioner?"

"That's what I mean, sire. He's missing his right hand."

"But he's been executed. Why take his hand, too?"

"The hand was done before—some other time."

Perhaps you're listening to my tale and you think my skull is numb. The truth is that I was trying to buy time. I hoped to give the corpse the opportunity he needed for his soul to escape.

"He has the left hand," the artist said.

"Indeed. His left hand suits him very well."

"Excellent. Now we are getting somewhere."

"You'd like to see the left hand."

"Yes, that is all I need to see, Fetchet." He drew out his purse and held it over his palm. "How many coins will it cost me to end this discourse so you'll allow me a few moments with this corpse?"

Now, you'll recall all I'd paid out that day: the haggling vendors, the fee for the paradise, the extra stivers to the magistrate for the new body, and the police escort. I already knew that Tulp would dock me some of my fee because of the missing hand and the scarred body. What profit had I made so far for all my efforts?

"Ten stivers?" Van Rijn guessed.

I thought it over for a moment without giving an answer.

"Fifteen," he offered, without waiting for my response.

I saw that my hesitation served me well. I kept quiet.

"You drive a hard bargain," he said, examining my face. "Eighteen."

"Master, Professor Tulp would not like it very much if he knew I had let you in."

"I do need to fill the censers with incense in the anatomy theater. How much time do you require? I also have other chores—to pack the peat for the furnace, stoke the fire in the gallery, fix the scented tapers in the candelabra . . ."

"Whatever time a guilder buys me I'll take. Incense and candelabras, I guess."

"Until the next church bell, then."

As I was walking out of the room, he added, "I must also ask you to be prudent with your words around Tulp."

"You know my word is . . ." I stopped myself, since my word had already proven its value as weak. "I assure you, my lips are fastened with sealing wax."

The artist turned to look at me. "One last thing. You mentioned to me earlier, Fetchet, that it is not only your job to prepare the body for dissection but also to bury the body parts after the lecture is done . . ."

"The arm," I said. "You'd like for me to hold the arm for you after the dissection is through?"

"Swiftly deduced," he said, clearly not thinking me capable of it.

He put a single shiny guilder in my palm, closed my hand around it. "Go, Fetchet. The tapers want very badly to meet their candelabra. You'll get it to me tonight?"

"I will, master, I will."

I silently backed out of the chamber and left the painter with the corpse.

THE EYES

I suppose it reflects on the poverty of the artist's mind that he cannot conjure his pictures straight out of his own imagination. He must rely upon the world, and the things in it, to remind him of how life operates: what light looks like slanting through old glass, how water seems to churn when it is lapping at a shore, how age can turn skin on a hand nearly translucent. This is precisely why I sketch, why I invite my subjects to sit for me, why I collect so many objects for my curio cabinet. I must start with source materials. In this case: flesh.

I will not call myself a Michelangelo or a Leonardo, but I have cared to know how form follows function in the human frame. I visit the gibbet on the Volewijk to sketch the dead, rotting away in the rain and tossed by the harbor winds. I go to the Kalverstraat shambles to sketch the oxen hanging from hooks at slaughter. I often bring women from the bawdy Breestraat to our studio to sketch them in the nude. I am not squeamish or licentious, only interested in the truth of life, artistry.

It was a tomblike room under that busy weigh house. On the other side of the great oak door, traders were doing business in grains and tobacco, gin and beer. But in that chamber where I'd met Fetchet, it was silent. The brick walls were slick and glistening with frost. There was a layer of frost on the windows, too, and so there emitted into the room a kind of shimmering, dusted light. It was colder inside than outside. My breath entered the air in great visible plumes.

After Fetchet left me alone, I gazed on the covered form, a landscape of hills with soft and sharp inclines. A muslin cloth was draped over the body. Stretched out on that bed of ice, with only his bare feet and the crown of his head and hair exposed, it struck me that the corpse looked like a kind of holy figure. In fact, the whole scene called to mind Mantegna's *Lamentation*.

Do you know it? If you come to my studio someday, I will show you my reproduction. Lastman gave it to me to teach me chiaroscuro in fabric folds. It is a portrait of Christ in the tomb, his feet toward the viewer, his head at the top of the frame, the whole of his body foreshortened. Two disciples sit over him and weep, but you barely see them. What you see is a moment of actual serenity; his Christ is not dead but—at rest.

I began to sketch with my charcoal. My thought was: start again with the mathematics, the correct proportions, the geometry, the width of his shoulders, the curve of the elbow and the length of the forearm.

I reached out and touched the edge of the muslin and began to fold it down on one side. My hands grazed the surface of his skin, which had the most unlikely texture, like brittle parchment. I could sense the stiffness of his flesh under my fingers. I used discipline to steel myself. I reminded myself to note the color of his skin, to ascertain which minerals would combine to produce the ashen gray hue.

I saw the other arm, with its stump, about which Fetchet had warned me. Where his hand had once been, his limb had been severed just above the wrist. The skin was pressed together like the end of a sausage casing. It was ugly and uneven and ragged where they'd sewn it back up. You could witness the cruelty of the executioner. I have seen a hand amputated once before. Or at least partially amputated. It was my brother's hand. He'd crushed it in a mill accident. That was when I was young, when Gerrit had only just taken over the mill. It was a hard time for my family: an accident that led to many difficult years.

I pulled back the muslin off the other hand. There it was, the thief's left hand. It was not as rough as I'd expected. The skin was callused, but the fingers were long and even a little elegant. He had done work with his hands, but it was not a laborer's hand. It had not plowed fields or fastened fishing lines, hauled up sails or sliced whale meat. It had wielded a knife, for eating, for tradesman's work, for fights, perhaps. But it was not a coarse hand, and the nails were freshly cleaned.

I sketched both arms. The stump and the hand. A study in contrast of the most gruesome sort. I stood and I drew, there in the frigid tomb, trying to prevent my thoughts from turning to Gerrit. I ran my charcoal along my pad and tried to capture these shapes. I drew from several angles, trying to get a feel for each form and a comparison of both forms. I felt sick and sad and hollowed out, but I went on drawing. I drew and I tried to prevent it, but my thoughts could not outrun the memories that these new sights so naturally evoked. One hand destroyed, another preserved.

⁓

The morning of Gerrit's accident was overcast, the sky thick and grainy, filtered through a thick haze. I had been given the chore of baling hay and carrying it to the cart. Even this light task had proved somewhat beyond my capacities, because instead of doing my work, I was standing just outside the barn, watching light play off the few aureate bundles I'd managed to bind so far.

It's funny how the mind collects details of certain sensations at particular moments: before something momentous is about to occur. Even now I can still remember the mesmerizing transition of color along each stalk, from a deep umber to weld, and the point where there was a pure spot of yellow ocher glowing hot like an oil lamp.

I heard my brother shouting—not Gerrit, who had assigned me my chores, but Cornelis—and then I heard the thudding of feet along the path.

"Get over here now. Now!"

I grabbed a pitchfork and pretended to be impaling the innocent grain. "I'm doing it. I'm—"

Cornelis was quickly upon me and his hand fell hard on my shoulder. "Drop that," his voice as firm as that hand. "We need you. Come now."

I followed swiftly as Cornelis ran back toward the mill. As we got nearer we could both hear Gerrit's voice, crying out in pain. As I got closer I heard that his words were incoherent, involuntary; and in between shouts he was yelping like a dog. It was an unbearable sound, and my first impulse was to turn back and disappear behind the haystacks.

Instead, I slowed, switching to long striding steps, while Cornelis ran ahead, spurred on by the cries. "Don't stop," Cornelis yelled at me, running back and grabbing my arm and slinging me through the door of the barn: "Don't be afraid. It's only Gerrit."

It was pure fear that surged through me then, hot and insistent, pulsing through my spine. My teeth clenched, my chest violently tightened. Already everyone but my mother was gathered around Gerrit, who lay on the dirt floor of the mill covered in what at first appeared to be a caking of bronze plaster, cracked with hairline fissures like the surface of a fallen Roman bust.

Then I understood that this effect was produced by my brother's blood, caked with the tawny dust of the mill's floor. And the blood, I saw, I came to see, was everywhere—on my father's breeches and shoes, splattered across my sister Lysbeth's dress and Machtelt's torn smock, and, I saw, too, on Cornelis's brow, an ominous spattering of uneven claret freckles.

"Let's get him up," I heard my father say, the familiar voice, round and authoritative. "Rembrandt, come to this side and take that shoulder." Once again I hesitated. When I tried to walk forward, my knees buckled as if I were steeped in marsh grass. "Now!" shouted my father so fiercely that my body finally obeyed.

I moved toward Gerrit and leaned down to position myself behind his head, as instructed by my father. It was then that I saw with horrifying clarity the catastrophe that had been wrought of Gerrit's hand. In the place of two of his fingers were mere stumps of flesh, bound up and crudely sealed by strips of fabric torn from Machtelt's smock. I could see the matching pattern still, but the makeshift dressing was soon seeped through, bright crimson. It did not entirely cover the flesh, which looked as if it had been bit and chewed by a dog.

I could not think, and I felt sick. I must simply follow orders and do as I was told to do. My father shouted, "Everyone, lift!" and I lifted Gerrit's shoulder even as he writhed and cursed and screamed my name. I had moved faster this time than the others, and jerked him unnecessarily. Then everyone else lifted him and when we had him up, I managed to lean down and press my lips upon my brother's brow and whisper, "It's okay. We're here. We're all right here, Gerrit."

As we carried him toward the cart, everyone was shouting instructions. Cornelis was telling Machtelt where to find the doctor in town if he were not to be found immediately at his home. My father, who was carrying the bulk of Gerrit's weight, was shouting toward the house at my mother, "Neeltje! Neeltje! Draw water from the well!" Lysbeth was weeping, saying something muffled through her tears.

I leaned close and spoke into his ear, "We're all here, Gerrit. We're all here. None of us is going anywhere." I said these words over and over as we moved toward the cottage and the more I said them, the more my voice seemed false, unsure.

"Hurry ahead," said my father, after we managed to place Gerrit in the hay cart. Getting no response from my mother, my father called to Lysbeth, who would not be consoled. "Mother must have taken the horse to the river. Go and get the bucket and bring water from the well."

Lysbeth lifted her skirt and ran on ahead. Father called after her, "If the doctor doesn't come in time, we'll continue on to town. Wait for Mother and tell her what has happened. Say it slowly, Lysbeth. This news will not meet her well."

My sister made off like a sprite across the hill, quieted, at last, by her purpose. I saw for the first time then that she, too, was covered in my brother's blood; it draped the back of her honey-colored dress.

The doctor had not come. The wheel on our hay cart was broken. My father and Cornelis and I had to carry Gerrit the whole way to town. The doctor treated him with true kindness, but his diagnosis was as swift as a sentence: Gerrit had already lost at least two of his fingers, shorn by the teeth in the mill's crank. To save the hand he would have to amputate one more, which had also been crushed beyond repair. If the hand healed as he hoped and did not become infected, Gerrit would still be able to use his index finger and thumb, the two vital digits for his work, but if the hand did not respond to surgery, the doctor would have to amputate even further, to the wrist.

This somber news passed through our family quickly and everyone descended into silence to wait. Though ten men were called upon to hold Gerrit down for the first operation, I was excused from this task because I was too young. Instead, I sat at the wooden table in the adjoining room, my head hanging, while my mother wept, smoothing her hand through my curls, as if it were I who deserved comfort. I wished only that I were an older, stronger, more capable man, as I carved my initials, RHL, into the soft surface pulp of the bench.

⌒≬⌒

In the days that followed, our family home on the Weddesteeg was full of people coming and going, faces drawn with worry. From my room in the house, I could hear Gerrit's soft moans through the starless nights, his turning in his bed. The hand had become infected and the pain burned up through his wrist. He begged the doctors to amputate it all to alleviate the terrible burning.

I offered to be the one to change the dressing on his hand. My mother saw that I needed something to do, to help, and she allowed me that task. I would unwrap his bandage slowly, doing my best to prevent it from sticking at any single point. But I was never entirely successful at this. I would accidentally tug too hard or pull too fast and he would cry out in pain.

Afterward, I tried to sit with my brother as much as he could bear my company. I told him, "You're going to be okay. The pain will pass soon." I didn't know if this was true. Looking at the hand, I didn't really believe it was true either.

Sleeping in the house and hearing his moans gave me nightmares. Once everyone else had retired, I crept out to the barn. But though I was out of the house, I had to face in my solitude my own torturous purgatory.

The fate of Gerrit's hand, you see, seemed intimately linked with my own fate. Gerrit, the eldest, had been trained to run the mill, which had been passed down through three generations of Van Rijns.

Cornelis was also capable of miller's work, but my brothers Willem and Adriaen had already pursued other trades. I had only just begun my apprenticeship with Jacob van Swanenburgh. I would be wanted back in only a few days to continue helping him with a large Italian-style painting of the punishments of hell.

If Gerrit couldn't run the mill, and Cornelis or Willem had to take over, I might be asked to suspend my apprenticeship. I thought my mother might ask me to come home for her comfort, for I was her youngest, and if she wanted that, I would of course oblige. That, too, would make my continued cultivation as a painter under Van Swanenburgh impossible.

Every night, my brother let me change his dressing. I was not a great nurse to him, but at least it was something I could do. You will think me very tender and caring when I tell you this. But I was only partially concerned about Gerrit's hand. Man is driven by his own interests, as you know, and those are often centered on one's self. The thoughts of my own future would not leave my mind. Throughout the days of Gerrit's recovery from the amputation of his fingers, I was hardly able to sleep at all, even in the barn. If it had been out of concern for my brother perhaps it would've been excusable, but it was for my own sake. Because I wanted so badly to continue my apprenticeship, to leave that house, to become a painter and a man of the world.

To my parents, painting was a worthy trade, not fit perhaps for an aristocrat or a merchant's son but sufficiently lucrative to support a miller's child. I already felt, however, that it was my calling to become a painter, and not only to be a tradesman but to be an artist, like Rubens or Titian. I felt a passion for the work, beyond anything I saw my brothers feel toward working their trades. To be able to express the conflicts and concerns of man through crushed stone applied with a brush: this is miracle maker's work. No less. I was awed by the task before me and uncertain I'd be able to master it.

You must know from where I speak, Monsieur Descartes. Here in this unassuming room, you work as I do in my painting studio, with no more than a slide rule, a few weights and measures, this handful of books, and your own mind. From these basic elements and your view out this small porthole onto the night sky, you produce titanic theories about the movement of objects, the circulation of the universe, and principles that guide nature. Neither you nor I will likely become wealthy from our endeavors, and yet we pursue them with the avidity of East India Company merchants seeking to conquer the New World. A discovery that elucidates perspective, or a new technique that allows us to illuminate a once-obscure human truth—these are what we both seek, as most people seek love or worldly riches.

Gerrit's accident made me want it even more. I was tormented each night in the barn by the thought that, as a consequence of the accident, I should need to stay at home at the mill and work as all my forebears had as a laborer and a tradesman dealing in grain. Losing the chance to be the painter I knew I must be.

But I was lucky: Gerrit's fever broke. The infection abated. The arm would be saved. There was a muted celebration in our house, everyone walking carefully across the floorboards and being utterly polite in case anything would disturb our good fortune.

My mother filled me in on the plans that had been arranged: Adriaen and Willem would both take leave from their jobs for another month to work at home through the summer. It had been decided that I would spend only a few more days at Weddesteeg before I returned to my apprenticeship. My elder brothers could manage until Gerrit was ready to take his rightful place beside my father again.

Greatly relieved by this turn of events and the consideration that had been given to my artistic progress, I wanted to prove to my father and brother that I would always do my part. I awoke at dawn and joined Cornelis in the mill, offering to crank and shovel and grade the wheat, or whatever else was needed.

My father and brother tolerated me through the morning, but by noon I sensed something wrong. I did not know if I had done my chores poorly or whether I worked too slowly, or what irked them. I tried even harder, begging for new tasks, demonstrating my willingness to help and improve.

At midafternoon, my mother sailed into the mill, flew directly at my father, and began to shout at him, as I'd never seen her do before in my life. All I heard was her constant refrain: "You promised me! You promised me!"

Finally she stormed back into the mill and toward me, as my father pleaded behind her, "I didn't think one day could do any harm." I thought my mother was about to reprimand me, but she grabbed my wrist and tore me away from the crank of the mill.

"You're a good boy, my son," she said. "You will be rewarded in heaven for trying to be a help. But your father gave me his word that he would not let you come anywhere near this mill from now on."

I really did not understand why she'd sought this absurd promise. I was a Van Rijn son, destined to take my turn at that crank. "But, Mother," I said, "I *must* help."

"Look what happened to Gerrit," she said, softening her tone. "What if that happened to you?"

She reached out and took both my hands, holding each one by the thumb and cupping my palms over her fists. "These gentle hands," she said, "are not going to be broken in a mill." She drew my left hand toward her lips and kissed the palm, then did the same with the right—each a benediction.

❦

I rubbed my eyes, feeling the fullness of those orbs through the thin shield of my lids. When I blinked back to sight, tiny pink and green dots clustered in my vision like gnats. There were the two hands. One amputated, one whole.

Here I was, in Amsterdam. Gerrit was dead, buried six months ago in Leiden, just about the time I moved here to run the academy. My brother had gone on to work the mill, but every day for him had been painful.

I put down my charcoal. My gaze continued to wander the body, like a traveler in an exotic land. Beyond the arms, past the severed limb. I rolled back the muslin and saw that the rest of the body was badly scarred: he had flogging scars on his shoulders and sides. I put down my pad and gently raised one shoulder off his bed of ice for just a moment. He was lighter than I imagined, but touching him seemed too much of a violation, and I let him down as quickly as I'd raised him. In that brief moment, though, I could see that the scars must have run the whole length of his back. They were hard, raw things, these scars—like carvings in a tree trunk, only raised rather than incised. I thought of the old tree and how it stands, in spite of these carvings, bearing those human cruelties with grace.

There were brands upon his neck and shoulders, both front and back. His stomach, though cleaner than his chest, had marks where he'd been stabbed. I imagined what kind of knife did those: the makeshift blades men fashion in jails, I thought. Some men wear their scars as badges of honor. I've seen university boys in Leiden who proudly cut their shirts to display their jousting scars. There are young men who seek to gain scars on their chin and neck. To toughen their flesh. To show they are men.

Leonardo wrote of *il concetto dell'anima*, the intention of the mind, revealed through the external elements—that the body is the house of the soul, and we can see into its inner chambers by way of its facade. If that is true, this man's soul was a house that was wrecked and sinking, discolored and chipped, the whole of the structure tipping to one side.

At last, I drew back the whole muslin and got a good look at his face. His eyes were closed, his jaw was slack, and his lips were dry and cracked. His beard was neat and his face clean. After imagining all the pain that had been inflicted on his body, I was surprised when I saw his face. It was at peace. His gaze was serene. There was no tension or sorrow or fear or pain. He was, you might say, a man without a ravaged body. A man given to complete tranquility.

I thought again about Mantegna's picture *The Lamentation of Christ*. And I thought again of my commission. The first glimpse of an idea for the Tulp painting came to me then. The trigger of inspiration: What if I would include more than just the arm of the dead man? What if I would paint the whole man? And no one in front of him to obscure him.

Yes, the whole corpse, in the center of the frame—at the base of the pyramid, even. To not just show the doctors and their proud moment with a single severed limb, but to show the man whose body they took for this endeavor. It was a man who had been scarred and punished, who had been beaten and executed, but whose face still showed this: this state of grace.

I have told you that I'm not a religious man, but that's not strictly true. I never attend church, and I don't care for men of the cloth. But I was taught the stories of the Bible and I regard them as a kind of human truth. I believe there are men who are tested with terrible losses like Job and men who are blinded by birds like Tobit. Real men, men we know. The Bible is not an historical text to me. It is a text for the living, which tells what happens to those of us right here, right now, among merchants and clergy and shopkeepers of Amsterdam. Among the rapscallions and butchers.

But men who suffer greatly, receive punishments beyond necessity, and yet they go on, continue to hope, to love, to spread their gospel. To go on until they are cut down. Christ was crucified among thieves. He died as a common criminal. Then could not a common criminal also be Christ?

I was excited by this revelation. Even there in the cold, dark, hateful tomb. Even there with the dead man in front of me. I began to become enlivened with this idea. I drew up my charcoal again to draw the face. To capture that sense of deep serenity.

As I was starting to sketch the face, I noticed another, smaller, more faded scar on his neck. I moved closer and saw that it was another brand but not the kind the executioner applies with hot pokers at the stake. Something more exact: something that looked like a prickly clover with a circle in its center. I knew that marking. It was the signature of the scabbard maker from Leiden, a man called Adriaenszoon.

It was no use trying to sketch after that. I used my handkerchief to wipe my brow—as I was suddenly sweating profusely—and grabbed my cloak and gloves, stuffing my sketch pad and charcoal back into my pockets. I threw the muslin back over the body, making sure to shroud his feet, his arms, the sides of his torso, his legs, tucking him in like a child. Then I fled the chamber into the daylight.

Outside, I drew the cold air deeply into my lungs, watching my breath on each exhale. Mercifully, the sun was still shining on the square. It was bitter cold when the wind blew, coming straight across the Nieuwmarkt from the IJ, but there was the sun, and the market was blessedly full of life. I drank in the sights and sounds—

all the swirling, beautiful activity—as if it were nourishment. I pushed my way into the crowded row of the fish stalls, where the air was thick with the stench of brine, and I inhaled.

I moved aimlessly along through the browsers and buyers, into the row of cheese sellers and bakers, and beyond them toward the vegetable stands and fishmongers. In a gap somewhere in the middle of the market, I turned around and looked at the building from which I'd just fled.

The Waag stood mutely like a proud castle in the middle of the bustle, its brick walls brilliant in the sunlight, its high turrets dusted with snow. Soon, all of Amsterdam would arrive here for the winter fest. All the guild nobles would come for the anatomy lesson and the crowds would descend for the torchlight parade.

I resolved that I needed to walk. Not just to be carried along through the streets but also to let the cold air fill me, to feel its sharp sting in my chest. I headed straight toward the wharf, letting the wind blow into my face. The sky was full of circling gulls, white and gray. The canal was dotted with black coots. Out beyond, the harbor was awash with ship masts. I walked, knowing I would walk for a long time.

XIII

THE BODY

I made it to Amsterdam by dint of my sharp nose, for all scents led
toward the city. I wandered around, gaping at the spices atop the
carts along the wharves, staring at the trollops on the quays, covet-
ing the boats in the canals, sampling every distiller's gin. I loved the
constant tolling of the church bells all around me, the thousands of
seagulls and pigeons everywhere overhead, the open windows pre-
senting wine-filled goblets and plentiful fruit platters and cheeses of
every color and crust, fine art, and silver. Even with all the trollops
and brigands, the garbage and the foul stench of the canals, Amsterdam was a thief's paradise.

I stole, it seemed, whatever was loose: copper, tin, and silver
spoons, platters, cups, plates, fruit, vases, tulips if they were cut,
brushes, spurs, blankets, bear hides—even shoes once, off a horse's
hooves. And I sought alms, too, using so many tricks I'd learned
along the way. Merchants here seemed to prefer to drop a coin into
the palm of a devout mendicant than spend a day at penance in

church. I acted the part of a saintly beggar, so enthralled by my recitation of prayers that I bumped into the fruit stands in the old market or upset a hot tray of veal collops, and left with pockets bulging.

On one of the days I was on the new canals, I met Jacob the Walloon, another vagabond. I told him of my woes and he said, "At least you're not living on the river. It's ten wide with rogues. There's so much pitiful flesh cramped side by side along the Amstel, it's like slaving on a galleon."

He put an arm over my shoulder and pulled me close like an old pal, guiding me away from the wharves and toward the town center. "You must be cold in that vest," he said. "I know of a way we can get you a nice, warm, tailored coat. I bet you'd like that."

Here's how the scam worked: We'd pick a tailor's shop where a gentleman was getting a fitting. He'd be disrobed while the tailor was taking his measurements, and his old coat would be hanging by the mirror, or maybe by the door. Jacob would run in and start shouting that he'd been robbed out in the street and that the thief had run past the shop. Usually, the gentleman would nobly chase out into the street, and the tailor would often follow. That's when I'd slip in and grab what had been left unattended. I'd take only the one used cloak, throwing it on over my jerkin, and walk back into the street as if it was always mine.

The first time I did it, I got a heavy wool cloak lined with purple velvet. To think, someone wanted to replace that for something new. I loved the feeling of the cloak so much, the comfort and warmth, that I told Jacob I'd keep it for myself. But he said that he deserved half so we'd have to sell it and split the cash. That's what we did—we went down to the market on the curve of the Amstel and sold it to a secondhand coat seller for six stivers, and each of us got three.

It went like that for a few weeks. We managed to steal a dozen coats from tailor's shops and then we got more brazen and went down to the stock exchange, where men were tossing off their cloaks in the heat of trading and leaving them on the floor. We did that only once, and the second time we were jailed and hauled up with irons.

It was a good enough trade, though, in secondhand coats, that we went back to it. Sometimes, I got to wear the coat for half a day until I met up with Jacob again, who wanted his spoils in stivers. Even if I had to give up the comfort of that coat, I could use what we'd earned to buy a near feast and sleep with a full belly. Later, we improved our game by focusing on barbershops. We'd sneak into the shop while some burgher or other was having his neck shaved. It was easy enough to snatch a coat without even being seen when the barber and the man were so focused on the blade.

On the sixteenth of November 1623, I was wearing one of my fine borrowed cloaks and trying to woo a pair of trollops beside the Oudezijds Voorburgwal, when I saw a lovely lady riding a black mare, her silk purse hanging loosely off her hip. Excusing myself from the trollops, I stepped out of the doorway and approached. "Madame," I said, "I am but a humble Leidener . . ." Before I even finished my opening salvo, the lady dropped her purse into my hands and urged her mare into a trot.

Not an hour later, the lady seemed to regret her generosity and sent a civil guard to search me out, accusing me of thievery. It's true that in my life I stole a good many things without any cause, but in this case the woman had wronged me. I was merely seeking alms! I was now nineteen, and so I was taken to the house of correction for questioning. I was very nervous. I sputtered some words. It was he, sir, who jotted down the first words on that piece of parchment you have in your hands—that, having stolen a purse, I was released from custody by the gentlemen of the tribunal on the affirmation that I would leave town forever on pain of imprisonment.

That evening, as I tried to stoke a fire along the banks of the Amstel with a crooked twig, I considered how I'd been wronged: my mother cruelly stolen from me at birth, my father knuckled under with his rage, our property taken over some meager dues. I had done my best to honorably beg and had only stolen things that no one would bother to miss, some bread or a pig's trotter here and there for a soup, and all the rest of Amsterdam sups on mutton while I sit empty bellied before a waning fire! My stomach ached that night like a lovesick man missing his mistress, and it howled at me as if I had stolen the lass myself.

That night, when I fell asleep against the log I'd pulled beside my fire, I had that terrible dream again. Once again, I was naked upon a table and could not lift my arms or move my head or open my eyes or scream, though I could feel the air on my lips and hear the murmurs of conversation taking place around me—without hearing the words.

This time, the nightmare took a new turn, which I only wish that I could forget. The man who stood above me, the one who resembled my father, was in this dream not wearing a coat but instead a butcher's apron, and he held in his hands not a pair of shears but a carving knife, which he used to flay me. I saw arrayed around me every manner of delicacy—the head of a succulent swine, a roasted rabbit and a larded dove, oysters in their shells, asparagus, grapes, apricots, pomegranates, lemons, and an array of colorful gourds. I—me, my body—was the centerpiece of a banquet. My father raised a goblet in a toast, pulled a chair up to the table, and then invited the other men to sit down and feast!

My luck wasn't all gone, for at that moment I awoke, and found myself very much whole, but still penniless and banished from Amsterdam, that city that had kept me fed. I swore not to close my eyes again until I had made my way all the way back to the Oudezijds Voorburgwal, where last I stood before my arrest.

⌒⟊⟊⟊⟊⌒

I made my way to Den Helder, where I sought, on the main, to feel the fresh crosswinds of the seas on my face. As a lad I was rather comely and ruddy cheeked, with locks of curly blond hair. Amsterdam had stunted me, though, and turned my pretty features mean. I had, in a short time, greatly aged. I could no longer run as fast or survive as long on a crust of bread and I slept less out in the elements. I knew that as soon as my eyes were shut some other vagabond could steal my things. I've been told my eyes are as bloodshot as the devil's own, and the purple rings beneath my eyes seem fixed in my face.

They say that he who sleeps well, sins not. But I have never slept well, Lord Schout, and perhaps that is why I'm always sinning. The less I slept, the more I came to curse those houses where Mother and Father called out, "Sleep tight, sleep tight" to their lucky babes in cozy cupboard beds. For the right to rest my head in peace and sleep a single night, I would've traded all I had in worldly possessions, but naturally I had nothing to trade.

In Alkmaar, I was arrested with a group of men and accused of mendicancy and banned from the state of Holland and West Friesland, for life. But where, indeed, was I to travel? Do I speak any other language than Dutch? Do I know any people other than my kinsmen?

There are gibbets just outside the city gates of every town in

Holland, bodies hanging like flightless crows; and every time I saw one, I thought of my future fate. I knew I should heed the message of those lifeless gallows birds, for I could see they were my brothers and sisters in luckless fate.

I joined up with the military service in Utrecht in 1629. They gave me a pair of shoes—the first I'd ever had in my life—and the pay was fair and the companions were jolly, but I offended my colonel more than once by failing to report on time. Since I knew I'd soon face a military tribunal if I erred again, I escaped that company without permission or papers of discharge.

For this I knew I'd be chased, so I headed to Houtten. There, a friend in cups named Jan Berentszoon took me to a house where two half crates stood below a window, inviting entry. He used an iron to break the lock, and I stood guard. This house provided us with clothes and linen, money and silver decoration, and we were able to sell the vest and buttons, and immediately expend the money on mutton and beer and pastries.

I regret nothing except that I do not still have that selfsame meal before me on a plate right now. Good Jan and I divided the rest of the plunder. So sated was I that I felt worthy of my new weal and left Houtten with the burgled clothes on my back. That was how I was found out in Utrecht, where a day watch became suspicious at the fancy tassels on my belt. I was again flagellated in public, branded with that town's name, and imprisoned in the house of correction.

The Utrecht house didn't hold me well, and twice I was able to break free. The first time, just digging with my hands, I removed a large stone from the wall that separated my cell from the church wall outside and kept digging out the wall until I managed to squirm out the hole. The second time, I stole a small handsaw from the rasp house and sawed through a window post to get out to the square.

When the guard caught me in the act that time, I threatened him with the saw blade. I didn't really plan to hurt the guard, as I told the judges there, and I will tell you again. It was only that I preferred to die rather than to stay any longer at that house of correction.

I didn't get my wish. I was flagellated there in the square. I know the good people of Utrecht must have seen quite enough of my bare back, because every one of my public lashings was attended by the full populace of that town, including the miller's rooster and the egg farmer's hen. It was at this time that the name of Aris the Kid was whispered from one town in Holland to the next. For it was said that I was some kind of sainted thief, as no amount of punishment or banishment or branding could deter me.

XIV

THE EYES

Where did I go after I left the corpse in the Waag? Time ceased to matter as I walked away from the Nieuwmarkt and all I know is soon I was outside the city limits. Snow was falling, the sky beginning to darken, and the wind, though strong as I walked along the banks of the IJ, had begun to abate. I must have crossed over the Sint Antoniesdijk, because I passed the line of mills and eventually found myself in a clearing.

There I stood, as the snowfall became thicker and faster, and the ground was soon patterned in shapes of old lace. I was cold but I don't remember that I shivered, so engrossed was I in thought. After a while, the clearing was no longer a detailed tapestry but a single sheet of linen, blanketing a landscape barren of man-made structures. At first the cows mottled the horizon, until they, too, were erased.

It was not so unusual, was it, that two men from Leiden should both find their way to Amsterdam, one beginning a life and the other losing it to the hangman?

I closed my eyes, feeling snowflakes fall upon my eyelashes and cheeks.

⌒⥿⌒

Soon, he stood there before me in the clearing, the youth I'd first met so many years ago, who was now the full-grown man who lay on the dissection table in the Waag. Blond, awkward, with knocking knees, he stumbled along the dry dirt path in Leiden, in front of our home, the Weddesteeg. Ahead of him was his father, his head covered in a flat black hat like a pie, and his mouth had the same shape. Flat and grim. He wore a black shirt with a double set of brass buttons down the front of an unadorned black cloak that came below his black knee breeches. His heavy boots hit the ground so hard when he walked that they sprayed dust into the face of his son, who stumbled blindly behind him through the dirt.

He was a study in contrast with my father, who was a giant of a man—tall, wickedly intelligent, wise, fair, and mild in all his dealings—and who wore a generous beard and a thick head of hair, tousled by the wind and colored by the sun. He was the rudder of our lives, as sturdy and purpose giving as the mill.

Adriaen's father seemed cold and small. He never spoke to me, but if my mother happened to be in the yard, he would always address her, not with neighborly greetings but with a rebuke. "Will we be seeing your boys in church this week, Mevrouw Van Rijn?" he'd ask, knowing the answer would be no.

She would patiently answer that church was not for everyone, though once the old man was out of earshot she would mutter curses at him under her breath. She was Roman Catholic though my father was a Calvinist, and he knew that full well. Nevertheless, she simply endured the old man's implied reprimand and we went on doing our Sunday chores.

As soon as they'd walked on, she'd remind us not to dislike the man, but we were allowed to feel some pity for the boy, since life could not be easy without a mother to comfort him.

Once I saw him walking down that path without his father. It was Sunday and he might've been going to church, but he didn't seem determined about it. I was out sitting on the fence, doing nothing in particular, waiting for some instruction on my chores. He walked up the road, then turned around and came back. Then walked again, turned around, and came back.

"Where's your father?" I asked him.

To look into his pale blue eyes was to tread into a kind of shallow puddle.

"He's gone off to be a sutler."

"Gone off?"

"To support Maurits in the campaign."

"When did he leave?"

"A few weeks ago."

His mother was dead, and now his father was gone, too.

"You're alone?"

He just nodded, though that puddle in his eyes took shape.

"And you're still going to church?"

He shook his head. "Not sure."

I was at the time something of a lonely boy myself. My brothers were my main companions, but they were all industrious workers, men who understood the value of a good day's labor. I was different.

I did my chores, but grudgingly; and often if I had a moment when I hadn't been given precise instructions, I would drift off into abstraction. My eyes would fix on the light coming over a bank of clouds, and I would stand watching it grow and then fade. Or I would gaze out along the mill line and observe the turning of the vanes and feel on my face the wind that made them spin simultaneously.

"Want to throw bones in the barn?" I asked him.

He stared at me like I'd offered him the first reprieve of his life.

***

The next Sunday, he came with some sheep's knucklebones he'd begged off a scullery maid in town. He showed me how to play the game by tossing a ball into the air and moving the knucklebones into groups, then picking up the bones. Only we didn't have a ball, so we used a rock from the garden instead. After that, I let him help me with my chores. He was faster at raking out the barn than I was and better at stacking hay. He could accomplish in a few moments what it took me an hour, and then he'd toss the knucklebones onto the ground and we'd play for a while.

Before the next Sunday, I showed my mother the knucklebones and she used some madder to dye them red. Then she baked me a *bikkel* ball, which we painted black. Properly equipped, I was happy to welcome him back when he came the next Sunday. Playing knucklebones became our regular pastime. He kept the set in the lining of his vest, and whenever we were done with my chores, he'd toss them out onto the floor.

Our friendship went on like that for a while. He seemed to have nothing else to do and no other obligations at home. I asked him about his father, and he'd tell me stories about his exploits in the

Gomarist war. Every time he told a tale, it seemed his father took a larger part.

He had done so much more than just become a sutler, it seems. He led the horde that forced its way into the Abbey Church in The Hague, and won an honorable place beside the stadtholder Maurits of Orange.

When Oldenbarneveldt went for his beheading, he claimed his father was at the front of the throng. "He got close enough to spit in the advocate's face just before he uttered those famous last words: 'Make it short, make it short.'"

I never knew if any of his tales were true, and I suspected they weren't. But they had real drama and battle scenes and that was what my young mind required.

Once I asked him about his father's shop. He said they were sheath makers, supplying civic militias and Gomarist warriors with leather scabbards for sabers and falchions and holsters for daggers and muskets. He rolled down the collar of this shirt and showed me a mark on the back of his neck. It looked like a prickly clover with a circle in its center. He said that was the shop's brand that they marked onto every scabbard and holster. "It's a beechnut in its husk," he said. "I collected them as a boy. They're bitter to eat, but you can use them for their tannins."

"Why is it on your back?" I asked.

He met my eyes and said, "It's from my father. He said he'd use it to know me when he saw me next."

I didn't ask him to elaborate. I saw that it was enough for him to tell me that much. His father had harmed him, scarred him, leaving him behind to tend a shop that supplied equipment to his religious army. We tossed the knucklebones that day until it got dark. But the next Sunday he didn't come again.

In the clearing, the sun had vanished over the horizon. A waxing moon illuminated the snow to a shimmering ghost white. I began to feel the sting of the cold for the first time, and pulled my cloak closer about my neck.

A vagabond passed along the path, leading a donkey laden with leather sacks. Where he was headed in this weather at that pace, I could not imagine; what town or inn lay in the distance I did not know. The old man did not look up at me, walking stooped with his gray head bent. I watched him pass and observed the sets of footprints leave imprints in the immaculate snow. The moonlight glanced off the donkey's black coat. They made their way across the clearing soundlessly, tracing a diagonal line through the field.

I hadn't intended to walk so far. There were pupils and apprentices at the studio waiting for my return. There was the anatomical lesson at the Waag. I had not given all of this any thought. My reason had been overruled by my meditation, and my memory still held sway.

The next time I saw Adriaen, I was already working with Lievens in Leiden. Maybe a decade had passed. We were busy at our studio, always painting, always competing for who could produce the best work. I was painting self-portraits. Over and over again, my own face. Lievens did it on occasion, too, but not with as much ardor as I did.

One particularly cold night I was working on a self-portrait and Lievens said to me, "Let's get you someone else to paint, so you don't have to paint yourself."

"Who should I paint, then, you?"

"Absolutely not. Not again."

A little while later there was someone at our studio door, asking for alms, asking for food. As I said, it was very cold, and more than anything he was looking for shelter. Lievens heard the door and went to answer it.

I heard him from the other room, speaking in a grave but tender voice. "It's bitter cold outside. Come in, come in."

When he came in, the man spoke briefly of his plight—the snow, his frost-bit feet, his hunger—but Lievens told him to take a seat beside the stove while he went to see if there was anything in the studio to eat. We sat together for a while. His face was hidden by his beard, and also by a broad-brimmed hat. I would not have known him. He'd changed in a hundred ways since I'd seen him last. I stood and stoked the stove and told him to move closer.

He did and soon his cheeks turned ruddy with the warmth. He took off his ratty shoes and warmed his feet by the crackling fire. I could see his eyes roaming the room to discover all our possessions. Mostly, they were items we used as props for our history paintings. Our hearth was arrayed with brass pokers and metal-handled brooms, and upon the wall, above our desk there was a gilded and bejeweled sword. In our cabinets were two gold flagons, a multitude of glass goblets, three silver platters, and several porcelain bowls. We had all manner of notebooks and papers scribbled with notes and sketches for our art.

Lievens returned with a jug of wine and a leg of turkey, holding them upon a pewter plate that nearly glinted in the light. The man was so grateful I could see tears coming into his eyes, but he held them back and merely nodded and thanked us. It was all he could do not to swallow that turkey leg in one bite.

Lievens and I took a seat beside him and we poured ourselves some wine as well. Lievens held up his cup. "To the courage to ask for help when it is needed," he said.

At first, it seemed the visitor wasn't sure the meaning of this, but then he lifted his cup. "To the generosity of strangers. I mean it with all my heart."

"Tell me, now," Lievens said, without taking his eyes off the man's face. "You told me something when you were coming in. You said you saw a man murdered this very night?"

"Indeed, I did, my lord, but it was none of my doing. I only sat nearby and was a witness."

"And who was this man, then?"

"No one, my lord, of any consequence. Just a vagabond and a thief, like myself."

"And what did he do to bring on his death?"

"It was a brawl. I believe it was over a few coins in a game of cards."

"A man was killed for a few coins?"

The visitor laughed. "I have seen a man drowned in the Amstel for a mushroom cap he foraged from the woods. And once I saw a man knifed for a piece of herring."

I could see the food in his teeth. I said, "You say you are a thief?"

He took a gulp of wine. "I am, my lord, a coat thief mostly. I steal other things on the occasion when I cannot get my bread by alms. A man must eat one way or another."

I asked, "And you don't mind saying you're a thief?"

"No, I suppose not. I didn't choose it. It chose me."

"Certainly you were not born a thief," Lievens said. His tone was one of complete equanimity. He didn't scold or provoke.

"I was born of my mother," he answered, "but once I was alive, she wasn't anymore. I killed her, you see. I started off a sinner."

Lievens laughed, and to my surprise, refilled the thief's goblet. "But you could not have killed her. You were a babe. But if, as you say, you have been a sinner all your life, that means that you have no remorse when you steal?" he asked, the wine gurgling into the cup.

"I used to. But I have none now. For I have seen many a man thieve, even those who have no need or want in the world. I have seen chandlers steal from oil sellers; I have seen priests rob the church coffers; I have watched noblemen refuse to pay the cobbler who fixed their boots. Is this not a kind of thievery, too? What of the merchants, who strut the avenues, plumes bobbing from their hats? Have they not made their wealth by thieving from those lands where no muskets protect their God-given goods? The world is full of thieves, my lord, and I am just the foolish and feckless kind who takes a little here and there, this day and that, who never improves his lot."

Lievens seemed very pleased by our visitor, and was thrilled to be having such a lively talk so late into the night. "You would condemn commerce, then? You would condemn the building of churches with tithes and alms? These are not examples of theft but of the ways of business and government in the modern world."

Our visitor sipped the wine slowly, and I could see that he was starting to consider his words.

"My point—and a very humble one it is indeed, for I am no man's judge—is that many a man has his hands in some other man's pocket. Thievery is a common sin. It is up to the thief to determine whether he lives by some moral code, and every thief must create some sense of his own morality. For myself, my lord, I have a few basic rules. I won't steal of a man poorer than myself, and I won't harm a man who does not seek to hurt me. If I can go two days without bread, I'll wait until the third to knock over a vendor's table in the public square. And once or twice when I was well off enough, I returned what I did steal."

"I see," said Lievens, very much intrigued. "And so, in this way, you feel that you are honorable, within your ignoble profession."

"Indeed," he said. "Every man is his own lord and master. Only God will determine his place in heaven or hell, and he does that before we take a single step upon this earth."

I leaned forward. "Have you come here to rob us tonight?" I said these words very simply, so that he would feel no shame in answering.

"I thought on it, my lord, for yours would be an easy house to rob. If one of you was alone here, or neither of you was here. It seems you have no way to defend yourselves save that fake sword you hang on your wall, and there's all that silver and those fine goblets in the cupboards. I'm certain there are many more treasures I haven't seen. Why do you keep them here? It's not a home but a place of work, it seems. But you have been kind to me, you see, and by my code of honor—though it may not seem terribly honorable to you—I cannot do you harm. I would not thieve of a generous soul who would willingly give so much comfort to a vagabond."

Lievens spoke next. "It's a good thing, then, that we took you in. For you have made us very wise to the ways of the world. And when you walk out that door again once you've warmed your feet and supped, you will put yourself into peril once again to steal something somewhere else?"

"Yes, my lord, I suspect I will," he said, finishing off the turkey leg and drinking the rest of the wine. "Though maybe not tonight. My father foretold that eternal damnation awaits me, and I have accepted my soul's curse."

"You accept that you cannot be any better than you are?"

"It makes no difference whether I accept it or not," he went on. "There was never any other path."

We did not argue with him. Our job was not to judge or to dispute morality with every passing stranger. We were, of course, not beyond reproach ourselves. We were busy trying to be painters, and we thought that art had little to do with morality. I was, at least, satisfied that he would not rob us while he visited, at least while both of us were in the room, and so I asked him if he would sit for me, for a *tronie*. I wanted to capture the peculiar mix of callowness and ruggedness in his face that is so characteristic of vagabonds.

"You want to paint me?" he asked. "It'll scare away the kids."

"It is not for children," I answered, with a laugh.

He did sit for me, and he was not a bad subject. He sat still and only moved his eyes to scan the room. I still did not recognize him, though, and I should not have if we hadn't gotten to talking about his past.

"You say your mother died at birth. Did you go to the orphanage?"

"No, my father did me that kindness. He kept me at home."

"And who reared you?"

"My father, himself. Reared me as cattle. Branded me here on my neck, as if I was a scabbard. He was a sheath maker and this was his brand."

He pulled down his collar to show me the brand—that beechnut I once took for a prickly clover. It was a scar you don't forget.

"He was a sutler in Maurits's army?" I said. "You lived here, not too far from the Weddesteeg?"

It seemed he knew me almost as soon as I knew him.

"Knucklebones," he said.

"Knucklebones," I said.

I wish I could say we stood to embrace, and laughed over old times. But we did not. Instead, the realization that we had known each other as youths made us both uncomfortable. He started to shift in his chair and asked if I was done. I put a few more quick jots onto the paper, and tore it from my book. I handed it to him. "No snake or fox."

He took some time to look at it. "I'm not as ugly as I think."

He tried to hand it back to me, but I told him to keep it.

"Trade it for your next supper. I've signed it there."

He laughed. "I guess they know you around here."

Adriaen left that cold night, and I didn't think on him after that, except to muse about how one man's fate is so different from another's. If he still had any plan to rob us, I knew he wouldn't, since I knew who he was.

Standing in that clearing in the snow, I imagined Adriaen's youthful face—the one I'd met years earlier—transposed upon that older, tired face of the thief in winter, and now on the cold, bluish-gray face of the dead man in the Waag. What a strange thing to have known a man in these three ways.

I stood for a long while, letting the snow continue to fall on me, letting it blanket my cloak and cover the red fabric in its sinless tint. There was nothing else to see on the horizon. Just various shades of white.

XV

THE HEART

I pounded on the door of that tower. The one that led up to the skinner's hall. I pounded and pounded and pounded. No one heard my calls. I ran round that weigh house, crying, screaming for anyone who'd hear. There were doors to guilds on every side—surgeons, painters, blacksmiths, masons—but no one opened any of them.

It were busy in that weigh house, full of men putting everything to the scales. Weighing grains and meats and butter and bags of worldly goods. Who knows what they weighed. No one had time to hear my cause. The dissection, they said, would start at sundown.

I pounded on the tower door and I cried out for anyone who'd hear me. The boy stood near, also crying. The boatman finally came and shushed us. He said he would take us somewhere warm, wait with us until they opened the hall. But I would not be moved. I sat myself down on the steps of that tower door.

This, here, is Adriaen's son. He is all I have in the world now, all that means anything. If I were to go back to Leiden, to go back to that mill house, the stones would always come, the boys would always jeer. The only way to keep my Carel safe, to give him any life at all, will be to do as Father van Thijn said. To bury Adriaen in our church. That were a chance he gave me.

Little by little they came. The people from Dam Square. They'd seen Adriaen go hanging and now they wanted to see him skinned. *Aris the Kid,* they called him, like he were their friend. That Kid, they said, who went to death so bold. The one who flexed his chest and bared his stump for all Dam Square to see. Tore off his shirt and stood naked in the cold.

The boatman stood by me and tried to shield me from their force. The boy said I were there to claim his body for holy burial. That's how word went through that market of who I were and why we'd come. I thought they'd try to stone me there, too, but that were not how it went.

The first thing that came to us were a link of sausage and then, right after, a hunk of bread. "For the lass," said the old baker who placed them in the boatman's hands. "She'll be hungry." Someone else saw what were brought and added to it butter. The boatman used his knife to cut the sausage and spread the butter. And then one came with cups of hot cider and gave them to the boy. "For Kindt's lass," he said. "No use freezing to death out here." More came. More food and more kindness. They called me "Kindt's lass," "Kindt's wench." They brought what they had, and shared it with me, the boatman, and the boy.

When we were done eating, a woman came up and asked to touch my belly. "There's luck in it," she said. "A babe with a strong mother like that." Others saw her and came, too. They called him

"Kindt's babe" and "Kindt's kin." One old lady bent down for a kiss. They came like that all day. They came with a shawl for me and gloves for the boy. They brought over a chair so I did not have to sit anymore on the steps by the tower door. They stood with us and talked with us and asked how I met "Aris." It were nothing like what I'd seen done in Leiden. And these were folks who had wanted his neck.

The boatman said, "She'll need your help to break into that tower. She'll need a mob to help her get his body back." He lit the idea like an edge of straw. They pushed forward, to the front of the line, where we sat at the foot of the tower and they told me they'd help. With the force of that whole crowd behind us, they promised, we'd manage to break the gate.

⋯⁂⋯

Some people thought I could save Adriaen. I could touch his soul through his wounds and turn them wounds into byways of grace. I could let his scars trace the course of his story. He did not tell me where he'd been and what he'd done, or why they'd flogged and banned him. I were not a confessor, and no redeemer. I started when we were young, the first time his father beat him, just before that wicked old man went off on his crusade.

"Mother says your father has joined Maurits's army." I stood at the door. It were almost evening. "She said I should check in and see if you'd supped."

"He's not a soldier. Just a sutler," he told me. I saw the dried blood around his mouth and eyes, his hand still cupping his chest. The blood on his mouth crusted in the small hairs of his first mustache. He were still young. No razor had ever touched his face.

"You're hurt," I said. He could barely see out of one eye. "You need care."

I were no older than he were. I made a poultice and fixed some soup. He could barely move his lips. His jaw were broken. We did not talk, but I fed him with a spoon. I stayed with him until the lantern went low. I wiped my hands on my apron and said, "Okay, then. Mother will be waiting."

He said nothing. "I will check on you tomorrow," I said before I left.

He tried to get used to the loneliness of his house with his father out of it. But he never managed that. In the evenings, he preferred the tavern. He loved the giddy sounds, tankard tapping tankard, the hurdy-gurdy men or the players of therobos and other lutes, the gamblers and vermin catchers. There were laughter in the taverns, and talk of journeys and adventures. He craved what he could not imagine and he drank down them ideas with the ale. I had mended him so he could get stronger and when he were strong he wanted the world. Soon, he were well enough to leave, and he packed fast and went.

It were nearly ten years before he came home after that. When he came back to me, all them years later, he were a rough man, a hard man, and a thief. I could see how he'd made his way. It were through filching and scrabbling. I could read his crimes on his skin and his hardships in his face. He had been hurt. I saw that, too. It were in his eyes, in his ways. He flinched if I reached out to touch him; he had a kind of twitch in his eyes. He were not that small and spindly boy who needed my ministering hands.

I tried to read Adriaen's story from his skin. Each of them flogging scars on his back and brandings burned into his neck and arms were a part of his story, part of the life he went and lived apart

from me for all them years after he left Leiden. When I were spong-
ing water over his wounds or sometimes when he were sleeping, I'd
touch them gently. Trace my fingers through the shapes.

He had the count's sword and stars for Haarlem and the lion
from Aalsmeer, them three Sint Andrew's crosses from Amsterdam,
and he had the shield of Utrecht, and the fresher ones were two
crossed keys for Leiden. Even when he were awake sometimes he let
me touch them, even though the skin were raw there and numb in
places. He squirmed sometimes, but he let me.

"Every town did claim you," I said. "Every one put its mark
upon your flesh."

"It was the other way around, Flora," he told me, as you might
explain to a child. "They branded me to keep me out."

"But they couldn't do it, could they? Still, here you are."

He didn't always want my touch. Sometimes, he'd turn over and
push me away. Sometimes he'd glare at me.

Maybe once you have that much of the world marked onto you,
you take yourself as the sum of your markings. I've seen sailors come
back from the seas with the ink in their skin they call *prikschilderen*.
They say they do that to stain themselves, to mark something of
their travels.

I traced my finger through his wounds where they told me a
story. I crossed the coat of arms for the city of Amsterdam. I touched
the groove where it marked out Utrecht's shield. I felt the long lines
of the whips along his back, the thin scars of the knife blades. It
were not for him I did this. It were for me. To know something of
his travels.

The white scars were thicker and longer. From the whippings.
Them were the ones he said were numb. The scars from the brands
were raised up. I moved my finger across the white ones and he

would squirm and wiggle. He said it felt like someone else's skin on his flesh. Like they'd given him different skin. I tried to be more gentle. But I did not pull my hand away. I let my fingers touch.

I dressed his wounds and kissed his forehead and brought food to his lips—that were what I could do. I could not save him and he would not save himself. There were something in Adriaen that liked a beating. After I'd nursed him them months in my house, I'd asked him why he kept going back to that tavern where he'd felt a thousand fists.

"I deserved it," he said. "It made me know I was alive." Then he cried like a babe. I let him curl into me, and I held him. He were gentle sometimes.

When he were well, up and about, and able to do his carousing, he were no different than he'd been before. A man's nature is his nature and a fish cannot turn to a sheep without witching. If I had that power, I would have done it: I would have changed him, saved him. I've never been any good at saving, only mending.

He'd leave my bed for the tavern, and later come back with his hands clenched to fists and sleep by himself on the doorstep. Sometimes he'd get angry when I tried to care for him, and he'd tell me I were no nun and my house were no convent. Sometimes, he'd just say, "Go find some soul worth saving."

Adriaen wanted to touch me, too. But he didn't. Not when he were still in bed with bruises. I touched him and he felt my hands. But he did not want to mishandle me, he said. He said he had too many misdeeds in his hands. They had too much ease for evil. He said his hands took more than they deserved. His hands claimed what were not his to take, and it always got him in trouble. He did not want to take me with those hands.

I wanted to feel his hands on me. Even if they were rough, even with a callused touch. On my back and on my breast. Maybe he thought that if he got that close, he'd never be able to leave again. Leaving were his nature, it were his way.

The day came at last. It were a warm day and there were a spot of sun in the garden. I were out back, tugging with a scuffle hoe at some weeds in the beds. The earth were sodden and rich from a few days of rain. I were going to plant a row of turnips and some vines of peas along the fence. I stopped for a moment and felt the sun fall on my face. Hard to think on it now, in this dead winter. To remember that it can be like that. Sometimes there is sun. Sometimes it is warm. I stood there and let the sun warm me, as if it were only for me.

When the sky shifted and the sun fell behind a cloud, I opened my eyes and saw Adriaen there in the doorway, leaning on a broomstick.

"Rain is on the way," he said.

"Always is," I said.

I picked up my scuffle hoe and went on digging.

"I wish I could do that for you," he said.

"You can. When you're well."

"I'd like to plant a few things and see them grow."

"Just a few months and it'll be a harvest. Turnips, potatoes, peas, carrots, and clover. I'll be drying the peas for winter soups soon."

"Already?"

"By September."

I could see in his eyes that he were imagining himself already gone by then. Where would he be? Under what bridge? Beside what city gate, on what river?

"Come inside before the rain," he said.

"A few more minutes."

When I got back inside, he were sitting up on the bed and he asked me to sit by him. "Flora, when I'm well, I'll go. You know that?"

I didn't answer him. I reached out and took his hand and brought it to my breast. I held it there until he knew it were his. Until he knew I knew he were not taking. I were giving. Then he touched me gently with no promises and no demands. He held my breast and moved his hand inside my blouse and up along my neck. He ran a finger along my chin and touched my lips. He pressed his palm against my cheek and put his fingers through my hair. He used both hands. He drew my face to his face and kissed me. He kissed me with full lips and a full heart, a heavy heart. I felt all his want. He moved his hand along my shoulders, down my back, over my hips. His hands took him on a journey he'd been long wanting to make.

I stood and took off my blouse, apron, and skirt, and stood before him so that he would know it were all his whether he stayed or not. We lay down together on the bed. In the same way I had let my fingers travel along his scars, his fingers traveled my skin. He watched where his fingers went, seeing all the crests and folds, the landscape of skin. They found the dark path from my breast down to my belly. They found the white rivulets of stretched skin upon my hips. They traced the blue tributaries of veins that wind along my legs. They moved slowly. They did not seek to take. They sought to touch, to see, to know. He had two good hands.

His smell were so familiar, a smell I had always known. It were the smell of the heath and the hay, of sweat and ale and burned wood. I relaxed into his arms and breathed him in. He smelled like a man and like a home.

✂⋆✂

The last time Adriaen left the mill house, we stood together at my cottage door. He didn't know about the babe then. Neither of us did. He said he wished he were a different kind of man. What I needed, he said, were someone who would live with me in the house beside the mill, and earn a living by the sweat of his brow.

"I wish I was like that," he said. "If I had it in me to be that way."

I should have told him he did have it in him. I should have told him he could have been any way he wanted to be. Or maybe I should have just said, "Don't go, Adriaen. Stay with me. Don't go." Odds are, he would have gone anyway.

✂⋆✂

A few weeks after that, they told me he were in the Leiden jail. He'd done a housebreaking with some other thief. They told me they were to saw off his hand. To take his hand for thieving. I didn't think they could do that, but they did. They did it right there in that sentencing hall. They brought a doctor in and had ten men hold him to the table. I screamed and cried and wept. What good did it do? What good does it ever do? Adriaen just went on like that.

When he came out of that hall, he would not let me guide him home. Not that time, he said, no more. "You won't want me now," he said. "You couldn't possibly want me now." But I did want him. I wanted him home. I wanted him by the hearth. I wanted to tend him and mend him and make my house our home.

XVI

THE MOUTH

I saw that they had come. By foot from Dam Square, by skate down the frozen canals, by barge across the Haarlemmermeer, by skiff from the wharf, by carriage from New Town, and by hook and by crook they had come to see Aris the Kid, who'd gone hanging in Dam Square. They'd heard of his bravery on the scaffold, of his brands and his stump and his naked, branded, breast. Now they wanted to see him on the chopping block. They wanted to howl for his flesh.

Nieuwmarkt was as busy as the Monday stock exchange, and just like the traders on that floor, everyone was waving hands in the air for a ticket.

Have you seen our anatomy hall, sir? It is a cramped space, high and circular and narrow and we can barely fit two hundred men in for the lectures, packed like herring into a herring buss. We are badly in need of a better hall, and the guild has already drafted up plans, but for the moment all we can do is strictly limit the tickets. Members of the guild, of course, have priority, after the magistrates and burghers and town councilmen. Tulp himself draws up the list and he is very precise about his guests. They must be men he seeks to cultivate as colleagues, sponsors, supporters, and friends. It's strictly politics, you see, who gets on the list.

By the time I heard the ruckus in the square outside, the crowd had grown so large you could've used it to man a ship. It was only me there—me against a roiling crowd—and I had no more tickets to sell. I heard them pounding, pounding at the door, and I stood behind it for a while, trembling, before I even dared look out the peephole.

My work was all done by then, the corpse prepared, the candelabras lit, the incense smoldering, the dissection table arrayed with all the necessary knives, saws, cleavers, scalpels, forceps, and ropes. I put one ear to the door and crouched beside it, listening, until at last it was too late anymore to keep waiting.

As dusk began to fall, the right and proper invitees—the barbers and surgeons, magistrates and merchants, traders and nobles in their finest doublets, stockings, and lace—at last arrived, pushing past the crowds, claiming their positions by the door. I hoped that the crowd might disperse, seeing the city fathers claiming their rightful places, but instead the crowd cackled and hissed and cursed the ticket holders and wouldn't let them pass. Then, too, I reasoned that somehow all the jostling would separate the wheat from the chaff, but I was wrong there, too. Immediately it went to fisticuffs as arguments erupted at the door.

I threw open the door and stood staring at the crowd with what little authority I could muster. "Ticket holders for the anatomy lesson of Dr. Tulp may now step forward and form a line right here," I announced. "Ticket holders only, please. I'm afraid tonight's dissection is sold out. Please, if you do not hold tickets, you must disperse."

The gentlemen composed themselves and tried to make a queue, but the crowd only became more agitated at the news that they could not get in. I was jostled and elbowed and yelled at to my face. I can still show you the bruises I received from that mob. Here, here's one on my arm and here on my hip. I'll roll down my hose to show you the welt upon my shin. That was where a lady kicked me, before demanding to be let in. A lady! I swear, I thought there would be a riot in Nieuwmarkt square.

Somehow, I got control of the door. I used it as a sieve and received each ticket holder one by one. A steady stream of cloaks and ruffs.

Once inside the anatomy chamber, I thought I'd finally achieve some sense of civility, but then, there, too, was more dispute. This time the jostling was among the guild members and other city nobles about where they'd take their seats.

Tulp's universe had its own logic, and it was manifest in the arrangement of guests in the rings: the optimal seats in the auditorium are those on the second ring—close enough to the dissection platform to observe every incision and movement of the forceps, yet far enough to shield the audience from the stench of tissue decomposition. City burghers would take the first row, because Tulp is running for city office and wants them to be especially familiar with his face.

Now, some surgeons claimed that they deserved to sit in the front row, in front of the city burghers, since it is their guild, but the burghers wouldn't budge. Already riled by the crowds outside, they seemed ready to roll up their sleeves again to claim their spots.

There was no winning with these men. Honor their status in whatever way you will and still they find reason to quibble. Well, at least they were finally all seated—and I managed to slip back down the stairs and see if I could sell the few final tickets for the standing room in the back.

※

I have, in a sense, always been a *famulus anatomicus*. My work is as close to my soul as my hand is just now to this tankard. I began this noble profession when I was five years old. My father worked for Carolus Clusius at the *hortus botanicus* at Leiden University. He was a specialist in tropical plants from the Indies and subtropical flowers from the Cape Colonies—a curio collector, too, in his way, but of the leafy vein.

My father performed yeoman's work in that garden, weeding wild grasses from the beds and deadheading overripe blooms. In the winter months, when the flower beds were fallow, he worked for the chief anatomist, Petrus Pauw, who liked to decorate the theater there with all kinds of frightful sights.

He had ten human skeletons: a skeleton rider on his skeleton horse, a skeleton playing the angel of death, a fateful scythe in his hand. A skeleton man and skeleton mate, side by side at a fruit-laden apple tree: the bony Adam and Eve. Six more around the amphitheater hoisted flags with deadly reminders in Latin: *Mors ultima linea rerum* (Death is the final end). One carried Horace's dictum, *Pulvis et umbra sumus* (We are but dust and shadow). I was only a boy, but I remember Pauw's chamber as well as my childhood cupboard bed. All my darkest nightmares came from there.

Both my parents died in a single week during the great pox of

1616. The only reason I lived on was fright. One day I found my parents both abed, their faces pale and hollowed, red blisters covering their necks and arms. My mother told me to stay away: "A monster has come," she said. "Quick, escape to the woods. We will come find you." I did as she said; I ran away and made my home in the woods for a week, terrified that the monster would get me. At last I got so hungry I had to go home. When I returned their bodies were already gone and a foreign woman was tending our hearth. I ran to Pauw, the only other person I knew. The great anatomist took me in as an additional set of hands.

Pauw didn't make me do much more than carry water and hold plants while he gave his famous lessons in botany. He preferred to do things by himself—things like cutting and bottling specimens. In spite of his preaching about how death was always among us, I never imagined I'd lose him, too. But he died at his desk as he was painting one of his banners. It would've said *Mors ultima ratio*, "Death is the final accounting." I was the one who found him, his face on his desk, his nose and cheeks covered with the black ink that had spilled from his pot.

I was alone there in the anatomical theater for a couple of weeks, sleeping in one of the skeleton boxes, before the successor came. He was Otto van Heurne, the one they call Heurnius, and he adopted me as if I were just another oddity in the *anatomicum*. He was a much more gentle soul than Pauw, and he moved Pauw's dusty skeletons and their moralizing banners upstairs.

Then he filled the anatomical theater with actual wonders: rocks and shells, coins and butterflies, Roman busts and burial urns, heads of Greek goddesses, carved African elephant tusks, wooden oars painted by South American tribes, ancient idols, whale bones, Japanese utensils for serving tea. If I stood in the center of Van Heurne's universe, the entirety of the world seemed to spin around me, from the archangels in the heavens, through the celestial dome, right down to the stones and rocks under Lucifer's feet.

Heurne persuaded merchants, sailors, and even ship surgeons to bring us earthly goods; and in this way, he taught me the rituals of my current faith: acquisitiveness.

If I'd once been afraid of death, who had taken three parents from me in two years' time, Heurnius's influence taught me to cultivate a pleased fascination with the dark messenger. Among the oddities and rarities that filled our chambers, Van Heurne kept specimens of the human dead. He bought dead children from an Englishman in Amsterdam, he asked his wonder hunters to seek for him the bodies of a giant. He was drawn to the ways of ancient Egypt, where it was believed that one never died but was simply "transfigured." He loved especially to collect mummies in sarcophagi.

As Leiden's chief anatomist, he also liked to examine the freshly dead. It was my job to fetch bodies for him. I was in my teens, and he sent me traveling the country freely by myself. Though the corpse cart emitted an awful stench, it didn't seem to prevent me from finding plenty of willing ladies.

The years with Heurnius passed quickly, but after nearly a decade pushing that corpse cart, it was time for me to make my way in the world on my own. I was just about to turn eighteen when I had the idea to come to Amsterdam and become a dealer using what skills he'd taught me. Soon enough I would buy a canal house and marry myself a beautiful Amsterdam girl.

We parted as father and son—in tears—and he gave me a purse and told me to waste no time in meeting the anatomist at the Amsterdam Surgeons' Guild. I secretly hoped that I wouldn't have to push the corpse cart anymore, so I avoided making that contact.

But by then it was already 1629 and Amsterdam was bustling with hungry curio dealers. I tried to sustain myself on buying and selling alone, but there was too much competition on the wharves and I was a mere Leidener fighting every other Amsterdam rogue for a steady supply of wonders. I was down to my last five stivers when Tulp came looking for me.

Since then, I've been his porter and body bearer and curator and culler. He is no Heurnius—no Heurnius, indeed. He keeps me busy with his chores while he works on the grand scale of moral philosophy, and yet he still counts all his coins very carefully. And though he has a small collection of his own curios, he is no hoarder like Pauw or Van Heurne. In the off-season, when the anatomies aren't in session, he lets me use the theater to display my wonders, and he pays for the quayside stables, too. He has asked me to procure for him an ape from the Australasias.

So now you see how whimsical this life can be? If I'd walked through the wood on my own two feet and come upon a crossing, I might have chosen the right path and not the left, but I was mounted upon an ass, which took its own haphazard course, so I landed where I am, as a collector of live animals and dead men.

❦

On the stairs winding down from the anatomical theater to the guildhall door, I said a prayer to my maker that the crowd had dispersed. Those who pray for only their own sake are rarely rewarded, though, and I was not so lucky either. The door, I swear, was bulging against the weight of that mob. They were pushing, punching, kicking, leaning into it, and their shouts were just as heavy as their hands. It is not a small door, you know, and the iron locks and latches were made by the city's best smiths. There must have been some thousand men out there trying to break it down.

I grabbed what was at hand—a long stick, a chair, a rug—and jammed them against the door, then said another hopeless prayer. I knew they'd find a way to get through; I only knew not when.

I ran up the stairs, locking doors at each landing and trying to shore up the final door to the anatomy hall. Soon, very soon, Tulp would take the center platform of the anatomy theater and begin his lecture. He would need me to act as his assistant. I would need to be inside. But I just ran up and down the stairs in a frenzy, trying to find a way to bolster our locks, to secure the doors, to prevent the throngs. It was only a matter of time before that whole crowd burst in.

XVII

THE HAND

Most excellent and ornate men of Amsterdam: Honorable Burgomaster Bicker, Amsterdam burghers, gentlemen of the stadtholder's
court, magistrates, inspectors *Collegii Medici*, physicians, barber-
surgeons, apothecaries, apprentices, and public visitors to our chamber, on behalf of the Amsterdam Surgeons' Guild, it is my greatest
honor to welcome you all to the Amsterdam *theatrum anatomicum* on
this, the opening night of the winter festival 1632.

At the request of the governors of our noble guild, I do humbly come before you to offer my annual lecture on the Human Body
and the Fabric of Nature. Tonight, gentlemen, we commence the
anatomical demonstration that will be the centerpiece of our city-
wide fête. This is an occasion of unparalleled import for the town
of Amsterdam and the Republic of Holland. Here shall we turn the
true eye of scientia to man's earthly form, so that we may come to
know our place in God's great universe through extensive ocular
testimony, lecture, and debate.

Our anatomical lesson shall be followed by a banquet for our guild members and honored guests in the great hall in the Waag's second tower. Our lecture will resume again tomorrow evening and continue throughout the week for five or six more evenings here in this tower. But later tonight the whole town will join together for public feasting and a spectacular torch parade through town, beginning in front of the Waag, continuing down the Nes, returning up the Damrak, and ending with fireworks in Dam Square.

I am Dr. Nicolaes Pieterszoon Tulpius, a son of Leiden. During the course of these proceedings, you may address me as Dr. Tulp or Tulpius. This occasion marks the second anniversary of my term as Amsterdam anatomist, lecturer, and praelector of our guild.

That guild of which I speak is one of the most highly respected of its kind in all Europe. Our *schul anatomicum* dates back to 1550, when we presented our first autopsia at the convent of the Eleven Thousand Maidens at Sint Ursula the Divine. The skin of the cadaver used in that effort—that of Suster Luyt, an executed thief—was carefully removed and treated and is currently exhibited in our guildhall, should any among you like to see it. Today, our guild doth represent eighty registered *doctoris medicinae*, two hundred and fifty barber-surgeons, and three hundred and ten apothecaries, providing treatment to one hundred and ten thousand residents of Amsterdam.

I count here at least a dozen members of our famed guild, including Warden Jacob Janszoon de Wit; Warden Hartman Hartmanszoon; Matthijs Calkoen; and our prized new apprentices, Adriaen Slabbraen and Jacob Block.

Gentlemen, 1632 is truly an annus mirabilis for Amsterdam. It has long been said that our city is strong in commerce but in all intellectual endeavors we are overpassed by Leiden, our neighbor town to the south and the home to a great university. This year, my friends, Amsterdam will rectify that state of affairs. In a mere three months' time, the new Atheneum Illustre, our very own university, will open right here in Old Town at the end of the Kloveniersburgwal, led by Amsterdam Surgeons' Guild member Caspar Barlaeus. The Atheneum shall be devoted to pursuits of all scientia, Latin, geologic arts, and, of course, natural philosophy. The Atheneum shall prove to the world that there is no place more illustrious on this globe than Amsterdam, and I know there are many among us tonight who would contribute to that honorable goal.

Ours is a city of rebirth, reclaimed from floodwaters and built upon the tireless industry of our engineers and craftsmen. Nowhere is our progress better represented than here, in the *theatrum anatomicum*. Even today, the great anatomists of Padua must conduct dissections in that city's concealed cellars, as the Vatican holds our scientia to be heretical. That church has silenced our friend and fellow philosopher Galileo Galilei, who proposes the view that the sun doth not move, but that earth revolves about it.

I would like to say, on behalf of the governors of our guild: let good Galilei come to Amsterdam, and we shall welcome him and his Copernican views! For ours is a free city, where the greatest minds of Europe may join together and celebrate true wisdom. See among us tonight, gentleman, that our town is already a haven for great thinkers. We have with us this very evening our dear friend and fellow philosopher René Descartes from Paris, who honors us with his presence in our humble anatomical theater. Please join me in welcoming him, sires, for he is an amateur anatomist in his own right.

Paris, Padua, Genoa, Venice, and Antwerp—all these cities may compete for prominence, my friends, but none matches Amsterdam's independence; our social, economic, intellectual liberty. We have among our citizens some of the greatest minds of all Europe, learned and skillful anatomists, painters, architects, draftsmen, engineers.

I observe among us tonight many of these dignitaries. Some of you I do regret I do not yet know, but throughout these proceedings you may think of this dissection theater as my living room.

Do not laugh, sires, for though we are in the company of death, yet we do celebrate life and all of God's glories.

Before me lies the body of a notorious criminal hanged by the neck this very day in front of city hall. Sentenced to death by four lord mayors and the honorable magistrates of Amsterdam, many of whom sit among us tonight, for misdeeds too numerous to count, the convict was penitent as he was led to the scaffold. With his final breaths he uttered the words, "May God have mercy on my eternal soul."

When looking upon his lifeless form, as we shall once I have removed this cloth, we should do well to remember the ancients' story of Marsyas, the satyr who claimed he could play the flute better than any man, mortal or immortal. He challenged Apollo to a musical contest, which the Muses would judge. Apollo and Marsyas proved both fine musicians, but Apollo outshone his immodest rival. Awarded the right to punish the satyr however he pleased, Apollo flayed Marsyas alive.

Whosoever, like this patient upon the dissecting table, believes that he outshines the Divine must pay the price. Let no man consider himself above moral law, outside the reach of God's law, else he be sacrificed to God's purpose.

All is not lost in this tale, gentlemen. This body, which conducted none but evil deeds during its earthly cycle, shall now be redeemed and made holy by its new purpose, which is to reveal to us the glories of creation.

Gentlemen, to commence my ocular demonstration on this fine winter's eve, I present you with a single tulip. The Violetten Admirael van Enkhuizen, gentlemen, is, as many of you do know, one of the finest tulips in the entire world round, surpassed in beauty and value only by the Semper Augustus. Note its color, finely striated in red, pink, and white, its faint golden tips a gilded halo to this throne. Behold then, the surprise at the bloom's center: a black iris within a blue eye! Give ocular testimony, too, to the unusual shape of its petals: they curve and bend like a strange melody.

My only misfortune, dear friends, is that this true specimen of God's divinity belongs not to me but to my friend here, the good poet and merchant Roemer Visscher. Thank you, Mijnheer Visscher, for lending it to me. This tulip, as you can see, as I walk it around the *theatrum anatomicum*, is the very exemplar of God's majestic handiwork. Would that I could pass it around for each of you to touch with your own hands, so that you might experience some portion of the pleasure I feel in its presence.

The bulb of an admirael, much like this I hold in my hands, sold this month at the flower auctions for the princely price of one of the new canal houses on the stately Herengracht. This one was cultivated in a hothouse so that it would bloom in time for our fête.

What makes this Violetten so exquisite? No, not its coloration, sires, nor even the delicate shapely petals. Why, if I should desire to do so, I should remove the bloom altogether.

There! It is done!

Gentlemen, what noise is this? Why do you gasp?

Have you never witnessed a tulip plucked from God's good earth and arranged in a vase upon the mantel? Gentlemen, I know many of you well enough to have seen your homes and know that all of your wives have done so!

Is it Mijnheer Visscher who would worry you?

No, no, he doth laugh!

Stand, my friend, and assure the crowd that you would not take offense! He knew what I would do!

There, gentlemen, you see! I do not deceive.

Gentlemen, gentlemen, be still! Resume your seats.

Please, honorable gentlemen, resume your seats!

Well, we must have a little fun at the winter fest, must we not?

Still, gentlemen, my amusing demonstration reveals a sober purpose. Why doth Mijnheer Visscher not object to my desecration of his priceless flower? For the life of this tulip lies not in the bloom that, whether planted or not, shall eventually wilt and wither. Rather the value of the admirael lies in its root, the bulb, which is returned to the earth so that it might bloom again. The petals, the iris, and the eye are but the outward manifestations of the glorious bulb. For it is the bulb that shall produce more tulips, the bulb that shall generate new life! The mother bulb lasts several years and may produce two or three clones, or offsets, annually.

In much the same way, gentlemen, human life is separated into two parts. The bloom of our human cycle is our body whilst it is young and strong and able. But as we all have observed, soon we, too, will wilt and wither, and ultimately our bodies are none but petals that do, lifeless, drop.

Our roots, gentlemen—the bulbs that do carry on past our flowering—are our souls. Our bodies are but the envelope of our souls here on earth.

The substance of my lecture is the division and also sympathy between man's body and his soul. It's a topic that should be familiar to those of you who have heard me sermonize here, on this pulpit, in this church of natural philosophy, in the past. Indeed, it was the subject of one of my first orations, *De animi et corporis sympathia*, at Leiden. I did not come to understand this matter on my own, of course. I inherited my understanding from the great ancient philosophers Plato and Aristotle, whose *observationis* have been passed down to us through Hippocrates and Galen.

They tell us to remember the Delphic oracle: *Nosce te ipsum, cognitio sui*. Know thyself. And its correlative: *Cognitio dei:* Know God.

Cognitio sui: Know thyself.

Cognitio dei: Know God.

We must understand the human body, our ephemeral encasement that we shed upon our deaths, in order to understand God and his larger purpose, his higher order. Man, as another of our ancients, the Greek philosopher Protagoras, related, is the measure of all things. He is greater than any other beast that walks upon this earth. He is God's ultimate conception. But what are the markings of our divinity? What separates us from all God's other creatures?

Let us now bring our attention again to my tulip, which I hold separated from its root. But instead of looking at the flower this time, I would ask you to direct your gaze just a bit lower, to this other remarkable specimen on display: the human hand that holds this stem. See how the hand twists, as I hold the tulip up to the candelabra. Note how the muscles within the arm do gently contract. See, honorable gentlemen, how the fingers do work independently of one another and yet also in harmony. How the thumb finds its way to meet the forefinger, and the remaining fingers open out like a bloom. These fingers grasp, press, and pluck! You have already seen how they plucked this fine bloom from its stem. To hold it aloft.

Like the tulip flower, this hand doth grow upon a stem. That stem, gentlemen, we shall call the cubitus, or forearm, comprised of two very different bones, which we shall call the radius and ulna, as per Vesalius, along with ligaments, nerves, veins and arteries, membranes and skin. Within our skin are flexor tendons and musculature that allow us to grasp this flower's stem, for example, to hold it betwixt our fingers, to twirl it so that we might observe all sides, as I am doing now.

This motion, this simple twirling of this flower, cannot be accomplished by any other species known on the earth. It is the gift of man and man alone. The horse, for all its strength and speed, cannot hold a gentle bloom with its hoof. The elephant, for all its vastness and power, has no hands to hold nor fingers to wave. Even the Indian satyr, that intelligent wild ape, has not the agility or grace of human hands.

Why would we alone be ordained with this skill? And, more importantly, what do we make of it? The same hand that should let us hold the admirael, or, for example, perform surgery or stroke our fair wives' hair in tenderness also enables us to steal, to strike, to knife, to kill. How do we use this hand? What do we owe to this appendage that would set us apart from barbarians and brutes?

The human hand, honorable gentlemen: the human arm. Wherefore is it God's gift? I dare not attempt the answer now, for this question deserves our profoundest consideration. Although this year's lecture shall explore many parts of the human body, the highlight of my presentation, I assure you, gentlemen, will be my discussion of the human arm and hand. I shall offer a demonstration of the mechanistic operation of the human arm, its major muscle groups, arteries, veins, and tendons—a subject which is particularly dear to my heart.

We shall begin, however, by cutting round with the surgeon's blade, to remove the skin.

Before I begin, let me make two apologies. First, especially for those standing in the back, I regret that our current chambers are not adequate. The Surgeons' Guild spent many months searching Amsterdam for new headquarters, and I'm pleased to announce that the governors have now decided to build an expansive new *theatrum anatomicum* right here in Sint Anthoniespoort. It shall be located in a large-bellied room in the new steeple currently under construction, and it shall accommodate twice as many spectators as our present chambers. At least, I hope, the close proximity among bodies shall keep some of you warm!

Secondly, as is the nature of all things corporeal, our patient, the focus of our attention tonight, shall inevitably begin its natural process of decay. That process, unfortunately, shall produce an unpleasant putrescence. As you perhaps have noted already, the many candelabras that hang above you to light the chamber are filled with scented oils and the censers burn with incense that should aid the olfactory experience.

You may have a particular sensitivity to putrescence. In which case, please position yourself closer to one of the small windows in the tower. As required by the Surgeons' Decree on the Anatomy Issue of 1606, I do ask that you attempt to maintain your seat throughout the proceeding. However, if you feel yourself becoming faint, may I suggest that you avert your gaze toward the anatomical text that you have brought with you or, if you have none, gaze at your hands or feet and contemplate my words rather than the patient.

However, if this doth not suffice and you find yourself overcome, raise your hand to notify our anatomical assistant—please step forward, Jan, so that our audience may know you—and he shall escort you out of the hall. There are chamber pots downstairs of which you may avail yourself. Once you have left the *theatrum anatomicum*, unfortunately, you shall not be able to return until the next evening's lesson.

In reverence to the tradition of anatomical lessons established by our worthy counterparts in Padua and Bologna, our discussion shall begin with a *quodlibet*, consisting of my lecture and recitation from the anatomical text. It shall be followed by a *disputatio*, in which members of the audience shall be permitted to submit questions and engage in debate about the material at hand. However, these comments must be respectful of the serious nature of the proceedings. Members of the audience should refrain from laughing or talking—or, indeed, applauding—during the lecture.

As per guild decree, I will pass around the auditorium various human organs that shall be dissected from the anatomical subject, so that you may inspect them at a closer vantage. They will be quite bloody, and though I will ask my *famulus anatomicus* to rinse them before we pass them around the audience, I must warn you that there will still be something of a mess. Please handle these organs carefully, observe them briefly, and pass them along to the person seated beside you. Should a member of the audience be caught attempting to abscond with the heart, kidney, liver, or any other organ, that person shall be fined six guilders and removed from the theater at once.

You laugh, gentlemen, but such attempts are not unknown.

Every year there is at least one foolish soul who seeks to leave with a souvenir. Last year, a young burgher put a liver into the pocket of his cloak. Had not the blood and black bile of this organ seeped through the lining, we would not have discovered the theft.

Let this year be the year that we reverse this trend. These organs would be reunited with the rest of the body for a proper Christian burial.

Now, then, I shall begin by removing this sheet over the patient. If you know yourself to be squeamish, please take a breath now, and breathe deeply for several moments. For the sight of the patient and its deathly pallor may be disquieting. I should prepare you, too, for the fact that this particular patient may prove even more unsightly than our usual fare, for his body is marred by the many markings of so many executioners' whips, chains, and branding scars. These, friends, are but the outward manifestation of his sinful path.

A final caveat: the right hand of this patient was amputated just above the wrist. This shall not hinder our discussion of his limbs, as we shall simply use the left arm, instead. However, it may prove disquieting to those of you who have never seen an unwhole human form.

Those of you who have brought along anatomical texts should be able to follow along with the demonstration quite easily. I shall be using two different texts to guide my instruction. The first is *De humani corporis fabrica* of Andreas Vesalius. Jan, please bring the text to me now. The useful illustration may be found on page two hundred and twenty-three.

I have removed the cloth. I shall take a moment to allow you all to view the body whole before I cut around with my surgeon's blade.

Tonight, I shall begin the anatomical lecture with a dissection of the patient's abdominal cavity, discussing all the major bodily organs. Then, following Vesalius, I will focus on the structure and function of the man's hand.

You shall see plainly that God has left his footprints here, within the body of this thief. Whence I begin to dissect the flesh and reveal those footprints, I ask you to think not only upon the appearance of the man, the shape or texture of the organs, but on the functioning of man's soul. We must give ocular testimony but search, too, with our souls. Observe!

XVIII

THE EYES

When I entered the anatomy theater through the side door, I was treated to such a strange sight. Dr. Tulp was holding in his hands what struck me as the head of a monkey or a small sea monster. It had no limbs, save the few cut tubes that ran out of its core. It had no eyes and no mouth, but a large indentation where its ears might have been.

He stood there holding it out to the audience in supplication. The room of men, all clad in black and white, seemed to me to be one man, whose single mouth was agape and whose eyes were fixed on the object before him. My gaze returned to Tulp, who stood at the center of the theater like the convener of a male coven.

Of course, I knew why I'd come here, and I knew the event was an anatomy. But some combination of the wind and the snow and the thoughts in my head had distorted my cognition, so everything I witnessed pointed to something else.

Before the praelector was the body on the dissection table,

though my mind registered it as a slain and quartered ox. It didn't immediately occur to me that the objects scattered about the stage were human organs. I saw them as curios from my *kunstkamer:* a dried snake, reef corals, a tortoise shell.

When the chamber door slammed behind me, all eyes turned in my direction, and my own awareness fell upon myself. I looked down and saw that I was quite a spectacle, as my cloak and shoes, my breeches, and even my hands were enveloped in white. I stamped off the snow and stood for a moment as the powder quickly turned into puddles. I bowed as deeply as I could.

For a moment, everyone was silent. I announced very clearly, "Sirs, I do apologize with all my heart." It seemed the entire congregation laughed at that moment. And in the sudden recognition that I had punned, I was able to reorder the elements of this picture to make better sense.

I had walked into the anatomy lesson so late that Tulp had already opened the chest cavity and was currently cupping Adriaen's bloody heart in his hands. A whole series of emotions rushed through me then, a confused tangle of feelings of pity and grief and a little bit of righteousness and ultimately powerlessness. I had left him on that table this afternoon, and I knew it would come to this, did I not?

Tulp stopped the proceedings and, with utter civility in spite of my tardiness, introduced me to his audience in glowing terms. I felt my whole body redden in mortification. Once I had spent what seemed like an endless amount of time receiving this unwarranted approbation, he told me where to take my seat. My eyes adjusted to the light and my mind took in the reality.

He was holding Adriaen's heart in his very hands, dispassionately explaining the structures and functions as if it were no differ-ent from the heart of a rabbit or a dog. His speech was appropriately dry and scholastic, but it was difficult for me to keep my eyes off the table where the body lay undressed, his chest cavity torn asunder, his organs laid bare, blood splattered about everywhere.

The memories so recently revived could not be reconciled with this picture painted before me in the present. Adriaen was cold and hungry when I'd seen him last in life. He'd been a bit dizzied by drink but he was nonetheless a man of vitality. I'd seen him in the tomb below earlier in the day, but even then he'd looked like a full man.

Tulp continued lecturing, speaking with theatricality and pomp that overstated his case. The words swept over me, though, for I wasn't in any mood to hear about physiognomy. I didn't realize Adri-aen's heart was being passed around the audience until my neighbor nudged me and deposited it in my hands. I had no time to reject the offer, and though I would not have taken it if I'd been given the choice, I did not give it back. It was a bit like having an infant thrust into your hands, so small and fragile, so oddly weightless.

To my surprise, though, it was cold as a seashell and hard as one, too. From a distance, I had imagined it warm and supple, full of the enriching blood of life. But it was clear that life had long since fled from this organ, in spite of all the blood.

Turning it several times, I found myself quickly spellbound by what holding it implied. I kept turning the organ over and over in my palms, feeling the way that its brittle texture felt against the moist, pliant flesh of my flesh. What could I learn from it, from hold-ing it? What meaning could I divine?

Finally, someone tapped me on my shoulder and told me I had

better pass it along. Others wished to see. I looked up, as if awakened from a dream, and handed it to the man sitting next to me. It was a muscle, I thought then, and its function was bodily, not oracular. No soul resided there anymore.

I looked around the room and saw some of the men who'd come to the studio to sit for my painting: the surgeon Adriaen Slabbraen, seated just at the edge of the dissection platform, craning over the railing to read Tulp's open copy of Vesalius's *Fabrica*, the apprentice Hartman Hartmanszoon standing up in the back row, holding his own copy of what seemed to be an illustrated anatomy book he'd brought along. Jacob Colevelt, the new guild member, was sitting all the way to the left of the dissection platform, his chin tucked down in a way that suggested he just might vomit. Van Loenen seemed to be contemplating something very profound.

I saw the consternation in the eyes of one guild member, the slight fear in the gaze of another, and the naive awe in the expression of a third. Living man's response to death, displayed there on the table before him, I thought, is not revealed through just one type of expression. This led me to thinking perhaps I could include this dynamic in the painting, each man reacting to the unfolding mortality play before him, each one taking it in in his own way.

Although I could no longer save Adriaen, perhaps I could give his body form in the painting, give his death some kind of reality, restoring, at the very least, a sense that he was a human man and not just a corpse. It was as I was contemplating all this that there was that terrible commotion outside the theater, and the door burst open and the crowd pushed its way in. What chaos in such an austere setting! What excitement! What a thrill. Of course you saw the woman who flew across the room and threw herself across the body of the dead man.

It was you, wasn't it, Monsieur Descartes, who'd tapped me on the shoulder to pass along the heart?

XIX

THE HEART

That were not a doctor's room. It were a butcher's hall. Adriaen lay naked with their knives and cleavers and clamps. I saw them weapons stabbed into the wood around him on the table. I saw his body cleaved open and his heart in some man's hands.

It were the force of that crowd that got us in that door. They pushed and pressed and pounded until the latch came loose and the locks did bend. I do not think they loved me but they loved the chance to try to save Adriaen. The kid. He were theirs now. His life were already some kind of lore.

We got in but it did not help. Them medical men and magistrates were no kinder to me than them who threw cobblestones, them who pelted. They showed no pity. They threw us all out and blockaded the door. They grabbed me on the belly, never mind about the babe. I screamed bloody murder but they did not stop, they did not bend. They tore me away from him and thrust us out of the room. They pushed the men back, the women back, the crowds. All of us were the same to them. We were all one man.

They shushed me with their gentlemanly ways. "He'll serve scholarship," they said. "He serves medicine." They said, "He's serving God." That's what they said, but all I saw were Adriaen, and no hope of salvation in that room.

Anyway it were too late. His body were open, his heart torn out. I were too late. I were too late to the hanging. I were too late to the magistrate. I were too late to that room.

I wept. I wept so hard I thought the babe would come out of my mouth. I were doubled over by the door, crying, weeping, but I would not convince them. It were too late. The only one who came were that Jan Fetchet. He took us some bread and ale from the surgeons' feast and told us to get warm and to rest.

"Sit, then. Take a seat here," he said. "Do not cry, for that there is not your Adriaen. He has long slipped his earthly noose. He never dwelt within that chamber, never felt the surgeon's blade. His body quit at noon; his spirit fled at two."

We sat and listened, because there were nothing else we could do. Fetchet sat with us and thought. After a while, he said, "His body is not, perhaps, his final fate. I have an idea. I will take you to the home of that artist, Harmenszoon van Rijn. He can give you what I cannot—the body's last part."

xx

THE BODY

I kept wandering from town to town, until I ended up back in the town I dreaded most, Leiden, my birthplace. The thought of returning home and seeing my father so repelled me that I spent a good many nights inside the town tavern, where I knew he'd never go. Some of the old guzzlers there remembered me from my youth, though the contours of my face were much changed, and they kept me well in cups. On the third or fourth night, I met there a man who recognized me from my father's workshop, and he walked up next to me and put a grave hand on my shoulder.

"Forgive me for not saying this in a more apt setting, but I'm very sorry for your loss," he said.

At first, I knew not his meaning, and I said, "Why, I've none to lose and therefore mourn not!"

The man's brow creased so woefully that I felt immediately penitent for my mirth. "Was your gentle father, that good and pious, none to you at all? Then his death falls very hard, indeed."

I gulped down the swig of beer. "Death, you say?" I dropped my cup. "My father dead?" I cried out. Little did I know that this would touch me thus. I cried out in agony and clutched the man who'd given me the news.

"Why, son, you didn't know? But he only died this week. Were you not here?"

I cried out again, and grabbed the man tighter in my rage. "You lie!" I said. "You lie! Your lips are the devil's own! Your tongue should be cut out!"

I didn't know it as I cried out, but in my rage and despair, I hit the man, my father's friend, and bloodied his nose. The tavern keeper parted him from me, and the other guzzlers leaped upon me. Still I tried to beat the man who'd talked with me, and the guzzlers put their fists upon me and threw me off my stool. As I cried out that the man was a liar, they pummeled me until I was no more alive than the sand on the tavern floor.

The other man they took directly to the town physician, and they rolled me out of the tavern door like a barrel. They left me there as a doormat, and I stayed and let them step on me even as the dawn came and they closed up shop and left.

This unfortunate affair did nonetheless lead to what was, in my adult life, the single brief respite from my ordeal. For, Flora, the miller's daughter I described at the start of my tale, learned of my beating, collected me from the base of the tavern steps, and brought me to her home to nurse me back to health.

No wench was ever kinder to a man. No gift that was ever given was as precious as this. While my wounds were new, I lived like a burgomaster under Flora's care. She poulticed me and fed me. She softly petted my brow and kissed me gently about my face. She never asked me once to account for the years that I had been gone;

she told me stories about the mill and about her parents—now both passed on as well. One day, she pulled out from under her bed a tight roll of leather that she placed in my hands. Within, I found my father's set of leatherworking tools she'd managed to save from our shop the day I'd fled from Leiden as a youth, and before the tax collector bolted our doors. I was nearly overcome with tears.

No woman—no one at all, as far as I can recall—ever showed me the face of grace. She was my mother, my sister, and my darling wife all at once. Flora alone knew my sorrow and anger over my father's death, and she swore to the townsfolk on my behalf that I had not meant to hurt my father's friend at the tavern, but only lashed out in the torment of my grief. On her good word—for she was beloved now in Leiden—other townsfolk provided for me, too: a new set of clothes to replace my vagabond's gray rags; a hand-carved walking cane to aid me as my ankle, broken in my attack, did mend; even a fancy cap to wear upon my head. I swear I would've become another man altogether, if I'd stayed with Flora for even a week more.

But when I was fully mended, she sent me out from under her roof, saying, "Alms to you is sin now that you are strong and well." She shooed me off with the broom, too, laughing so her bosom quavered. "Find work and return to me with a plump goose to roast on Sint Bonaventure's Day."

I stopped in for a quick goblet at the very tavern where I'd received my beating. For I had been a thief and a mendicant so long I knew not how to seek an honest wage. The tavern keeper's eye weighed heavy on my face as I complained of this sad truth to my fellow knave at the bar. He said the same was true for him. How can a man work if he was never trained? I told him I'd squandered the training my father had given me in the sheath-maker's trade and showed him the set of tools Flora had given me in the leather case. He told me that if I wanted now to put those to good use, he at least knew how we could employ them.

In a low voice, he said he'd come to know a childless merchant who kept a stately house and a stable of horses he sold to the Americas. He kept the rest of his treasures in a cellar that didn't rightly shut. I told him I didn't believe it to be true and bade he take me to the place.

He found the place and we used my father's carving knife to pry the cellar door, but found no treasure. Instead, we burst in upon a man who was taking his bath in a barrel below the stairs. He came at us, in all his naked glory, and we ran to free ourselves from his soggy embrace. This so-called merchant, it seems, was no merchant at all, but instead a constable of the Leiden court.

For this offense, I was flagellated in public in the square in Leiden, as poor Flora watched and wept, along with all the other townsfolk she had tried to convince of my goodness. Then I was branded with the blunt end of an iron—you can see the scar from that day here on my shoulder—and banned again from Holland and West Friesland for twenty-five years. I was forced from my birthplace by pitchfork, in a torch parade, and stripped of my new clothes and fancy cap. I would not have felt quite so much shame if it weren't for the sound of Flora's wailing, which played in my ears for many weeks as I walked and walked and walked. I was banished from Leiden, and yet still, I ended up back there.

So golden-hearted is that wench that I suspected she would await my return no matter how much I'd sinned. Poor is the wench who tries to convert a thief into a gentleman with kindness. I could not help myself from continuing along my well-worn, and pernicious, path.

My last offense was to trespass on a house near the Stevenshof in Leiden. I lifted some windowpanes to attempt to filch a purse that was sitting near the glass, but was caught in the act, because the windows fell down upon my hands and I howled noisily.

I hope I will never in my life see that hellish city of my birth again, for the worst violence was done to me there. The justice of the court took no pity for this minor offense, and seeing the long list of misdeeds on my record, he screwed up his face. I was speechless when he announced that my right hand was to be sawed off at the wrist. And I was still not awake when this horrifying punishment began. But when that rusty blade took the first bite of my flesh, I awakened. Ten men had to hold me down, and one put a plank of balsam between my teeth so I would not bite through my own tongue. But pain is a curious demon and in that moment I had so much of it I soon became almost calmed. A strange thought passed through my mind in this moment of stupor. This was, indeed, the very lifelike incarnation of the nightmare that had kept me from sleep all those years. My arm was being sliced open to the cold air. Though I did scream and kick and repent with all my heart to get them to stop this torture, some part of me believed that now that the deed was truly done, I'd no longer suffer from that dream.

Then I lifted my head and saw what they had done to me and I died my first death. I won't speak more on this because the torment of that day is enough for one man to bear. As you can see, Your Honor, the skin has now closed around the cut, and the arm is but a fleshy club where once I had a hand. No more thumb have I to hold a pen nor index finger to pick my nose. I miss each of the other fingers just as much, for now I know how much good they could've done for me had I used them well.

These brands and whipping scars from my ankles to my neck, this stump that hangs useless from an able limb are all testament to my depravity. I was a pretty boy. I might've grown up to be a handsome man, but my form now represents my wretched soul. No man alive, not even a blind man, can fail to observe my wickedness.

XXI

THE MIND

January 31, 1632
Dear Mersenne,

I write to you again tonight in a rare state of agitation, having just returned from the anatomical lesson. I have at this moment arrived at my lodging at the Oud Prins, and I feel a desire to relate all that I have seen, for it has given me a great deal of new insight into the questions of the body and soul that have so preoccupied me of late.

I have torn off my gloves, though I still wear my cloak and my hat. Let me remove my coat and hat and I will continue with more solemnity.

There it is. I am defrocked, as it were.

I write to tell you of a fascinating performance at the anatomy hall this evening, when that Tulpius, of whom I jotted earlier, dissected a human hand. The lecture was otherwise uninteresting—Tulp is more moralist than philosopher, and used a great portion of the evening to search the poor criminal's corpse, in vain, for evidence of despoilment. The liver was not black, the heart was not shrunken or distended, and neither the small nor large intestine contained polyps, no matter how long he spent examining their every turn and curve. I thought at one point he'd wrap the dead man's digestive tract around his neck and use it as a scarf.

In any case, he took particular care with the portion of the lecture in which he focused on the hand, as I believe this is the only area where he differs with Galen, who mostly dissected Barbary apes and never managed to dissect a human hand. Instead Tulp sided with Vesalius, saying that the hand is the only distinctively human feature of a man.

First, Tulpius covered all but the limb, and asked his assistant to hold it steady at the shoulder. Using his scalpel, he sliced through the center of the forearm and the skin folded back and rolled away.

He presented to us the muscles and tendons that wrap around the radius and ulna—these bones I have previously observed only in skeletons. By holding the elbow steady and turning the arm laterally, Tulp demonstrated how these various muscles operate together to allow for the very complex mobility of the forearm. Some groups work for extension and others for supination, and then the tendons work for pronation and flexion.

The radius and ulna are only two bones but they are miraculous, really. Because there are two bones in the forearm, unlike in the upper part of the arm or in the legs, the forearm is not fixed; it can twist and corkscrew. In that way, we can move our hand in various directions. You could go so far as to say that these two bones, the radius and ulna, make almost all human endeavors possible, because they allow for the torquing motion that makes all hand movements possible. Turning a doorknob. Stabbing with a knife. Operating a crank.

Then Dr. Tulp sliced horizontally across the wrist and pulled down the skin of the palm over the tips of the fingers, as if the skin were a glove. He snipped off the skin at the fingertips just below the nails, like a butcher would trim sausage from a long band. It was all very neatly done, I must say. As I mentioned, Tulp certainly knows his way around a blade.

A funny thing occurred to me when the interior of the hand was at last revealed: it very much resembled the inner workings of a harpsichord. The hand has a whole system of pulleys and sliding structures that make it possible to bend each finger. You know how, as you press a key in a harpsichord, the corresponding string within the instrument will sound when the plectrum plucks the string? It was like this with the fingers, which could move on their own as he drew back each flexor tendon.

Then Tulp gave us a very clever demonstration of the operation of these flexor tendons. He used his forceps to grasp the tendons in the wrist, creating tension in the arm so that the fingers of the corpse began to curl.

It was macabre and scintillating at the same time. Every one of the onlookers gasped. A few admitted afterward that they'd thought for a moment that the dead man's soul had returned to his body.

Tulp was only playing puppeteer. All he had done was put pressure on the mechanism using his own hand. Yet it was quite extraordinary to see it. How can I put it accurately? It was proof that the body is a machine and that the muscles and bones all act in accordance with mechanical principles. I shall not forget it.

After he had done it, Tulp let a few of us also try grasping the
flexor tendons ourselves, so we could feel the motion within the
arm. I was very pleased to have this opportunity, as I might not
have completely believed what I had seen without testing it. But
it was very simple, Mersenne. The human body is constructed,
it seems to me, with a very clear mechanical purpose in mind. All
these parts work in harmony, and all is apparent once you are able
to gaze upon these elements individually.

The hand is part of that machine, but the machine operates at
the dictates of the soul. If a corpse's hand can be reanimated in
death, then it must be by some other living soul and not itself.
I could directly observe through Tulp's anatomy that most of
the vital functions, such as digestion of food in the stomach
and so on, do not involve the soul at all—that is, the part that
thinks, understands, wills, imagines, remembers, and has sensory
perceptions.

Permit me to suggest that the soul is very much like the corona
of a candle flame. It is apparent to the observer, but it is illusory.
It changes depending upon the way it is viewed. It is there, and yet
we cannot touch or feel it. The candle allows for the corona to
exist; the candle flame is extinguished when the body dies. I believe
this candle flame must be found in the brain, for that is the seat
of the will which drives the hand and all the other bodily
mechanisms to perform acts. But the corona of the flame is what
happens inside the brain. In other words, thinking.

The rest of Tulp's lecture was not so spirited. He speaks much
about the importance of ocular testimony, yet his theological
lenses obscure his sight. The lecture included such a perverse
assortment of claims, mingling science of the ancients with his
Calvinist theology, that I found my thoughts twisted about in

all directions and ultimately nowhere at all. Never have I heard
a single modern surgeon so often quote Hippocrates, Pythagoras,
and Celsus. It's as if it were yet 1522. Poor Galen should only be
lifted directly from his grave and brought to stand before the entire
assembled mass of Amsterdam surgeons for a more vivid display of
sycophancy. Tulp deforms his own logic to make empirical enquiry
reflect his personal theology, no doubt the result of his education
under Petrus Pauw, that strict predestinationist who found human
beings so irredeemable.

After the performance with the arm, the guild members went off
to their banquet. Since his strict religiosity forbids him to partake,
Tulpius welcomed us into his private chambers. There, I suggested
to Tulp that the brain, and specifically the pineal gland, might
be the location of the soul; he responded that Galen had already
disproved all theories about regulation of psychic pneuma. Well, I
just left it at that. As you know, no one else on the continent has
even spoken of psychic pneuma since Niccolò Massa.

My friend, that is my story for this evening. I shall put down my
pen for now, for the fire has gone out and my chamber has grown
cold. I will write more reflectively tomorrow in response to your
observations on the corona of a candle flame. For now at least, I
must blow out my own candle and sleep.

Your true and loving friend,
René Descartes

XXII

THE EYES

I was summoned to join the banquet with the magistrates, noblemen, barbers, and surgeons and I could hardly decline as I'd already
come so late. I did not see you there, Monsieur Descartes; perhaps
you are one of the few men in town who does not have the stomach
to feast after a dissection.

They held it in the grand hall of the medical guild at a long
wood table made, I was told, from a single giant oak that had been
shipped all the way from the New World. That was only the first of
many extravagances prepared for this particular feast. Silver trays
of Gouda and Edam cheeses, lamb, goat, pig, fish, beef, and lobster
were delivered to the table, and it seemed as if the autopsy was
quickly forgotten.

I didn't have much of an appetite upon leaving the dissection
chamber, and my head was swimming with memories of my brother
and the boy from Leiden. I was thinking, too, of that woman who
rushed into the anatomy theater during the dissection, and how she

had the force of the crowd behind her. How they had pressed their way into that room so that she could see him one last time. But like that . . . to see him like that . . .

No one else seemed the least bit interested in this or anything having to do with the anatomy lesson. Once they delivered the casks of Rhenish wine, the conversation quickly turned bawdy. Some gruesome jokes about innards were made at the dead man's expense, and the men stabbed their knives into their meats with far more dexterity than Tulp had used his blade. It was about the time when the banqueters began singing and crashing their tankards against the table that I was tapped on the shoulder to see Dr. Tulp in his private chambers upstairs. This was a great relief to me by that point.

Tulp received me warmly when I entered his office.

"They're toasting you at the banquet," I said, sitting down across from him. He was behind a large wood desk on a chair that seemed more like a throne. "Don't you want to join the festivities?"

"I dislike liquor and abhor tobacco," he said with a gentle smile. "I am an antisumptuary but I don't seem to be able to prevent the guild members from partaking. I pay for the banquet out of the guild's purse. I simply choose to remain apart."

"I am honored to be invited to your private chambers. Let me express my heartfelt apologies that I was so tardy tonight. If it could have been prevented, it would have."

He offered me some more of his herbal brew and I accepted it.

"I wondered what had become of you," he conceded without scolding. "But I was pleased that you arrived when you did. You did not miss the most important part. That part you'll need for the portrait."

"Your dissection of the hand was masterfully done," I said. "All the guild members are saying so. I should think Professor Pauw would be very proud of his star pupil."

Tulp bowed his head, I think, to blush. "That is a generous compliment, indeed." He looked up at me again. "I think he should be disappointed with me; I was not able to locate the source of the criminal's corruption in his soul."

"Where did you suspect it would reside?"

"I should have thought to find it in his heart or at least his liver."

"And not in his hand?"

The doctor shook his head. "Moral philosophy and criminal justice diverge dramatically when it comes to offending organs. Judges and magistrates punish the hand because it is the most effective way to prevent the repetition of the criminal act. But there is no medical evidence that the hand itself contains the source of the thief's soul corruption any more than the tongue is to blame for the liar's prevarications. Our moral philosophy teaches that all soul corruption resides in one of the vital organs of the thorax."

"And could there be no other medical explanation?"

"All men of scientia must come up with new theories, or else we should never have any lively debates in our profession and no new published works. Some men believe that new knowledge is always the best knowledge. I prefer to stick with the ancients. The mortal soul is clearly to be found in the thorax. Now there is a debate, of course, between Plato and Aristotle about whether there is further division and that the immortal soul can be found in the neck and head. Yet, for a thief I think one must focus on the mortal soul to discover the source of corruption. It would be in the thorax. I must have overlooked something during this dissection. I am just not sure yet what."

He was momentarily distracted, jotting down a note for himself.

I began to move slowly around the room, taking in all that he had on display. It was a formal study and everything had its place. The shelves were lined with mustard- and rust-colored leather-bound tomes. In the cabinets were a handful of anatomical preservations in glass jars: small samplings of animal and human tissue in pale liquid, labeled with their precise contents. The colors of the specimens were fleshy reds and pinks. There was a small slice of what appeared to be a human lung latticed with holes like a fisherman's net. Another jar held a lobe of a brain, its contours gray and brown with age. The cabinet also contained smaller jars of what seemed to be medicines and ointments, items from his developing pharmacopeia, I guessed.

On another wall was an anatomical drawing of an ape. The lines of the drawing were weak and thin, the shapes that made the body too round and inexact to be a credible likeness. The ape looked more human than he should, yet not at all natural. To one side of his cabinet there was a wall marked in the shapes of his medical tools— forceps, scalpels, retractors—some of which lay on the shelf below.

He finished writing and returned his focus to me.

"It is an important question," he said. "Where the soul resides. You must have an opinion of your own on the matter."

"I have been told often that my portraits do not accurately depict my patrons. And many of my subjects do not see in themselves what I put on the canvas. When I view a man, I do not study so much the color of his eyes or the precise folds of the particular wrinkles about his mouth. Their noses are too wide, or their eyebrows too large; they say my skills in creating likenesses is sometimes wanting." I paused to collect my thoughts. "As a portrait painter, it is my job to try and capture not only a man's likeness but also a man's soul. Men of learning, like you, search for the soul that lies within. The artist is trained to view what is without and to reflect it as faithfully as possible. But how many of us are able to use what we see on the outside as a way to glimpse what is within?"

Tulp smiled wryly. "And yet your self-portraits do depict you faithfully."

"There it is," I said. "But what do I look like? I don't know. Every self-portrait is a different man. I see my subjects and their features surely, but my job is not to depict these precise features or any accumulation of parts, only to depict the man himself. That requires going beyond the qualities of his edifice and gazing, somehow, more acutely into his soul."

"Aha," said Tulp. "Then you think a soul can be viewed from outside?"

"This is what puzzles me, because I believe I do," I said. "What is it that can make manifest the stuff of a man's soul? As you point out, the courts would have us view a man's body as a map of his misdeeds. The thief's brands tell us where he has sinned. His whipping scars tell us how egregiously. Then we cut open his body and examine his internal organs to discover what corruption lies within. But as a painter of portraits, I must follow the advice of Leonardo, who instructs us to seek the soul through the external elements. I must see the man as a man first, and guess at the soul within."

Tulp spent a moment considering this. "You are very learned," he said.

"For an artist . . ." I finished his thought a little wickedly.

"I had not expected it. But I am glad for it."

"Thank you."

"We anatomists believe that a man is redeemed through our dissection because his body becomes useful for human inquiry. Do you find any truth in that?" he asked me.

"That suggests a soul can be redeemed. I hope that is the case."

"A politic answer. You impress me, Master van Rijn. I am glad you came to speak with me."

I swallowed the last of the tea he had poured me. The taste was still bitter but I could see how it might yet work wonders in me. "Surely, you didn't invite me here merely for a discourse on the soul?"

"No," he said. "I wanted to discuss a practical matter, about the portrait."

"Of course."

"We had discussed using the arm in the portrait," he began, "like the Vesalius woodcut."

"Yes."

"It is maybe a petty concern, but it is important to me. In the Vesalius portrait the arm depicted is the patient's right arm. This patient, as you saw, had no right hand. It was taken by some other executioner. For my dissection I had to use the left arm."

"Yes, I noticed."

"It is important to me—though I understand that it complicates matters for your portrait. But I would like you to paint the right arm, rather than the left arm. I would like it to look like Vesalius's arm. Is that possible?"

My mind was already full of so many other thoughts about the painting that I could think of no reasonable reply except to agree. I did not tell him then that I was considering portraying the whole man. I knew it would upset him if I did. "I will do my best to faithfully represent the right arm," I told him, "although my model is missing the right hand."

"Excellent," he said, taking my cup and his own and putting them both on a silver tray. "Do you have any other questions?"

I stood, recognizing this signal that our session had come to a close. "I have only one. Can you tell me who that woman was who entered the chamber during the dissection? Was she his wife?"

He stood as well. "A very sad case it was. She is not his wife but a woman who carries his child. She has left now, though. I think she has gone home."

Painting diagnosis: Rembrandt's *Anatomy Lesson of*
Dr. Nicolaes Tulp, 1632

I believe I now have corroborative evidence to support a rather important discovery in the painting: I have examined two very small paint samples from the right hand of the corpse, in the underpainting and in the overpainted section. Looking at it under the microscope, it is clear to me that the overpainted section seems to have a significantly higher density of lead white than the pigment below it.

Even more important, perhaps, the uppermost layer of paint appears to have been applied with much greater density. Rembrandt appears to be trying to fix a problem, to be eradicating an earlier choice as he paints a fully formed, elegant hand over a stump. Meantime, I asked my studio assistant to check through the *justitieboek* that informs our present inquiry. This was written four days before Aris Kindt was hanged in Dam Square. That's 27 January 1632. He apparently gave his confession after being "hauled up with two hundred pound weights." Here's the actual wording:

Adriaen Adriaenszoon from Leiden, alias Aris Kindt or Arend Kint placed by aldermen in the hands of my Lord Schout in order, through being put to the rack, to speak the truth on that of what he has been accused of. Two hundred pounds of weight were bound his legs, as he was unwilling to confess to have helped the cloak thief . . .

Another entry:

He has committed many thefts, purse snatchings, housebreakings, and other evil acts, for which he in this town as in other towns has been frequently arrested, then released and discharged from jail, under the expectation he would mend his ways. He was several times severely punished, thus persisting in denying and lying lie upon lie, he is by the Lords Aldermen placed in the hands of Lord Schout. Says to have been flogged with the others in Den Helder and Alkmaar, after he had been branded in Leiden four to five days before. Therefore the Lord Schout of Leiden, having learned of the misdeeds of this cloak thief, has decreed that he should have his right hand sawed off at the wrist. . . .

This is the fifth Rembrandt painting I have had the privilege of examining and restoring. I worked on two in the Metropolitan, one at the Hermitage, and another at the Rijksmuseum. They were all painted at different stages in Rembrandt's career, and I have been able to see, through very close scrutiny, how the master applied his pigments to achieve his illusionism.

In Rembrandt's later work especially, there's always a very strong sense of focus in the fragments. That is, you don't have to think very much about where to look, because Rembrandt is very deliberate in showing you. Rembrandt understood that the eye is drawn to texture, and so he builds up his paint in the key passages. And when he wants to correct something, he goes back in and uses pentimento. I will be giving special attention to his pentimenti— those layered dabs of paint—to try to make sense of his intention.

Actually, it's not just the thickness of the paint that directs the viewer's attention. It's a perfect combination of texture and light: it's the lighter colors to draw your attention to a single point of focus. The drama of the painting—that famous spotlight effect.

I was able to explore this more deeply with his later paintings, in particular the *Prophetess Hannah*, when I was working for the

Rijksmuseum. The one that some scholars believe is Rembrandt's mother. In that one she's holding a very large book, the Bible most likely, and she is using her hands to touch the place in the book where she's trying to read a passage. It's clearly an important passage. It seems her eyesight is not good. The old lady's hands on the book are both cast in light and finely detailed. You see every wrinkle in her hands, every minute fold of skin. Nothing is left to the imagination: you can almost count how many washes she did in the river, how many garments she sewed back to life by the light of a single candle. You can sense what it would be like to take that hand into your own, the way the skin would softly slide away under your touch.

Everything else in that portrait fades away as you look at the hands. There is simply less pigment and less light in other parts of the painting. You see her face, but the eyes are mere dots, the nose is a simple slant, the tilt of the head is her only expression. As you move back from the picture, away from those hands, the paint is looser, more general, even kind of slapdash at the edges, as if Rembrandt couldn't care less at that point about line, about shape.

There's intelligence to the way he brings your focus into what matters: those old lady's hands literally trying to absorb through her fingertips the significance of that text.

But to return to this question of Aris Kindt's hands. What's interesting is that this evidence suggests that Rembrandt saw the dead man in person, and that he may have originally painted the hand as he saw it, as a stump. That is, he planned to include the suffering of the thief, to show his punishment as well as his dissection. At some point, though, Rembrandt changed his mind and invented a hand for Adriaen. Restored to the thief the hand that was taken from him. And not only that. He seems to have restored the flesh elsewhere, too. Kindt would have been covered with scars from all his punishments. Brandings. Whipping scars.

So was this some bold act of compassion on Rembrandt's part to restore the man? Or did he do it to protect Tulp from infamy? Or what could be the reason that he went back and "fixed" Aris. Why would he have done that?

I want to put into the record the final words from the *justitieboek* on Aris Kindt's final conviction in Amsterdam:

These evil facts and their serious consequences are not to be tolerated in a town of justice and honesty but to be punished by law and by this be an example to others. It is therefore that the lords of justice, having heard the sentence, demanded and the resolution of the bailiff, also the confession of this prisoner, have sentenced him as they sentence him by now—to be led to the scaffold in front of the town hall of this town in order to be executed by the hangman to the rope till death [follows]. Accordingly, the corpse to be buried in the earth and they declare all his goods, if there are such, be confiscated to the disposal of the lords. Actum 27 January 1632 . . . and to be executed on the last day of January.

A final note about the signature. Rembrandt himself must have considered this work to be a significant leap forward from his previous work. Before this painting, he always signed his canvasses with the initials "RHL" for Rembrandt Harmenszoon van Leiden. Rembrandt, son of Harmen of Leiden. This is the first painting he signed simply "Rembrandt."

XXIII

THE EYES

When I got back to the studio, the workday had already come to a close. All the pupils and apprentices had gone home. Lit only by my single lantern, the room was the color of cobalt, the shadows layered and rich. The silence was silken. I carried my lantern into the center of the studio and stood for a moment, watching.

The room had seen the arrivals and departures of multitudes. Everywhere I could see the results of a productive academy that had managed to keep running smoothly in my absence. Tomas had gotten further with his copy of my *Jesus at Emmaus*. In the etching studio, Isaac had completed the run of the prints I'd asked for. There were about fifty of them strung from lines crisscrossing the ceiling and another batch already dried and stacked on the table. He'd left the copper plate in the press, cleaned and readied for another round of printing.

I plucked one of the prints off the drying line and held it in my hands. It was the image I'd requested: my mother at home at Weddesteeg in her mourning attire, the week of Gerrit's death. I hadn't drawn her; I'd etched the plate from memory.

The paper from Isaac's etching was still damp, the ink tacky. There was a lot of black in the print, but cross-hatching seemed to have worked. It made the textures distinct: the fur trim of her shawl, the gloss of her black mittens, and the rough cushions of the chair that props her up.

My mother won't like this portrait. I've captured her in the depth of her grief, her eyes unfocused, her mind distant, her whole body slumped under the weight of her sadness. She had loved Gerrit more than the rest of us, I think. Maybe not before the accident but certainly after his hand was crushed.

After I went back to my apprenticeship in The Hague, and later opened my studio with Jan Lievens back in Leiden, she no longer worried about me. I would be self-sufficient, while her oldest son would need a mother's focused care.

At the funeral, though, my mother had held me so tightly it felt as if she were trying to bind me to her through her grip. She never met my eyes when I tried to touch her pale skin, her translucent cheeks, so worn with time's passing. Her eyes darted away from my gaze.

Maybe she didn't want to share this grief with me. Maybe she was trying to protect me from the power of her love, but I did not think of that at the time; during the funeral, all I could think was that she was angry with me for continuing to live and thrive after her favored son had perished. One should not believe that a parent is able to love all sons equally. Some sons are easier to love than others.

I reached up and pinned the print back on the drying line. I took a deep breath and let the smell of the etching acid fill my nostrils, stinging just a little bit.

Taking the lantern with me, I returned to the painting studio. The snow had made the sky brighter and I could hear some of the revelers from the festival already in the streets.

I went to Tomas's copy of *Emmaus* on the floor, and lifted it to eye level. The apprentice was nearly finished with the painting now, and it would be his first completed work. Tomas had managed to give Cleopas a strong expression of fear, even if the gaping mouth he'd rendered veered a little bit toward the comical.

The problem was the way Tomas had handled the light. In my study, I had placed Christ in deep shadow, the revelation casting Cleopas into light. Tomas had given an equal amount of light to the disciple and Christ. He'd managed to bring clarity to Jesus's features, but that wasn't the point. It was the choice of light that was most important—instead of bringing the viewer's eye to Christ, I wanted to call attention to those who witnessed Christ's resurrection. It was the witnesses who mattered in this particular story. This was their story, not Christ's. His return wasn't about his form or his face or how he looked as a man. It was about Cleopas recognizing God in this stranger. The emphasis had to be on Cleopas, the disciple, and his experience of discovery. His sudden recognition that the stranger was in fact Christ—that was the miracle.

I let the painting rest again against the wall. Maybe Tomas knew already it wasn't working. Maybe that's why he'd taken it down from the easel.

It was time, at last, to sit down and paint. I knew that I had been finding ways to put it off all day and now the moment had come to sit down and truly begin. I had to demand true concentration of myself—real discipline. No more distractions. Only the painting at hand.

I drew up a chair and positioned myself in front of that massive stretch of linen. I saw the lines and shapes I had brushed onto the canvas that morning. They looked aimless and weak. Even the consistency of the paint seemed noncommittal. The brushstrokes had no authority, no direction. Only a set of shapes. The work of an amateur.

Things had changed in me since I'd made my first attempt that morning. Now I at least had an idea for the overall composition and a strong concept for the image. I was sure of what I would try to do, and I wasn't sure if I would achieve it. Including the dead man in the portrait would be a risk, but it was a risk worth taking because it would add so much more drama and tension to the piece. It would create a narrative, where no narrative existed.

I found myself a wider paintbrush and picked up my palette again. I dabbed my paintbrush in the Kassel earth, and I started again. I moved the composition of guild members higher so that I could place the corpse at the base of the canvas. I started to paint an outline of the thief front and center, at the bottom of my pyramid. I outlined his overall shape, a large ovoid containing head, torso, legs, feet. I moved the figure of Van Loenen to the top of the pyramid and put Dr. Tulp to the side on the right. But I gave him a great deal of space, so that he had pride of place and room to move his hands.

I looked at the figure of the thief. I considered turning him forward like Mantegna's Christ, but looking at it within my pyramid, it didn't seem right. I decided on a compromise. I should turn him diagonally within the frame, so that his feet would be a bit foregrounded and his head higher in the perspectival plane. As I outlined, though, I saw that this would require me to make him somewhat foreshortened, to make the proportions unusual between his torso and legs.

I outlined a general shape of Dr. Tulp, standing over the body, making his cuts. That was my idea—to show Tulp standing over the open cavity of the dead man's body, searching for the soul. All the other surgeons and apprentices would be standing alongside him, gaping into the body cavity, observing Tulp's dissection. Adriaen would be wide open at the center, a kind of plundered landscape, with the doctors mining his organs.

It seemed like the right kind of image to make a point. The tearing down of the temple to chase after the thief within. It would be a modern allegory of scientia. The marks on the thief's body would tell the story of his crimes; the stump would illustrate his punishment. The repose of the body would speak of his unearthly suffering.

I liked it as a concept, and my hand moved swiftly across the canvas with the brush. I worked in the detail of the body. I outlined both arms. The anatomized arm and the stump. The specifics of the muscles and tendons and veins of the anatomized arm would have to wait for later, until I could get that arm from Fetchet. But I could work on the other arm based on my morning's sketches. I went to my cloak and found my notepad.

I brought it to the easel and tried to work from the sketches. Now, though, I had to consider the stump. The partial arm, hand missing at the wrist. How realistic should I try to make it? And what was I conveying with that shape?

I found, however, that all this thought was becoming hard for me. It was too technical, too dry. And with each brushstroke, I found myself becoming more and more upset. It pained me to think about that hand. The thief's hand. Adriaen's hand. Because I also thought of Gerrit's hand. My mother's kiss. I remembered Adriaen's hand holding the wine goblet that Lievens had given him. How he'd brought that glass to his lips with that hand and had waved goodbye that night after he'd supped.

Each stroke made me ask myself: Was it further cruelty what I was doing? Making a man's great loss, great suffering, so manifest? Would it tell the story I wanted it to tell? Or was it too literal minded, too directly on the mark?

My own hand slowed. I pushed myself away from the easel. I crossed my arms and took in what I'd done. This, I thought, was a portrait of human cruelty. It told of how men ravage one another in search of truth. How they carve each other up in the name of justice, and how they fail to see their own brutality.

I put down my brush. I had a choice now, and it was an important one. Would I use my gift to echo this brutality? Would I be no better than the executioner to put the man's sufferings on display as spectacle? When she'd kissed my hands, had my mother blessed them for this?

I sat there for a long time in front of the canvas in the dark. I stood, walked away from the easel, and thought. I walked back to the easel, walked around it, and then found my seat in front of it again.

I got up from the easel and walked to the windows, looking out over the city and toward the IJ. Down in the streets below there were a few passersby already lighting their torches for the midnight parade. A group of revelers stood below my window, pouring out their cups of ale from a tankard, singing a drinking song. The women raised their skirts, kicking their feet in the air and laughing. All the way up Sint Antoniesbreestraat I could see crowds lining up for the parade. Already some men were shooting off Chinese sparks from nearby rooftops.

What a strange evening. Out there, it was festival time. I stood and watched the figures walking, dancing, skipping toward the Waag, but I did not feel as cynical about all this as you might imagine. I thought about the cycles of life and death and how celebrating execution and dissection was one way of acknowledging life. Who feels more alive, after all, than a man who has recently witnessed a death?

When I heard the rap at the door I was not surprised. Something in me knew that I should be expecting what happened next.

"Enter," I said.

"Master, you are here then." It was only Femke. "I thought I heard you return earlier, but I was not sure if you'd gone to bed."

"No, I'm working. It's the only moment when I get a bit of silence."

She stepped farther into the room and I could see that there was another figure behind her in the doorway.

"Please forgive me, master," she continued, leaning forward to whisper. "I told her it was an unusual hour for callers, but she would not be sent away. I thought you would see her. The others stayed below."

"She?"

"She has come from Leiden, she says . . ." Femke said, unable to continue. She drew her apron to her face and dabbed her eyes. I saw that she had been crying.

"Tell me what upsets you."

"She is, well . . . Master, she is . . ." Femke swallowed hard but could not speak. She moved closer and I offered her my hand.

"What is it?"

She sputtered, "I can't say. You must speak to her. She will tell you." Femke's smeared face seemed to come into a strange kind of focus. "That rapscallion Jan Fetchet brought them here."

She blew her nose into her apron noisily. I covered the easel again with my cloth. "Thank you, Femke. Tell her to come in. You must only bring us another lantern and something warm to drink. Can you manage that?"

"Yes, of course, master. Yes, I'll do it right away."

⌇⁕⌇

The door edged open slowly and I saw that it was that same woman from the dissection. The one who had run in and tried to cover the body with her own. Her head was covered in a thick wool shawl, her face shrouded, her eyes downcast. She wore peasant clothes, over her large, pregnant belly. Her movements were labored and slow. I was sorry that she'd had to climb the stairs.

I asked her to sit and offered to take her mantle. "I dare not dirty your fine furniture, sire. I need only a moment of your time."

"My furniture is not so fine. And in any case, if you're going to speak with me, you must feel at ease," I said. "Please, take the seat."

She handed me her mantle, and once she was settled she also removed her shawl. Her hair was pinned up under a cap, but I could see that it was thick and fair. Her face was pleasantly round, her skin smooth.

We sat together in the studio as the lantern flickered. I did not feel uneasy, though I had many questions for her. She did not seem ready to speak to me yet, but I knew there was much she wanted to say and I should wait for her to begin. Femke returned with a second lantern and a cup of warm milk for each of us. She lit the stove and asked if she could do any more service. I told her she could retire for the night.

"Tell me your story," I said to the woman once we were alone again. "And why you came tonight to the anatomy."

228

"I'm the one they call Aris Kindt's wench," she said.

"And what do you call yourself?"

"Flora. Flora of Leiden."

"Flora." The goddess of springtime. "You came for the hanging?"

"I came to try to save Adriaen. To plead his case."

"I see."

"They said I came too late. They said I did not have the right papers. We never married."

I nodded.

"They'll call him a bastard child," she said, putting her hands to her belly. "The convict's son. I would have come earlier if I had known about it sooner. But Adriaen has been gone a long time. He left Leiden in the summer, and now the canals are freezing through."

"No one told you? He didn't send word when he was sentenced?"

"No. He would have been too ashamed. When I saw him last he were being lashed in the Leiden jail."

"How did you find out?"

She looked at me, as if remembering it for the first time. "The stones. The boys threw them at my home. So many stones came." She spoke softly and slowly, as if she was trying to remember all of it, every detail.

"Your house was stoned?"

"They pulled the cobblestones out of the lane and pelted my house and broke windows, sent things flying. It were this morning, but now it seems a lifetime ago. *Witch!* they called me. *Crone!* So many curses. *Hag!* they screamed. *Whore.*"

As she spoke, I painted her face in my mind, and I saw increasing beauty in her plain features. I asked her if she would be willing to remove her bonnet. She gazed at me for a moment, trying to understand my meaning, wondering at my intent. And then, as if she understood everything, and without saying a word, she reached up and removed the pins from her cap.

She carefully drew her hair across her shoulders, as if preparing for a sitting. As if somehow she intuitively understood. I was looking at her to plan a painting. But how could she know?

Her hair was lovely. It was ample and full of curls. If I were to paint it, I'd use lead-tin yellow, unmixed. But I would ask her to pin up half of it and leave some flowing in ringlets. I'd fill her hair with wild spring flowers, like Flora of the myths. Her eyes, I'd paint with raw umber and a tinge of madder lake. Her skin tone, a mixture of sienna, red ocher, and lead white. I would paint her pregnant, too, her hand resting on her full belly. I'd dress her in vernal silks. I would try to do her justice. She was a beautiful woman of the world, in spite of her hardships. Her body was voluptuous and robust, her magnificence undeniable.

She went on talking and talked for some time and I listened while I tried to imagine her in oils. She told me the whole of her tale, from the stones thrown through her windows up until she'd tried to storm the anatomy tower to claim Adriaen's body.

I let her speak, and I memorized her features, her kindness, her faith. When she reached some points in her tale she would stop and cry, a soft quiet cry, like a slow unburdening. Then she would go on with her tale.

I knew of Adriaen's beginnings and saw him at the end. I knew who he'd been but only the outlines, a sketch. Her tale filled in the details, explained who he'd been to her. She painted him in rich pigments, with the kind of texture that gave him substance. She had come all this way to claim him, and no one had allowed her to stake her claim. She had gone to the hanging and to the magistrate and to the surgeons and then to Fetchet. And he had sent her to me. Was it to ask for the final limb? The limb I had requested for my examination? Or was it for something else?

Finally, she asked for what she wanted, and what she wanted was simple. "I want a way to make him whole again."

XXIV

THE BODY

Yes, Lord Schout. It's as the bailiff said. The night watch found me under the quay on my back in a leaky skiff. I was hiding there since before the dawn, hoping to cloak myself in its pitch.

No, sire, please! No, no more weights. Truly, sire, we only wanted the burgher's cloak. I never meant to harm the man. He lives still, I'm told. I'm told he's not harmed. Surely that means we can be released, Your Honor? It was only his coat we wanted. I'm a coat thief, sire. I steal them and sell them in the open-air market behind the Amstel.

The coat had a fine fur collar. That's what I noticed first. It was black, heavy wool, from a skilled tailor. I have made something of a study of coats, Your Honor, and can tell from a distance which ones are stitched by the Ferdinand Janssens of this city and those flung together for sea-bound sailors at the wharves. I can tell you just about every character of a man by his cloak, by how he chooses his tailor and what he'll spend to purchase his winter warmth.

This one, I wasn't going to sell at the Amstel. This one, I wanted for myself. Only to hang across my shoulders and give me shelter from the chill. Only to spend a night in the comfort of its enveloping arms. I did not mean to harm the man, sire. I respected the good lame burgher.

It was Hendrick who hit him on the head with the rock. Hendrick Janszoon of Leeuwarden. Yes, the same one that is here in the rasp house. You saw how big he is? With his fierce uneven teeth, he can make a woman drop her purse just by yawning. I've known him for ten years and we've been in and out of the jails together as many times in as many years. The other accomplice was Jacob Martszoon, the Walloon. I know Jacob from the outskirts; we met ten years ago. I never once saw him do violence. He keeps an extra knife in his pocket to skin rabbits, sire, and I've seen him be as gentle to the poor creatures he's about to eat as a nursemaid is to a babe.

Hendrick and Jacob and I were in the tavern, the two of them singing in the back, keeping the barkeep company. It was a freezing night, Your Honor. There were ice drifts on the canals.

Hendrick was wearing a big brown cloak that I'd stolen a few weeks back. That was an easy job. The door was open and the cloak was just hanging there in the doorway. Someone had just gone in, or someone was on the way out. It was a low-hanging apple, Your Honor. I reached in and nabbed it.

Then on the way back to the tavern Hendrick claimed it. He said it was his spoils since he'd bought me beers that night. Hendrick is twice my height and three belt sizes bigger. I dare not argue with him unless I want cobblestones up my nose.

I was sitting in the tavern window. The night boats were moving slow through the ice. They sent out skiffs, with all their lanterns. All those lights in the dark.

Every time I shivered, the sadder I got. The Walloon tried to bring me another tankard. "Don't fret," said Jacob. "We'll find you a coat as fine as Hendrick's."

"There would not be that luck again," I said.

He answered, "We will make our own luck. Look out that window and play the burgomaster's wife, and look upon the men in these canal byways as salesmen, modeling cloaks that are yours at any price. Choose what you like and we will make sure you get it."

The Walloon is like this when he's two sheets to the wind. His pale face goes red and his fangs show. He was in the mood for an evil jaunt. He turned back to the barman, to sing the final verses of a song. "The wenches drew their skirts to the hip . . . and the captain went down with his ship, yes, lads, the captain went down with his ship." He left me at the window.

There were not many men went by, for it was hard to keep a lantern lit. Those that passed went under cover of wide-brimmed hats. Then I saw the guildhall doors open and out came all the men who'd been inside there. They were not tanners or smiths or ships' carpenters. They were dressed like near royalty: doublets, garters, snow-white starched ruffs. In their lanterns I saw round faces. Their coats were wool, fur lined.

Imagine me in one of those coats, I thought. Perhaps this one of deep purple wool? Or that with the red felt trim? I thought perhaps this was too greedy. How would Flora feel if she saw me arriving down the path in such a grand garment?

Then, the door of the guild shut, and with it the light went out. The men scattered into the black night. I felt the sting of the freezing damp again. Amsterdam winters are merciless, my lord, and yet so many men never worry over warmth. They go about in grand cloaks, warm hats, and leather gloves from Italy, never feeling the sting of that wind that bites at me every minute.

Then the guildhall door opened once again. This time, it didn't swing wide, but I saw a figure in the light of the hallway. I could not see the man's face, only his back and his arms, which were raised as he tried to light his lantern on the stoop. In that lantern light: the fur collar. It was the nicest of all the coats I'd seen on the men outside the guildhall, its fur trim the color of Turkish honey.

This burgher was the last man out of the guildhall. He was alone now; all the other men had already made their way down the lane. My sight is poor, Your Honor, but I watched him move down the street toward me, slowly, very slowly.

"You've chosen one, then, have you?" said Jacob. He was standing behind me all of a sudden and reading my thoughts. He placed his hand hard upon my back.

I saw then that the man's gait was uneven, and it may have been that one foot was smaller than the other or one leg longer. Something was not right in his walk.

"No, not him," I said to Jacob, but he'd already called Hendrick to the tavern door.

"What a prince you'll be in that cloak," declared Hendrick.

"Yes, you'll prance about like a very Brabanter," said the Walloon. "Why, you'll waltz along the quays, sampling the herring."

"The Kid in a burgomaster's wool," said Hendrick. "He may drown within it, but it should be his."

"Not him," I said. "He's lame. Don't you see?"

Hendrick taunted, "What? Can you not stand to rob one of your kind?"

I said nothing after that. We went out into the night. The rain had stopped, but the streets were slick with ice and the air was thick with misty, chilling drizzle. We three followed the burgher down the byway toward the Nieuwezijds Kolk. Our mark slowed, then stopped. The further we got, the worse the poor burgher's walk got. He moved, it seemed to me, like a badly wounded donkey. Not one foot and then the other, but one step and sort of falling forward, as if with any given step he might collapse.

Jacob and Hendrick didn't bother hiding as we followed close behind him. They played that we were sailors off a merchant sea ship, on a weekend leave. There are many such packs of men out carousing on the streets in that part of town. The burgher never once looked back.

Just as we neared the Heerenlocke, the good burgher stopped before a high door. He took his keys from his belt. While fiddling with the lock, the rain started again and his lantern went out. It was in that rain and that darkness, I'm sure, that the fear finally hit him.

He leaned down to tend the flame, and while his fingers fussed, Hendrick made his move. He put his chisel to the burgher's neck and whispered in his ear. The burgher dropped his lantern. Hendrick told him to put his key back in the lock slowly and quietly, but his hands shook too much, and the keys, too, fell down onto the cobblestones. Hendrick pushed him into the doorway and held him by the chin with his bare hands. Jacob used the chisel to pry open the metal clasp instead. Then we three stepped inside the darkened entry hall, and that's where we tried to uncloak him.

I tried to be kind. "Be still, good sir, and it will take but a minute."

He squirmed in Hendrick's clutch and his eyes fell on me with a dreadful pleading.

"Be still, good sir," I said again. I always try to go about my thieving in the pleasantest possible way, Your Honor. It's not such a terrible thing to lose a coat. It's the fear that does the worst harm. "I only want your coat," I told him. "It will take but a minute."

He got even more jumpy. He would not be still. He wrestled and pulled and then began to shout, and as soon as his scream passed his lips, I reached out to silence him with what I had: a rag inside my vest. The man had the shrill cry of a newborn, Your Honor, loud enough to wake all New Town. I felt sorry for the burgher but I needed him to be quiet. I pushed the rag between his lips and begged him to be still.

I tried my best to protect the good lame burgher, Your Honor, but Hendrick knocked him over the head. I looked up to see what he'd used: a large stone he must've picked up from the alley.

I yelled at Hendrick, "Why did you do that?"

He hissed back at me: "Shut up. Take his arm."

Then we all heard heavy footsteps coming up the alley and a hard voice calling, "Who goes there? State your name and your business."

The door to the house was open. Jacob and Hendrick dragged the burgher inside and we all went in. The night watchman called again, "Who goes there? Answer or I will ring an alarm."

We were still trying to get the cloak. I lifted the burgher's arm, but he was too heavy, and Jacob and Hendrick decided to run off. I thought to run into the house, but there was yet another gate. I looked down one last time to see the burgher, who was now moaning. His eyes looked up at me in frightful terror. I felt so sorry for him then, I wished I'd never left the tavern, never talked to Hendrick once in my life. I begged him to keep quiet. I left that house and ran in the direction Hendrick and Jacob had gone. There was a body in the alley, too: they'd struck down the night watchman, who was groaning and trying to find his feet. We made it all the way back into Old Town before he caught up with us.

I was lucky to find a workman's ladder on the Geldersekade and a small boat at the ready. I untied the skiff and, using the ladder as a gondolier's pole, I pressed the boat from its mooring and down the canal toward the Waag. There's a tunnel beneath the weigh hall quay. I leaned my ladder against the embankment and lay down in the skiff. Then I pushed myself by hand into that tiny passage.

I breathed a long sigh at last, hiding in that pitch-black warren, for dawn was just about rising and I'd easily have been given away. I lay there until an hour later, when I was awakened by something tossing the canal waters about my skiff.

You know the rest, Your Honor. How the night watchman climbed down my gondolier's pole to find me. How I dunked him in the canal. I got as far as the Sint Agnieten monastery, where your civic guards were waiting, muskets aimed. It was panic that encouraged me to swim—I thought I still had both my hands; I could feel them paddling in the water. But one hand is all I have and I cannot swim with just one—nor swim at all, truth be told—so I was thankful the civic guards trawled me with the net. I was sputtering when they got me to the bank.

This I do admit, Your Honor. We were wrong to try and snatch a coat off the lame New Town burgher. The attempt was made worse still when I tried to stifle the man's screams. But it was Hendrick hit him with that stone. I swear I wanted nothing from that burgher other than the source of his warmth.

Yes, Your Honor, you're right. I have gone astray. I could have been a sheath maker with my training. Yet I am a coat thief. I steal and I cavort with violent thieves. But I swear I am not violent. I'm not ripe for hanging, sire. What could the public want with my body? I am nothing. No one. I'm no more harmful than a crow that comes down into the farmer's field and plucks away the grain. They don't kill crows in the fields in Leiden. They scare them off with sticks.

Can you loosen the weights now, sire? I have told you my accomplices; I have confessed to my deeds. I'm sorry for the burgher and glad to hear that he is now well. I'm a stupid and useless man, Lord Schout, but there is no evil in my breast.

At least one drop of water, then, Your Honor? With a little moisture on my tongue I can go on. I will answer all your questions. I will convince you of the purity of my soul. Only the mercy of a raindrop . . .

THE EYES

Flora left my studio with a note in her hand for Fetchet: he could give her the item I'd purchased from him that afternoon—Kindt's arm—and he could also keep my coins. But as I was placing the note in her hand, I said one thing:

"I have another way to make him whole again. You must give me time, and I will summon you again when I'm done. Stay in Amsterdam, and perhaps things will turn out all right."

Paint, I thought to myself, once Flora had departed the studio. You must, at last, paint. It is only crushed minerals and oils. What can it do to reverse cruelty or reveal truth or transform life into something more sacred? I wasn't sure yet. But I wanted to see if I could try to make something more powerful of this painting. Something I'd never done yet.

He was a man, and he was flesh and bones and mind and soul. She had loved him, Fetchet bought him, Dr. Tulp had claimed him for science, and I had wanted him for art. All of us sought his flesh. All of us have wanted to make something of this man's body. But he did not belong to any of us. He was only Aris the thief.

I turned toward my easel and once more addressed the canvas. I saw my own brushstrokes, the loose curves at the hand for the stump, the hole I'd outlined in his chest. Before Flora's visit, I had envisioned depicting Adriaen as he was when I'd seen him: his skin scarred and beaten, his lopped hand, the mark of the rope still visible on his neck. I had planned to show him mid-dissection, with his whole body cavity open, and perhaps with his organs removed. It would be an image of an anonymous body, marked as such by all his brandings, stripped bare, supine, and subdued under the intelligent gaze of the surgeons.

But would it satisfy Flora? And would it satisfy me?

Now that I had heard Flora's tale, I regarded the figure in the center of the frame differently. Yes, a destroyed body would be too literal. It would only elicit discomfort and shock from anyone who saw the picture. People would not see a man. He would remain a body, a poor convict taken apart. Flora was right: people didn't mind seeing other people's suffering.

I thought again about Emmaus, and how Christ walked among his disciples for a while before he revealed himself to them. They walked in the dark, on a path through the forest, and finally came upon an inn. They went inside to sup, and still he did not reveal himself to them. It was only once they had reclined at the table, and received their sustenance, that his image became manifest. A single candle illuminated his face, and his identity was revealed.

I brought my lantern close to the easel again. What if I were to illuminate Adriaen, to bring him into light? If he were not sliced open and degraded but instead elevated and lit? What if I did not show the power of the men over him but his own power over them?

All the other guild members would be like Cleopas, each in a different way, observing the effect of the body, learning something from it, expressing that discovery through their faces. But each would be discovering it in his own way. One would be awed, another frightened, another confused, another repelled. Each face would reflect part of the experience of facing death.

I knew at the time, of course, that if I took this course I might be upsetting Tulp or the other members of the Surgeons' Guild by creating an allegory on their commemorative canvas. I knew that if the praelector didn't appreciate this, did not like the portrait, he might withdraw his payment or refuse to hang it in the guildhall. I did think about that at the time. However, I knew that I needed to make a painting that meant something. Too many events had transpired that told me there was weight here. There was importance in this image. It was a kind of test.

I drew my brush out of the *pincelier* again and started to work on the thief's body. I added details, colors, to the flesh, I added texture and substance to the skin. I worked all the way across the torso and down the arm until I got to the stump.

My instinct told me to replace it—to restore the hand. I cannot say it was a conscious choice. My own hand simply continued to dab my paintbrush into the paints and to add details. The cut went away, and in its place stood a fine, manicured, gentleman's hand. Then it occurred to me that I had a certain power in creating this image, to replace what had been taken from him.

I thought about Tulp's search for the soul in the body, and how we all go looking for the soul in different parts. But what if the soul can't be found in the organs or the limbs? What if the soul of a man is found in his very life? What if the soul is not material but active? What if it's somehow connected to how we make use of our gifts?

If I could restore the stolen limb, I could also unscar the body, remove the exterior signs of his malfeasance. He would no longer be Aris Kindt, criminal and evildoer; he would be like any man who was deserving of dignity in death.

I could close up his chest, so no one would try peering into his organs to detect evidence of his soul's corruption. I could restore his human form so that he was a man again and not a patient. I would allow Tulp to dissect his functioning arm, to see the mechanism of that graceful limb, which allows a man to point and reach.

As I continued to dab my paintbrush into the Kassel earth and bone black, I recognized what was possible through this portrait. I could make a broken man whole. I added some lead white to my palette and painted on, adding details to the skin fold, until the hand was whole, moving on to adding color to the flesh so that it was pristine.

But there would be a sense of clear sacrifice in this image. The man has given up part of his serenity to serve scientia. No, to serve understanding, to provoke compassion.

As I was restoring Adriaen to his former shape, I realized that I was not painting a Christ figure at all. I was painting a Lazarus of Bethany, resurrected from death after four days in the tomb. Christ had not come soon enough. Flora had not come soon enough. Adriaen was already dead, and there was no way to save him. But we could raise him, in a way, from his deathbed and give him something else: immortality.

You hear me speak and this is one further heresy, is it not? I have not only claimed to be able to paint a Christ figure, I have claimed to *be* a Christ figure. I believe that with my crushed minerals and my linseed oil and my ground and my canvas and brush, I have the power to resurrect. This is why I should not go before that panel, why it will be difficult to state my case. Because it's true that I am arrogant and it's possible that this is what I'll say.

There is a nuance here, though, which I know that you can understand. I do not believe that I have the power to restore, the authority to resurrect. I am not a miracle maker, not I myself. No. It is art that has the power to do that job. It is art that can restore a broken body, return a dead man to life. It is the fiction created by the paintbrush, the pigments, the mathematical structure, the capacity to shine light. . . .

My job is to serve the art, to be the hand that wields the paintbrush, the eye that is capable of seeing what needs to be presented in paint. I am a mere conduit—through which art can accomplish its aims. A few crushed minerals with oil and turpentine, some strokes of a brush, and an artist has that extraordinary ability to stop time, to reverse time, to immortalize and resurrect.

It is why people sit for portraits in the first place, isn't it? So that they can be captured at the height of their fame or youth or wealth. A portrait can freeze time, prevent aging, remove wrinkles and imperfections, and even dispense with death altogether if the sitter manages to live on in paint. Tulp knows this. That is why he has commissioned this portrait to commemorate his lesson. But we do not choose to use this art for vanity, for superficial fixes of a man's skin. The power of our art is wasted if we use it to subtract from reality or erase a part of life.

It was not Adriaen I wanted to preserve, restore, resurrect. He was no saint, no man of terrific honor. He was, it was true, a common thief, who lived by the laws of the street and stole what he needed to get by. But I also saw that, if Aris Kindt the thief could be given a reprieve, if he was restored with beauty and love and light, then we could all be reprieved. All of us would be resurrected, forgiven, illuminated in his flesh.

This idea enlivened me, excited me, and I painted on, thrilled and busy with the incredible sense of purpose it contained. This work. It was not just painting, it was making art.

⌒⟡⌒

I could hear the sounds of the festival in the streets getting more riotous as I relaxed into the freedom of painting what I wanted to paint. Outside in the street I could hear a lute player. The slurred song of a drunken singer trying desperately to remember the words.

I worked on the guild figures, creating the expressions in each face, giving them variety and simplicity, but singularity. One awed, one frightened, one philosophical, one full of hope. I continued to work more diligently on Adriaen's left hand—the one I needed to represent with its anatomy revealed—adding a few details to the arm based on what I could still remember from Tulp's lesson.

Tulp's hand needs to apply the forceps to demonstrate the movement of Adriaen's muscles and tendons. So I began to outline his hand, leaving the rest of his figure merely in sketch. It was an extraordinary feeling to paint one man's hand using an instrument to operate another man's hand.

I thought of Michelangelo's Sistine Chapel and God's hand reaching out to Adam. There is irony in letting a pair of forceps intervene between the surgeon's hand and the hand he will animate through his touch. But just when I thought this, I looked down and saw my own hand, holding the paintbrush, and the brush itself, like the forceps, was an instrument of reanimation as well.

I wish I could tell you that a kind of fire burned through my hand just then, feeling my mother's benediction on my skin, but I can't. All I can say is that I knew it was the right thing. That, right there, would be the center of the painting. The artist's invisible hand presents the surgeon's living hand, to reanimate the hand of the dead convicted thief. And in that way, to resurrect all humanity.

I heard the singing grow louder outside my windows as the parade took shape along my street. I knew that I had finally found my way into this painting, and that it would be no mere portrait but one of my greatest works. I would illuminate Adriaen's body. I would cast the damned man into light.

XXVI

THE MOUTH

Watch your step as you climb the stairs and hold the rope fast. Come, then, let me take your mind off your daily worries, and step, instead, into my chamber of wonders.

Now that the Waag is an attraction, I get hundreds of visitors each day. Like you, they want to see that portrait by Van Rijn—I still can't manage to call him what they call him, just "Rembrandt"— and the anatomy theater depicted in his painting. It's inside the theater that I keep my chamber of wonders when the anatomy isn't in session. I've got such rarities there as no man's ever seen.

Oh, yes, I am the only one—apart from Tulp—who has the keys to the chamber where the painting now lives. I could not possibly let anyone in there, seeing as I'd run a great risk of losing my position as *famulus anatomicus* if it were discovered.

Come, now, don't press ahead. The stairs can be slippery when they're wet. Oh, yes, I've seen it many times. Perhaps more than even Tulp. And of course I know the painter; he is one of my best clients. One of my true connoisseurs. Indeed, he is a brusque sort. Not at all like dear Professor Tulp. That's why he has caused such a controversy for the guild. He prefers to call his work "art," and seems to forget it is a commission.

Oh, yes, it is praised! I have heard some say it is greater than Raphael's paintings. That our very own Amsterdam master has outdone the Italian greats. I am no *liefhebber*, so I cannot give you my own opinion. A shame they don't take it out of that storage chamber behind that door right there and let the public see. Then every man and woman could make up their own mind.

There, the door to my chamber of wonders is unlocked. Come in, come into my cabinet. Within my cabinet are some of the most singular objects and relics ever known to the world, and yet very few men are aware of my holdings. Only the truly curious—and the truly deserving—are given an opportunity to tour my finds. Typically, I charge a fine fee for access to these chambers. You, however, have won over my trust to such a degree that I no longer seek your coinage. Come, if you will, join me within.

To the left you will find my *naturalia*, all the wonders of nature's kingdom: dried herbs to cure any worldly ills and a rare assemblage of shells from the farthest earthly shores. A conch shell dotted so evenly with brown freckles along its curves one imagines a painter has taken his brush to this surface.

To the right, I'll show you my *animalia:* birds and mammals of sea, land, and sky, from here to the Australasias and as far as the New World. Farther into the room, you'll find the pride of my collection: preservations of human flesh, including mummies from ancient Egypt I was able to purchase from Heurnius's troves.

Above, you'll see my armadillo and crocodile, a boar's head and sea monkey. See spears from tribal Africa on this wall, and horns and antlers from more than twenty different species. There you have seats made out of bones and cowhide; here there are drinking cups made of ivory. See my whole elephant tusks, too, and here a coat made of leopard pelts.

Earlier, I told you of a marvelous creature, the bird of paradise, that true rarity of rarities, which inspires awe through its beauty and through the fact that it, alone among winged creatures, can never alight upon the earth. One can only assume that this constant need for flight is a burden to this ethereal fowl. And yet even flight, this eternal flapping of wings, is essential to its soul. For when caught, it soon dies, so well does it love the free air. The great wonder hunters of all Europe have tried, and failed, to capture one alive. But it will not be snared, nor tethered to earth. For the *paradiseus*, its form is its destiny.

Here, then, feast your eyes on this true wonder. This marvelous creature that evades earthly captivity. This one is, of course, dead, but from its incredible plumage you can imagine how it must've looked while it was alive.

Oh, yes. There's the door there, yes. Right behind that door is the Rembrandt portrait. And it's true, I do have the key. As I mentioned, it would be a serious risk to my position as the *famulus anatomicus* to allow anyone past that door. . . . It would have to be something very interesting to make it worth the risk.

Oh, well, maybe. I might be able to consider a donation . . . for my collecting. Yes, in the interest of science . . . I could maybe allow you in for just a moment, if you promise not to tell. . . .

Right this way, then, right this way.

You know I had a hand in the conception of that masterpiece? It's a long tale, but I'll tell it for an extra stiver if you'd truly like to hear.

Well, yes, I know that Van Rijn personally. Ask any burgher in Amsterdam and he'll tell you: if there's an oddity or rarity you seek, I can put it into your hands. I'm a barterer, a trader, and a broker in God's great bounty. Should you desire a clawless otter from the Cape of Good Hope or a bull's horn to be played like a trumpet, merely inquire here. Maybe you want a tortoise shell worn as a German helmet in our roiling Spanish wars? Just say my name: Jan Fetchet . . .

XXVII

A WINTER FESTIVAL

The whole city around them celebrates. As Flora and the boy head toward the skiff the boatman has tied to the edge of the canal, they must push their way through the rowdy masses. Flora takes the boy's hand and elbows her way to the canal edge. She drops and seats herself on the bank, then draws the boy onto her lap and passes him along to the boatman. He carefully guides them down.

Revelers troll the streets, bearing lanterns and long wood poles wrapped with cloth and set aflame. As they begin to drift slowly among the other boats in the water, Flora watches the celebrants, thinking this must be a foretaste of hell, the grotesque figures dancing and laughing and drunk with vengeance. *Adriaen*, she thinks, *I hope the man was right and that you are already long gone.*

The church bells are sounding out the final hour of 31 January 1632, and these bells are subdued and kind, like a hand gently caressing a wound. Each chime from the towers overhead drives another shovel into the ground, burying the day bit by bit. *Bong, bong, bong.*

No melody to the chimes this time, only a slow and steady ringing of finality. Adriaen's day has ended.

Flora watches the lines of dark figures make their grim procession through the street above, now in a sudden sweep of enthusiasm, shouting and raising their torches high. Some people are singing, some drunkenly staggering in the streets, their torches burning wayward circles in the air. If it were not so unreal, Flora would cry. But she is done crying for today; she cried out all her tears as she told her tale to the painter. Tomorrow she will surely cry again, but for today her tears are spent.

Alongside their skiff, other boats pass with their own lanterns lit, making a double pageant of light as each flame is reflected against the black surface of the canal waters. The crowd bawls and bellows, and some men jokingly try to climb down into their craft. The boatman warns them away with the blunt end of his paddle. "Back off or you'll end up in the soup."

She is glad for him, this stranger who became her protector. Where did he come from and why has he, of all the people in this city, managed to be so kind?

Ice has formed in only some places along this canal, and there are a few drifts, especially near the bridges, not yet thick enough to prevent their motion but suggesting the hazards to come in narrower channels.

"Where to?" asks the boatman, and Flora cannot say. She has decided not to return to Fetchet, not to deliver the painter's note, not to take the limb, or any of the rest of the body. It is too terrible a task. Too horrendous even to think about. She will not try to piece Adriaen back together in this way. She will do as the painter suggested. She will stay in Amsterdam and she will wait.

Where to? All day, her destiny has led her from one station of the cross to the next and now there are no more stations. Without the purpose of seeking Adriaen, she must act on her own free will. It will be the first of many hard and lonely choices, she thinks. It will be a lifetime of choices ahead.

"I know a place," says the boatman, relieving her of her silence. "It's no castle, but the linens are clean and the keeper is honest. And it will be off the main streets, so you won't hear the parade. He is a friend and will not charge you too dearly. You and the boy will be safe."

Flora nods, content to have this decision, at least, made for her. "Where will you go?" she asks, feeling a flash of panic that her guide will leave her, too.

"I will not go far," he tells her. "I will come and check on you in the morning, and you can tell me what you want then. Tonight, you should only sleep, and let the weight of sleep clear your head, forget all you have seen today; forget these torches. Tomorrow, you will set a new course and I will take you where you need to go."

"You do more for us than you should," she answers. "In all this time, you haven't told me your name."

Here, he turns his face away from Flora and watches the lights flit off the water for some time. "Jacob," he says. "Some call me Jacob the Walloon."

THE HANDS

Margaretha is still awake and threading her final green stem into her new curtains when her husband at last returns. She is already in her box bed, clad in her sleeping gown and cap, but she has been unable to sleep, knowing the festival has taken over the town, seeing the beautiful, glistening lights play across the water and reflect in the windows of the mansions along the canal. It is a magical night, the city lit up to glittering, and all in celebration of her husband's success. She is aglow with pride.

She is alert to any creak of the floorboards or rustling outside her door, hoping soon to hear her husband's footsteps so that she can receive his firsthand report of the lecture and debate. She does not want to startle him as he arrives, for certainly he expects her to already be abed—the Westerkerk bell has now chimed again, after all, long past her usual bedtime—and yet she hopes he will rap on the door of her chamber nonetheless.

Just as she is setting the green floss on the nightstand, she hears at last the unmistakable groan of the stairs under his step. Yes, she will go to the door and prevent him from seeking his own chamber. She cannot stand to wait until morning to hear his report.

"My love," she calls from her doorway, her ardor in her voice surprising herself. "Come join me. Tell me everything."

Her husband is weary, she can see already from the tilt of his chin. He glances up at her, not surprised to find her awake but pleased to have such a warm welcome. His eyes are reddened, the soft flesh beneath them purple and in tiny folds. What a long day it has been already, preceded by a few weeks of frantic preparation and sleepless pacing. If she were a good wife, she'd guide him straight to his chamber, undress him, and tuck him in for the night, demanding nothing, providing only comfort and succor from the world.

But she is too curious, too eager to share in his success. He moves toward her across the corridor and she places her hand in his, leading him into her room and gently closing the door behind her. Now standing, she has a better view of the procession below, a joyful and haphazard dance of lights glittering across the canals and trailing plumes of white smoke.

"They are celebrating you, my love," Margaretha says, motioning to her husband to sit in the nearest chair, the one upholstered in red velvet, closest to her bed.

Tulp laughs, modestly. "No, my dearest, they are celebrating merely because they have been given leave to celebrate. No Amsterdammer needs much of an excuse to raise their tankards, especially in these dark nights."

"You are too self-abnegating," Margaretha says, circling behind her husband to loosen his lace collar from his shirt. Once she has unclasped it and placed it on the commode, she puts her warm hands to the back of his neck to release the tension where she knows it dwells. He groans with appreciation. She unbuttons the front of his doublet and takes the meat of his shoulders within her hands, gently massaging there. "Have the guild members finished the banquet?"

"I doubt it very much. When I left they were still pounding the table for more oxheads of wine. I left Fetchet with the keys to the stores. He will manage in my stead."

"He is a useful servant, I think."

"Yes, indeed. Tonight we had very special circumstances. When I left, I placed a purse of three guilders beside the corpse and a note of gratitude. I suspect he will find it when he goes to bury the parts."

Margaretha moves around her husband and sits on the wooden edge of her box bed. She takes his hands in her own and begins to gently massage his palms. She can see in the light of her bedside lantern that his face is truly drawn and his expression somehow dispirited. "My dearest, you seem unhappy. Did it not all go as planned?"

He glances up at her and a smile of admiration passes his lips. "It did not go as planned, no," he says, "not all. But I have no reason to be unhappy except that I am drained from all the activity. I suspect, in fact, that this evening has achieved precisely what I intended, and that tomorrow I shall awaken with a fresh set of pleasures to attend."

Encouraged by these words, Margaretha presses her fingers more deeply into her husband's exhausted flesh. "I shall not keep you up late," she says, "but do indulge me in some part of the tale. Perhaps it is unwomanly, but I do want to know all that transpired. I want to know all that the nobles said. I am pregnant with curiosity."

This time his smile was a full smile, brightening his kind eyes and turning his soft cheeks ruddy. "I had private conferences after the lecture with several fascinating men," he tells her. "There is the French mathematician of whom I have told you in the past, and I was also visited by Johannes Wtenbogaert and several burgomasters, who promised to support me in tomorrow's election. Some decried the fact that I have not yet been selected for the board of the Atheneum. Another told me it was only a matter of time before I should be a strong candidate for mayor."

"Truly?"

"Indeed," he says, looking down as if only acknowledging these words to himself for the first time. "It was meant as a compliment more than a prediction, I suppose."

"Take it for a prediction, though. You will, my love. You will someday be Amsterdam's mayor."

In spite of his obvious pleasure in sharing these details of the night, Margaretha can see that she is wearing her husband out. Before she can offer to dismiss him from her chamber, though, he says, "My wife, may I stay with you in your bed tonight? I'm afraid

I have no more energy even to make it to my own chamber. If I am propped in bed, at least, I can talk until we fall asleep."

"Yes, of course, my love," she says. "Then let me help you out of your clothes. Here you go. We will climb together into sleep's kind arms."

"Thank you, Margaretha. You are my gold."

THE MOUTH

Normally, Fetchet would be drunk by now, so soused he'd be doing a dance in the middle of the Kloveniersburgwal, maybe trying to get dunked in the canal. Last year during winter festival, he got some partyers to do a little game with him, where he asked them to pass their torches under his feet, so he could prove how high he could jump. Luckily, he'd only been fully aware of this death-defying bravery the next day, after he'd been regaled with his own exploits by a ruby-haired, green-eyed bedmate. If only Fetchet could woo women so successfully when sober.

While the torchlight parade is in full swing on the nearby streets of De Wallen this year, he is digging a grave in the Oude Kerk yard. The church tower has now struck midnight, and still the Leiden woman has not returned for Aris's remains—he's glad of that—and now it is up to him to dispose of them. The body will get a Christian burial, though not in the strictest sense of the word.

Some of his parts lie on the ground beside Fetchet in a burlap sack. The organs that were passed around the audience are in a pot on the other side of the hole. He's prepared to plant them all into this raw earth beneath him, to be mixed together like some kind of unholy stew.

Does it qualify, really, as a Christian burial? Fetchet wonders for the first time as he continues to shovel the dirt. Not being a believer, he was sure he couldn't know. Next time he runs into a priest, he thinks, maybe he'll ask. Or maybe he'll just keep doing his job and not think about it too much. He stops digging and stands the shovel upright in the dirt next to him. He wipes his brow on his coat sleeve and feels the coarse hairs of his wool jacket prickle his face.

He reaches into his right pocket and draws out the three shiny guilders Tulp left for him. They are some of the newest-looking coins he's ever seen, as if Tulp had gone straight to the mint and taken them from the press. Who paid doctors with such fresh currency? They are certainly satisfying to the touch. He brings one to his lips and places it between his teeth, biting down. It tastes vaguely metallic for a moment, before he tastes the soil from his fingers instead.

He slides the coins back into his pocket and wipes his hands on his pants. He lifts the shovel again. What did Tulp pay him for, exactly? It wasn't reimbursement for the extra expenses he'd had to pay the vendors in the morning. He hadn't even told Tulp about all that yet. It wasn't for what he'd lost on the paradise. Rembrandt had made up for that. It was for managing Kindt's wench, for keeping her out of the anatomy chamber so he could go on with his dirty business before all those clean men.

No, thinks Fetchet, as he digs his shovel into the ground, I shouldn't think that. There is nothing dirty about the anatomy. I love the anatomy; it is my birthright, my legacy, my very parentage. I love its ceremony and its pomp; I love the doctor's feigned authority and the spectators' awe and civility. But amid all the bloodletting, cutting, lecturing, banqueting, torch-lighting, and debauchery, the scientists—his beloved Pauw and Heurnius and now Tulp—are doing something important. Like the Egyptians before them, they are building the foundations of a civilization.

That's what he tells himself as he pitches his blade into the hard ground a few more times and thinks about Flora. He keeps shoveling until the hole is deep enough to prevent dogs from unearthing this grave. He's glad he sent her to the artist. He had a feeling that Van Rijn would find a way to make her forget the arm. It would've been cruel to make her go home with a bag full of parts. A man is not his flesh, anyway. A man is a man.

He picks up the burlap sack and empties it into the hole. Turning his face away, he shovels the fresh dirt back into the hole. Using the back of his spade, he packs it down as firmly as he can, or at least enough that it won't attract dogs. He feels painfully sober, and cold. The wind is picking up.

Without knowing why, Fetchet kneels in the dirt, his hands on either side of him touching the cold ground. He looks at the black soil and then up at the black sky. The celebrants are nearby, singing and dancing like he usually would. He can smell the smoke of their torches, pungent and fresh. He takes a fistful of dirt into his palm and tosses it on top of the grave he's made.

"Well, then," he says. "Sleep tight, Aris." He makes some motions with his hands—not exactly prayerful gestures, but some kind of gestures nonetheless. Then he stands, listening to the church bells finally chime midnight, not bothering to wipe the dirt from his pants.

THE MIND

Descartes has finally put down his pen and screwed tight the lid of his inkpot, since the innkeeper has rapped on his door. He has stained the sleeve of his nightshirt with a blot that has taken the shape of a butterfly's wing. He curses quietly, and resolves to find a wife who can help him manage such troubles. But whom will he find if he never leaves the Oud Prins?

Outside, he hears a faint shouting that is quickly overpowered by the sound of the midnight bells in the church closer to his hearing. He knows the festival is out there somewhere, but he was able to get back to his inn before the majority of the revelers took to the streets.

Tomorrow the streets will be littered with burned wood and flint, empty tankards and broken glass. He will keep to himself in his rooms until they've swept the debris into the canals. Tonight, he must find some way to sleep, though his mind is still astir with all the comings and goings of this eventful day. He wonders where he put that wad of cotton he uses to plug his ears.

He goes to his basin and draws some cold water up to his face, using a bit of soap to rinse his teeth. Using a hand towel next to the basin, he pats his cheeks and forehead dry, and lets the rest of the water sit for a moment chilling his face. The fire seems to have gone out; he does not wish to worry the innkeeper at this hour, so he opens the iron door and peers within. There are still embers glowing in the back. It is merely a question of adding some kindling and a log or two. That should hold him through the night.

He takes some wood out of the basket next to the stove. How much time he spent writing those long letters to Mersenne, he thinks, bending down, lifting his kindling. What possessed him to write so profusely? His friend surely would not be interested in it all. Perhaps he could keep the pages for himself and simply pen a shorter version, more to the point? Or, he could simply toss those pages all into the fire and begin again in the morning once he finds a clearer head.

He presses the frailest twig into the stove, positioning it atop the hot embers to try and make it catch. The embers glow but seem not to take to the twig, which has no frayed edges desirable to the fire. He chooses another twig, split down the center and shedding its bark. This one should do, he thinks, as he introduces it to the heat. This time the ember licks at the edges and seems to like what it tastes. A small flame erupts along the very end of the branch and then begins eating its way along the twig. Success in so small an endeavor, thinks Descartes, makes it feel as though the whole universe operates in harmony.

Once he is satisfied that the other kindling has caught, he presents a small log in the center of the stove and decides that will be sufficient. If the fire dies, the chill will wake him and he can get started with his work before dawn. The carcass he bought at the butcher's is in the kitchen, preserved on ice. He will get up early enough so as not to wake the cook and confuse the servants further. The lamb will still be nearly fresh, and he can begin by dissecting its limb to see how closely that resembles the man's.

Yes, tomorrow he will begin afresh, pursuing his own anatomies with the lessons he has learned today. He will begin with the lamb.

THE EYES

Rembrandt paints. He holds his palette in his left hand, his thumb in the hole, his fingers balancing the board. Cologne earth, Kassel earth, lead white, umber, red lake, vermilion, yellow ocher, red ocher, bone black.

He chooses a small round brush and dabs it into the Kassel earth, then draws a bit of lead white and red lake into the mixture. The resulting color is brownish pink for the muscles of the dissected hand. With very light strokes, he fills in the shadows of the hand, the contours between where the fingers would have been. Then he adds more white to the mixture, and dabs in another layer, where the edges of the fingers and knuckles would be. He is building up the layers, building a hand from no hand, giving it detail.

Then he cleans his brush and dabs it into white, mixes in a touch of umber. Light falling on the hand, on the wrist, on the corpse's side. Light falling on the belly, on the ribs, on the chest, on the lips. He adds white to the face—not the whole face, because half of it falls into shadow, under the bodies of the surgeons who are leaning over Aris's head to get a glimpse of Tulp's demonstration of the hand. A touch of white, to make a glint of light on the edge of the forceps. The tips of Tulp's fingers and the dead man's left hand.

There is much more to do. He will go on painting until he gets it all right. Until there are layers and layers of pigment that will never be diminished. Not by his death, not by his time, not by any time. Cologne earth, Kassel earth, lead white, umber, red lake, vermilion, yellow ocher, red ocher, bone black.

THE BODY

Aris hears his own name called from the gate. His name and all his aliases. *Adriaen Adriaenszoon. Aris Kindt. Kindt. Aris the Kid! Your hour has come.*

The same words called by the executioner with barbarous clarity. Adriaen Adriaenszoon, alias Arendt Adriaenszoon, alias Aris Kindt, alias Aris the Kid. Your time is nigh.

Then other voices join in—other men, in other cells, other guards: Aris, Aris! Aris Kindt! Aris Kindt! The jailhouse echoes with it mercilessly, and then the crowd calling his name doubles the sound. Aris Kindt! Aris! Aris! All these voices mingle into one insistent mass of voices, indistinguishable as a chorus, all at once. Aris, Aris, Aris, come! Aris Kindt! It's your hour.

Where is he now? He is not shackled. He is not walking. In fact, he can discover neither his hands nor his feet. The voices outside are also crying within. *Adriaen!* One cries. *My Adriaen! Where can I find you?*

That voice there is unmistakable; it is Flora. She is calling out for him. Where was she, then? Nearby? Has she made her way to Amsterdam? Will she come and claim him?

He senses hands upon him. They do not seem to be human hands, though they are human voices. Are they the executioner's hands? Or God's hands? The devil's hands? Why can he feel the pressure of hands but not his own body being grasped?

As their force surrounds him, lifting him and moving him through the night as if he had no substance, he sees no men, no hands, and no figures of any kind. It is only these voices and a sense of heat somewhere, a sense of flame that lifts him.

There comes a rush of memories, all rearing up like stallions in the confines of his mind. His father towering over him at the pine workbench in the shop. The soft, pungent leathers pressed through his tiny child's hands. The tall reeds that made fence posts along the worn path to church. His father's mumbled scolding. The windmill with a roof made of thatch. Flora through the window playing on the heath. Flora. Her cool cloth pressed into his hot wounds. Her bucket of water and her basket of herbs.

The sting of the blade of the first knife that cut him, the way he gasped. The weight of one fist on his chin, then many more. The ache of his ribs kicked and shattered. His father standing before a large, darkened door. The bill of deed on the shop door. The pitiful trawling all over town for day labor. The dead old crone with her bucket of sand. The cool redemption of a swim in the river. The terror of escaping a galley by diving into the sea. The pain when he hit the water, the reward of freedom when he surfaced. The supple forgiveness of Flora's flesh. Flora. Flora and her basket of bandages and herbs.

He is drawn through the square weightlessly, feeling no body, sensing no self, and the sky is starless and clear, no clouds mounting, no threat of rain. In fact, there is heat, like a thousand torches burning, filling the night air with their subtle smoky scent.

He flies over Dam Square, past the Oude Kerk graveyard, past the gibbet at the Volewijk and he sees the crowds below, a flow of people like rivers from one street to the next. He hears the crowds: the masses of people who stand and dance and revel and call and curse. They cry his name. Their voices are now softened, calmed, soothed until they are no longer shouting his name but singing it: *Aris Kindt!* Like a lullaby. *Aris! Aris! Where are you now?*

He knows at last what he must do. He must confess everything, the whole truth of it to whoever is ready to listen. It does not matter if he is saved—no, he knows he will not be saved in spite of all this floating. Speaking is merely a step toward whatever will next unfold, but he wants to speak, he wants to explain, to tell his story because now, at last, someone—some more than one—seems to be listening.

ACKNOWLEDGMENTS

This novel, six years in the making, would not have been possible without the generous support of a US Fulbright Fellowship in Creative Writing (2006–2007) and the Jack Leggett Fellowship from the Iowa Writers' Workshop (2007–2008) as well as support from the Netherlands America Foundation, the Ludwig Vogelstein Foundation, and two heavenly writing residencies at the MacDowell Colony in New Hampshire.

It would take a proper bibliography to credit every book that helped prepare me to write this novel, but I'd like to mention those that were particularly influential and inspirational: *Rembrandt's Anatomy of Dr. Nicolaas Tulp*, by William S. Heckscher; *Rembrandt: The Painter at Work* and *Rembrandt: Quest of a Genius*, by Ernst van de Wetering; *The Body Emblazoned: Dissection and the Human Body in Renaissance Culture*, by Jonathan Sawday; *Rembrandt Under the Scalpel: The Anatomy Lesson of Dr. Nicolaes Tulp Dissected*, by Norbert Middlekoop, Marlies Enklaar, and Peter van der Ploeg; *The Philosophical Writings of Descartes* translated by John Cottingham, Robert Stoothoff, and Dugald Murdoch; *The Anatomical Renaissance: The Resurrection of the Anatomical Projects of the Ancients*, by Andrew Cunningham; *The Spectacle of Suffering: Executions and the Evolution of Repression: from a Pre-industrial Metropolis to the European Experience*, by Pieter Spierenburg; *The Embarrassment of Riches: An Interpretation of Dutch Culture in the Golden Age*, by Simon Schama; *Amsterdam: A Brief Life of the City*, by Geert Mak; *Everything That Rises: A Book of Convergences*, by Lawrence Weschler; and *Spectacular Bodies: The Art and Science of the Human Body from Leonardo to Now*, by Martin Kemp and Marina Wallace.

I also want to acknowledge the support and guidance of particular historians and scholars: William Heckscher; William Schupbach; Norbert Middlekoop; Tim Huisman; Dolores Mitchell; Robert C. van de Graaf; Jaap van der Veen; and the terrific conservator who worked on the painting at the Mauritshuis, Petria Noble. I want to thank Bas Pauw from the Foundation for the Production and Translation of Dutch Literature for lending me some seventeenth-century Dutch plays in translation (particularly the Bredero!).

I'd like to thank the wonderful researcher Ruud Koopman for retrieving for me the *confessieboek* and *justitieboek* documents related to Aris Kindt's criminal history in the Amsterdam municipal archives, and his son, Karsten, and Jaap Wit who translated the seventeenth-century Dutch texts. These laid the foundation for the Kindt narrative, which was also inspired by G. A. Bredero's social satire, *The Spanish Brabanter*, which, in turn, was based on the sixteenth-century picaresque novel *Lazarillo de Tormes*.

But primarily, I wish to thank Ernst van de Wetering, the world's leading Rembrandt scholar and author of six volumes of the *Corpus of Rembrandt Paintings*, for being my guide and mentor during the early days of writing this book. He gave me my Rembrandt reading lists, suggested contacts in other historical arenas—seventeenth-century Dutch social, criminal, and aesthetic history—and provided me with his thoughtful feedback on chapters and repeatedly enlightened me with his considerable wisdom on Rembrandt, the man and the myth. I am deeply indebted to this brilliant art historian.

I'd like to thank my generous readers: Leslie Jamison, Erik Raschke, Patricia Paludanus, Jim Lake, Dina Nayeri, Christopher Saxe, Amal Chatterjee, Marian Krauskopf, Julie Phillips, Joshua Kendall, Emily Raboteau, and Josh Rolnick. I want to thank Benjamin Roberts, a historian of seventeenth-century Dutch society and culture, for fact-checking the final draft. For various sorts of cheering on: Jeremy, Tom, Mickael, Bajah, Josh, Alex, and Itamar.

Finally, thanks to my incredible agent, Marly Rusoff, her partner Michael Radulescu, to my wonderful publisher, Nan Talese, her assistant, Daniel Meyer, as well as to David and Rebecca and Dad and Carol for the love and encouragement that helped me get through the rough spots. And to my daughter, Sonia, for giving me the incentive to finish it.

A NOTE ABOUT THE AUTHOR

Nina Siegal received her MFA in fiction from the Iowa
Writers' Workshop. She is the recipient of the Jack Leggett
Fellowship from Iowa, a Fulbright Fellowship in Creative
Writing, two MacDowell Colony Fellowships, and other
grants and awards. She has covered fine art and culture for
The New York Times, Bloomberg News, the *International Herald
Tribune*, *W*, *Art in America*, and many other art publications.

A NOTE ABOUT THE TYPE

The text of this book was set in Van Dijck, a modern revival of a typeface attributed to the Dutch master punchcutter Christoffel van Dyck, c. 1606–69. The revival was produced by the Monotype Corporation in 1937–38 with the assistance, and perhaps over the objection, of the Dutch typographer Jan van Krimpen. Never in wide use, Monotype Van Dijck nonetheless has the familiar and comfortable qualities of the types of William Caslon, who used the original Van Dijck as the model for his famous type.